Sydney West

by

David B. McKinsey

Sydney West

Published in Seattle, Washington, USA by Blackbird Parlor.
First Edition.

LCCN: 2022921178

ISBN Paperback: 979-8-9873013-0-2
ISBN Hardback: 979-8-9873013-1-9
ISBN eBook: 979-8-9873013-2-6

Cover design and other illustrations
by David Blackbird McKinsey
www.blackbirdparlor.com

Support your local independent bookstore,
and stop helping billionaires go to space.

For Breanna.

I'm glad you're here.

This novel contains themes of trauma, mental health, paranoia and unreality. Reader discretion is advised.

Death

ONE

For once in longer than he cared to admit, Jacob was early. He surveyed the long line of patrons trying to squeeze what little else they might from the day's caffeine allowance before the shop closed.

She was buried on the other side.

Finally, he caught her eye from behind the crowd, where she sat behind the counter on her bar stool, flying through orders. She was always easy to spot with a head of pastel pink hair, but tonight the small woman was nearly lost under it all.

Her dark eyes registered his blue and his quick head flick to the right. She nodded behind the black mask over her mouth and nose, looped around her ears.

Jacob waded through the Sunday evening crowd, over to the row of wooden tables against the wall, but stopped short.

The entire room buzzed with people he wasn't listening to, but he did his best to remain polite in his quest for a place to sit. Most others had been more extreme in ignoring the man sitting further down, across from the only empty space.

Jacob caught himself staring and looked away, he hoped, before the dark-haired man in the long coat looked up from his book. Jacob had seen him lurking further down the campus hall or across the yard from time to time, but they had never had the opportunity to meet.

He wasn't even sure he wanted to, despite wondering why he'd never seen him talking to anyone else. Only floating through–the shadow no one seemed to look directly at.

Keeping his eyes from the floor, Jacob strode over and sat.

He set down his tablet and folding keyboard, as well as his backpack, before the massive lump of black in front of him shifted. And still, no acknowledgement came. He was in the clear and opened a text document.

"Dear *God*, they don't still make people read that?"

"*Wha?*" Jacob squawked. His head snapped up so violently, his black-rimmed glasses jumped from his nose. He reached up and reset them.

The patron squinted only slightly before he returned to neutral–almost as if he wasn't fully awake, but hadn't sagged yet. The moment wasn't helped as Jacob caught himself staring again.

He couldn't pull himself out of it this time.

The man wasn't flamboyant but, the more Jacob looked, the more he began to edge toward the unsettling. His nearly floor-length, black wool trench coat was drawn up close to his neck, a camouflage for a towering frame. When Jacob finally realized he was stared back at, the general shape of light skin and straight black hair with a deep undercut all the way around snapped into sharp focus.

He was proud he didn't jump again, but that probably didn't matter. The man squinted his dark grey eyes again, then turned his gaze over the side of the table.

Jacob looked down to his spilled backpack. His notebook and other books had slid out in a long pile, The Heart of Darkness clear among the rubble.

"Ah!" Jacob added to his animal sound a moment ago. He leaned over to tidy his mess.

Then came the quiet, oddly artificial sound of a page turning. He sat back up to see the stranger had received a text message. In one hand, he held his book. In the other, he held the wide, flat shape of his phone and stared into it, stone-faced.

He looked up to Jacob and then back, and started to look a little sick. The shift was obviously from whatever he was seeing on the screen, but there was no explanation for the particularly horrendous shade of grey his face had turned.

"Hey, you okay?" Jacob asked.

The stranger in black didn't immediately look up but, even then, only for a second, then back to the phone and up again. He stared at Jacob and didn't appear to be breathing.

Jacob forced himself to remember his own absolutely necessary oxygen flow.

The dark student's eyes drifted from Jacob's face, into the crowd behind him. His line of sight drifted even further, toward the entry to the back sitting area before his gaze slowly drifted back.

Jacob's attention fell to the man's phone which had just received the messages. There was just enough time to make out a few full sentences, though inverted.

Okay, Sydney, you go on your little adventure.

Pretend you're as smart as you think you are and this won't backfire. You won't come crawling back.

And then the recent message came after.

Maybe we should see if that little Hipster Boy you're talking to can take your place? He blends in a bit more, don't you think?

Sydney's color hadn't returned. He let go of his book and cast a quick look across the crowd again, then abruptly stood.

"Don't talk to strangers," he muttered, before he strode away behind Jacob, pulling his collar tighter around his neck.

"*Hey!* You–" Jacob snatched up Sydney's copy of *The Hound of the Baskervilles* and spun himself up and out of his chair.

Sydney stumbled halfway to the front door, but recovered and didn't look back. He curled himself over as if already fighting the cold outside in the dark rather than the last stretch of business hours inside a scuffed red and gold café.

Jacob's will to follow all but died. He stood there with the little paperback in one hand as he mutely watched Sydney disappear back through the window-paned door. No one else turned, even as the icy air crept through from the momentary opening.

He stared down at the book, then slowly returned to his seat. Those text messages had also been labelled The Cat, an absurd nickname to bother him. Maybe it was more about the way Sydney had looked around the room in horror.

Jacob stared into his tablet screen and finished a few more words over the next fifteen minutes. By the time the small woman with pink hair tapped him on the shoulder, he nearly jumped so high he fell out of his chair.

It was never a simple thing to lie to his girlfriend, and he avoided it as a rule. He kissed the top of her head to placate his guilt.

There was nothing the matter, technically. Nothing at all. But the rest of the night was high-strung in everything from dark shapes in the snowy alleys they passed, to the faint sound of ambulance sirens in the distance.

Monday dawned with mediocre coffee and the indistinct flavor of creeping dread. Though typical, Jacob rubbed his sore nose for the fifth time in five minutes to check if he was bleeding. He'd rolled the wrong way out of bed and, bashed awake on the wall, took the opportunity to leave before the other two tenants came out of hiding.

That dread didn't dissipate, at least at first. Whether embedded in the day from his rude awakening or a carry-over from last night, neither mattered.

At lunchtime coffee, he was struck with the fact he'd enjoyed a moment's peace for the first time in hours. He dug a few more coins out of his backpack and bought another.

He did, however, look up and down the hall before he ran off with his cup to enjoy himself in peace. He hadn't seen Sydney at all today, if the name in the text messages was accurate. Lack of that tall, imposing figure down the hall or in the yard wasn't as helpful to his mood as expected, but he pushed any lurking concerns away.

He even found it in himself to enjoy the first half of English class, as he thought he'd ought. Professor Suleman didn't quite drone, but held an air of disgruntled YouTube video commentator, speaking out through the screen rather than to the adults in the room.

Jacob added a polka-dotted tie to the stick figure at the edge of his notes, caught between the jaws of a marshmallowy T-Rex. The hydraulic door at the back end of the room hissed, but the footsteps were faint.

Suleman kept going, oddly enough. He took every opportunity to spotlight delinquent behavior, whatever it meant to him any given day.

Jacob checked in every few minutes to listen to him rant about *Frankenstein* some more. About how people tried to muddy the waters of science with beliefs. About how all the students should take this opportunity to apply the lessons to their own lives. About how stupid people were if the supernatural was anything more than allegory, though he would say he never *technically* said that, and kids these days were oddly sensitive.

Jacob didn't raise his hand so much anymore.

And then Suleman stopped. Jacob looked up to see him looking back to the back row. Several students up front cast a look over their shoulder, as did Jacob a moment later.

The absurdly tall man from yesterday sat in the last row, hand held high in a short, black leather glove. The grey pallor from yesterday hadn't gone away, and he stared straight ahead at Professor Suleman and almost through him, like he was trying to nail him to the whiteboard.

Jacob looked back to Suleman, who'd begun to crack and let some personal annoyance bleed through. The Professor waved a hand.

"Well?" he said.

Sydney dropped his hand.

"She was a teenager when she started writing it, though," he said.

"What? You've been here for two weeks, this is the first time you decide to–remind me your name?" Suleman started.

"Sydney West," he answered. "And now that we have that out of the way–why are you trying to make Mary Shelley out to be something she's not? She was eighteen when she started it."

Suleman began to speak but Sydney spoke faster, though no louder, and overpowered him.

"That's really no way to encourage the next author of a classic. Of any age."

The professor's anger visibly sparked.

"And that's really no way to treat your elders, Mr. West. I advise you come here to learn, or you're wasting your time."

From the corner of Jacob's eye, another hand shot up. A woman with messy brown curls wrangled to the back of her head wiggled her black-nailed fingers.

"Yes, Ms. Diaz?"

Her hand dropped.

"It's easy to forget Mary Shelley was so young, since the book is so popular, in hindsight."

"Also true," Suleman conceded. He looked back at Sydney. Jacob didn't look behind him again.

The professor took a breath to speak, but hesitated only for a second.

"Anyone else have something to say? Or may we continue?"

The entire room was silent, except for a faint tapping at the back. Sydney stopped tapping his fingers.

Class continued, the interruption having no notable effect Jacob could identify. The period droned on, students inserting their hasty answers where requested and appropriate.

Jacob eventually squinted at the clock over the whiteboard. The second hand passed twelve and the room erupted.

Mr. Suleman resigned himself to the flurry, and stacked his papers with a decisive *crunch* before he sat down behind his desk. No one objected, or wasted any time making themselves scarce.

Jacob scooped up his books and notebooks and shoved them unceremoniously into his backpack in effort to join the flow at its peak. A deep green waffle-weave top slid by him and he glanced up as Diaz disappeared in the small mob.

On impulse he looked back to where Sydney had been sitting. He was still there, slumped over the desktop with one arm out, like a big black cat stretched out in a sunbeam.

A woman jumped over the desktop to Sydney's left with a clatter, and he jolted awake as she slid over to the floor without a thought of him. He blinked widely a few times and pulled his gloved hand back from open air.

Someone's cell phone went off with a digital roar near the doors at the front of the room and Jacob spun back around to his desk. When he looked to the back again, Sydney was already gone, though the hydraulic door behind where he had been had yet to close completely.

Jacob wrenched his backpack clumsily over his flannel shoulder and ran out to see where he might have disappeared to.

Just like he knew to look down in search of Katrina and her pink hair, he looked up across the heads to catch Sydney as he stepped into the stairwell.

Jacob jogged. Then he ran. Then he hesitated at the fireproof door before he pushed through. Sydney didn't seem to want to talk yesterday, there was no reason he would want to talk now.

Still, Jacob had to know what had unnerved him so much.

He skipped three steps up at a time and caught up with Sydney at the next landing in the chilly stairwell.

"Hey, you okay?" Jacob asked through deep breaths and let his backpack fall down to one shoulder.

Sydney glanced over his own shoulder as he ascended the next flight.

"Fine. Why?"

Jacob's phone exploded in digital fanfare and he scrambled to fish it out of his pocket. He quietly informed the caller they had dialed the wrong number, then caught up once again.

"I know it's not my business or anything, just wanted to make sure everything's okay," Jacob explained.

Sydney stopped, stone-still, staring straight ahead. Jacob retreated a few steps down, which only served to intensify Sydney's turn and glare down at him.

The most alarming feature of the enormous man was the total lack of recognition in his face.

"Sorry," Sydney began, his face almost wincing at the word. He took a deep breath. "Who are you?"

"We talked yesterday, at The Red Cheshire. You seemed kind of… I dunno, really worried about something, then you left in a rush."

Sydney's eyes widened a bit.

"And where is that, exactly?"

"What, you mean The Red Cheshire? Where you were last night?" Jacob replied.

Sydney rolled his eyes.

"Never mind that, I guess. What did we talk about? Did I say anything?"

Jacob didn't answer as quickly.

"A bit," he said.

"What did I say?" Sydney shot back. Jacob resisted the urge to take another step down.

"You hate the book The Heart of Darkness, and, uh, told me not to talk to strangers."

If there was some kind of skirmish between Sydney and an ex, Jacob wanted no part of it. He also shied away from the idea of confessing he'd taken a look at his text messages. Upside down. Accidentally. Yeah, that would totally be a good excuse.

Sydney's eyebrow quirked.

"You're no help," he muttered, then turned and ascended.

"*Wait,* I–" Jacob called after him, scrambling for the zipper of his backpack. He was being outrun and, backpack half-open, he jumped up the steps to follow.

"*Are* you okay, though?" he asked. Sydney turned so quickly Jacob nearly crashed into his shoulders.

"*Why* are you still here?"

"I just want to make sure you're fine. You looked really upset when you left, and it's been bothering me all morning." The sentence picked up momentum Jacob didn't intend, and culminated in difficulty looking Sydney in the eye.

When he managed to do so, if only for a second, Sydney had an uncomfortable look on his face, pinched to the side and brows lowered, like he'd discovered a rock in his shoe he wouldn't have the opportunity to remove for quite some time.

"Thank you for… trying to be kind," Sydney started. Jacob braced for a reprimand. "I don't want to talk about it, but I have a request."

"If I can, sure," Jacob answered. He let his backpack slide down his arm and sit on the floor.

Sydney's turn came to brace, which didn't give Jacob any relief.

"I'd like a ride to–home. I've been having some… issues, and I'd like to make sure I get there without… other problems. But I feel fine. Don't worry."

Jacob brightened up. Only one obstacle came to mind.

"What are you going to do about your car, though?"

"I don't have one," Sydney answered, and shifted his weight. The conversation was running longer than anticipated.

"Ah. I used to ride the bus a lot, too," Jacob said and

lifted his backpack again, "until I got some help with a–"

"I don't like the bus, much," Sydney interrupted. "And I'd like to get home." He pulled a black leather wallet from his coat pocket and wrestled with removing the license from the sleeve.

"I don't need to see that. You can just tell me the road and give me directions, don't–" he noted Sydney glance over his shoulder at the windows to the rest of the campus and snap back, the wallet lowering with his hand.

Jacob glanced back at the windows, saw nothing, then reached into his backpack and pulled out Sydney's copy of *The Hound of the Baskervilles.*

The sky was overcast and half-reflected the stairwell in high-contrast shapes, but there was nothing particularly notable there.

"You don't need to–" Jacob started again.

"West Barrow Street," Sydney interrupted and Jacob's sentence died. Sydney folded the wallet and put it away.

"You *walked from downtown?*"

He held out Sydney's book.

Sydney rolled his eyes harder in the most expression Jacob had seen from him since they met. He then turned and climbed the stairs again.

"I mean yeah, I can take you. There's time between classes, but *jeez*, man. Garage is–garage is down. Sydney."

Sydney turned and followed him back down the stairwell.

Jacob held the book out again. That same disturbing lack of recognition sat behind Sydney's eyes. Jacob shook the book and Sydney hesitantly took it.

Jacob then led the odd student back out and toward the parking garage, ignoring the occasional second, echoing set of footfalls that were frequent enough for him to be sure they were there, but rare enough for him to wonder why he was so bothered.

TWO

"Myrna. *Myrna...*"

Myrna Diaz looked up from furiously typing on her phone. Her faux-fur collared bomber was drawn up high around her ears and the fuzzy, skull-shaped earmuffs didn't help much for sound, either.

"What?" she burst.

The woman at the other end of the bench pointed as well as she could through bright woolen mittens, down to Jacob trudging down the edge of the parking lot. Sydney trailed in his wake like an omen of death.

"Is that the guy? The one from like two years ago, you were talking about?" asked the owner of the tight mass of red curls. Her knitted hood barely contained her hair.

Myrna's dark eyes flicked up over her phone and back down. She didn't move from her wide-kneed slouch against the back of the bench.

"Yep," was all she answered with a pop of her *P*.

"You're not going to talk to him?"

Myrna's eyes flashed. She sat up straighter only from the tension.

"Yeah, sure. But I'd prefer not to instantly punch him in the face, so I'm gonna go ahead and wait, don't you think?"

The other woman paused, fiddling with her own phone in the pocket of her parka. She leaned back further on the bench and brushed a few curls out of her olive, freckled face.

"Good point," she conceded, then pulled out her wooden-cased phone. Her lock screen background was set to a photo of herself with a lanky, white-haired man around her own age, with light skin and black sunglasses.

No new messages.

The ride to West Barrow Street was quiet. Jacob wouldn't have minded, except that Sydney was totally silent but for when he turned his little blue Mini Cooper down the street.

"Thirteen," was all Sydney said.

Jacob mumbled a "*cool*," mentally kicked himself,

and continued pushing away the guilt of cramming Sydney into the passenger seat.

His knees rattled against the glove box and his head brushed the ceiling when he sat up straight. He therefore slouched to an extent incredibly uncomfortable to look at.

Jacob had thought over and over about what he might ask, and what they might talk about but, as seconds ticked by, his enthusiasm for small-talk died. He tapped his thumbs on the steering wheel.

At least Sydney hadn't complained about folding himself up to fit in the car.

"No, I mean, it's back there," Sydney explained, pointing over his shoulder.

Jacob pulled into the next driveway and backed up to head back the way they came.

He pulled next to the curb, down at the end of the sidewalk. No later had the parking brake creaked on did Sydney jump from the passenger side door and make long strides down the icy pavement.

He stopped in front of number thirteen, where the plain, pale yellow townhouse unceremoniously met the sidewalk.

Jacob reached for his gear shift, but let his hand lay there another moment. Sydney was just standing there on the sidewalk, staring at his front door.

He pulled his hands up and, from where Jacob sat, looked like he was fighting the urge to wring them. Jacob reached up to turn the car off, instead, then jumped out his door and narrowly missed a speeding motorcycle.

Jacob slammed his door behind him and trudged up the sidewalk, where he stood next to Sydney, but not too close. Sydney didn't seem to even notice he was there.

Jacob did, however, take a pause as he faced the large metal door knocker head-on. The hardware was shaped like a bat, wings outspread with the ring hanging below in its feet.

Sydney held up one finger to silence him before he even spoke. Jacob swallowed whatever words hadn't yet formed.

Sydney took one giant step forward, grasped the bat

by each wing, and swung the whole piece up to the side, pivoting on the top screw. A tiny, shining bit of metal fell from behind it, onto the blank coconut fiber mat. He stooped to retrieve the key, unlocked the battered brass knob, and still hesitated.

Sydney took a small breath and turned.

"You want a drink or something?"

The dark doorway yawned behind him, barely containing his stature. He would have to drop slightly to fit inside.

Where Jacob expected a pool of warm air, or even some kind of light, he found what was closer to an open cellar door.

Sydney's hand strayed just inside the darkness. Jacob jumped as the overhead light inside came alive.

"Ah… sure. I've got time," Jacob answered and followed Sydney inside, noting the missing screw from the bottom of the bat-shaped knocker. An odd place to keep the spare key, sandwiched between iron and wood.

The air inside wasn't much warmer.

Sydney stepped into the open kitchen further down the right side of the room, with a long cutout in the wall angled back toward the fireplace at the left. A staircase jutted out from the long, white wall to the left, just beyond the fireplace, and on the other side of the railing was another empty space that ate the linoleum up in darkness.

Jacob stepped in further, but slowly, listening to Sydney open and close cabinets and drawers in rapid succession.

His hand slid along the back of the long white sofa, one of the only furniture pieces, and there was little décor. A black pinstripe armchair sat at the end of the glass coffee table, facing the wide window at the front of the house. A narrow wooden table sat to Jacob's right, just before the entrance to the kitchen, hardly big enough to eat dinner at, though there was one wooden chair.

That was it.

There wasn't even a roll of paper towels he could see.

Sydney pulled the black plastic electric kettle from its stand on the bar and set two pastel ceramic mugs next to it in plain view.

"Hey," Jacob started with a croak. "Is there something you're not telling me?"

Sydney looked up from the countertop Jacob couldn't see. He ripped two green paper tea bags open at once and dropped each one into a cup.

"We met twenty-four hours ago and you expect me to tell you my life story? *Less* than twenty-four hours, actually." Sydney's face didn't change, and it was becoming increasingly difficult for Jacob to tell what he defined as humor.

"Er, no. I just–you're being weird about this, is all." Jacob heard him pop the lid off the kettle before he swung the faucet lever upward.

Sydney then waved up and down his own body within view, in answer to Jacob's statement.

Jacob wasn't quite sure how to interpret the reply, but thought it best not to make further comments on his appearance. Welling anxiety pushed more words out anyway.

"Well, good. Self-awareness is good. I'm glad we've established you're a weirdo, I just–"

Sydney's eyebrows screwed up toward the middle and he looked back down to the faucet. He swung the lever in the opposite direction. That was the last straw Jacob could take.

"This isn't your house, is it?" Jacob blurted. He gripped the back of the sofa a bit tighter. Sydney's eyes flickered, but barely.

"Of course it is. Do you want tea or don't you?"

If Jacob hadn't seen him rip the top off the packets, verifying the seal, he would have declined then and there. He still hesitated to answer.

"You want me to show you where it says on my driver's license?" Sydney pressed. "It has a photo of me and everything." He set the kettle back on the stand and pushed the switch. The red glow blinked on in the distinctly greyscale room.

"This is your house just because it says on your–"

"I could also show you the closet, if you like. With

all the shirts that would make you look the size of a nine-year-old. And the skeletons. Let's not forget the skelet–"

"I *get it!*" Jacob interrupted, in turn.

Sydney opened his mouth to speak, but the words stuck in his throat as his eye line was pulled toward the ceiling. Jacob heard nothing, but held his breath as Sydney followed something with his eyes.

All at once, Sydney rounded the back end of the kitchen and darted up the stairs, only a "*Drink your tea*" left hanging in the air.

Jacob waited a long moment. The tea, regardless of type, probably wouldn't sit well with him after this. After another pause, he slowly crept up the stairs, stopping to peer around the bend of the empty landing before he ascended further.

The top floor was dim, but a window at each end of the hall illuminated the hollow passage in shades of yellow-grey. The sunny winter afternoon held more color than Sydney's entire house so far, if it really was his.

He acted like he had never been there before, searching cabinets and having to hesitate before even opening the front door.

The door to the left was ajar, and Jacob barely registered the bedroom. He crept a little further down the hall and poked his head into the door there, where he found another black armchair in the center of the room and every wall, except for the space with the window, covered in stuffed book-shelves.

A brief clatter made him jump. He placed Sydney in the bathroom at the head of the stairs, next to the louvered doors of the linen closet. There came sounds of more scrambling, like Sydney wasn't quite picking up his feet, but picking up something else.

The bathroom quieted and, as Jacob crept back toward the staircase, he was hit with a wave of guilt like a faint bad smell. It was unfair to demand Sydney tell him more, when he wasn't even sharing everything from Sunday. He would have to ask about The Cat and those text messages.

The most reasonable explanation was that Sydney

had been talking to an ex. Then again, that ex seemed angry, as exes were wont to be. And a little stalker-y from time to time. The question was, an ex-what?

That person also knew Sydney was talking to Jacob yesterday, precisely when they were talking. Maybe they were an ex that Jacob didn't want to know about, but Sydney might want a bit more context for their only previous interaction.

The bathroom popped open, Sydney speaking almost before he stepped out.

"I realize I've been rude," he said.

"Again, with the self-awareness. Bravo," Jacob answered, once he'd recovered from the spike in adrenaline. He clapped quietly with the tips of his fingers against the palm of his other hand.

In the corner of his eye, he noted the bathroom was also decorated in shades of black and grey. He looked with more purpose and found the medicine cabinet half-open, bare on the inside and a black bath towel hanging over the mirrored door that faced the sheer curtained window.

"There are just… a lot of personal things going on. And then, with the–" Sydney waved his hand dismissively, "–personal things yesterday, I'm not really thinking clearly. I had the class reminder in my phone already. My memory isn't great lately, which is embarrassing, and I–"

"Listen, I know you don't really know me," Jacob wedged in, "but you left me with a *really* weird feeling yesterday. Are you sure you're okay?"

Sydney fell silent. He relaxed his shoulders and slowly lifted his eyes to look at Jacob squarely.

"I passed out on the street and someone called an ambulance for me."

Jacob's eyebrows flew high.

"What? *Why?*"

"No idea. I spent last night and this morning in the hospital," Sydney answered. "Hungry and dehydrated, but nothing else they could see."

"They let you out of the hospital when you're having memory problems?" Jacob pushed.

Sydney's shoulders fell further.

"They didn't let you out, did they? They wanted to keep you in?" Jacob asked.

Sydney took a deep breath.

"I take it you don't have a hospital phobia. No one *likes* hospitals, but for some reason I apparently can't–"

Jacob scoffed and shook his head side to side. He descended the stairs in a rolling rumble.

He heard Sydney follow, again with that haunting, second set of footfalls Jacob had heard in the school stairwell, though quieter on the carpet. He didn't expect anyone to follow Sydney down, but the suspicion was there.

"Who's The Cat, by the way?" Jacob called back to his shadow.

"What are you talking about?" Sydney complained.

"It's not something you said, but I saw you were texting someone labelled The Cat in your phone."

Sydney pressed the fingerprint scanner on the back of his cell phone and opened his text messages as Jacob crossed over to the narrow dining table.

"Maybe they could help. I mean they didn't seem very–" Jacob's explanation cut short as he turned around. Sydney held his phone up for Jacob to see clearly there were no texts.

Jacob started to speak, but Sydney flicked a few screens over and displayed his contacts list. The screen was also empty.

Jacob stared at it some more. Sydney shifted his weight with an exasperated sigh. Jacob looked up to his face, then back to the phone.

"Oh. Okay, weird. But listen–" he said, following Sydney back into the narrow strip of the kitchen. The electric kettle had already turned off.

"If it doesn't get any better, go back to the hospital. I don't know what your money's like, and I'm not asking. But there's definitely something going on I'm not gonna get nosy… nosier about. And there's bill assistance stuff, especially for students.

"You're some guy I talked to for like… thirty seconds at The Red Cheshire, then ran off somewhere. I feel like I could have helped with something, so I wanted to make sure you're okay, at least. But *seriously,* I have limits."

He held onto each side of the countertop, waiting for a response. He then let go upon acceptance his words were enough declaration he was leaving.

Yet, he stayed there and watched Sydney slowly pour water into one of the mugs. Sydney sighed as he set the kettle back on the stand, and then turned.

"I know," he said quietly. "Thanks, though. I owe you a drink." He lifted one of the mugs, tag hanging out, and dipped it forward as if in *cheers*.

"Sure. Sounds fine. I'll see you around." Still, Jacob hesitated. He forced himself to turn on his heel and march back out to his car.

Sydney stood there in the quiet kitchen until the buzz of appliances rose out of the silence.

He took his mug of tea up both flights of stairs and into the bedroom, where he set it down on the desk. Tentatively, he pried the black textured laptop open and hit the power button before he sat in the vinyl rolling chair.

Relieved at the lack of password screen but disappointed by near total lack of desktop icons, he double-clicked on the web browser. From there, he typed *Sydney West Colorado Springs* into every search engine he could remember.

Everything he saw wanted to tell him about West Sydney, Australia. Then came Sydney Terrace, somewhere in Colorado Springs, which wasn't too far away from the house. There were over a hundred professional profiles with some variation of his name, which he skipped over entirely. Then came a travel website telling him he would travel roughly eight thousand miles from where he sat to his namesake in Oceania. And still, he pressed on.

Finally, his eyes began to swim and the text blurred, turning almost into totally different shapes. He pushed the chair back with his legs and rubbed his eyes with his thumb and index finger.

The floor creaked and ceramic gently met wood. He opened his eyes, then jumped and pushed his chair into the side of the bed.

A second human shape was reflected in the window above his desk, outlined by the hall light. His eyes were fixed on the tall, dark shape as he pushed back even further and crawled backward off the chair, toward the end of the bed.

Sydney took a deep breath, casting a glance down to his desk and back up. The second reflection was gone. He looked back down to his computer.

On the right sat the mug he'd brought up on his own. On the left sat the second, full of steeping tea with the tag hanging over the side.

THREE

Jacob trudged through the stone passageway between the school and dormitories. Eerie haze of the evening had already begun to gather, obscuring the lampposts as they rose into the air from deep snowdrifts. The orange-yellow lights seemed to float on either side of the path as he pushed on toward his home away from home.

After a few quiet, less chilly minutes to himself, he threw his parka onto his bed, over a pile of laundry, then turned to the blanket draped figure on the bed at the other end of the room. Not a muscle there moved.

He returned to the cluttered living room and fell backward over the brown corduroy sofa.

The person sitting inches to his left was wrapped in a cocoon of fluffy blankets, engrossed in an odd, pixelated game on the television. Jacob's glasses dropped down onto his forehead, but he left them there and took in the landscape of blurry squares.

The second roommate shifted under his cover, hardly a patch of skin to be seen. His brown hand slowly slid up and out of the cocoon like an enormous tongue. Jacob, sensing the approach, opened his mouth and hoped he wouldn't have any regrets.

A handful of potato chips dropped inside. A few bounced out and over his forehead, onto the floor.

"*Why I' a' squa'es?*" Jacob attempted. He received a blank stare from the carefully crafted breathing space.

Jacob chewed and caught his glasses before they fell the rest of the way off his forehead.

"Why is it all squares?" he asked again.

"You can't tell me you've never seen Minecraft."

Jacob pushed himself the rest of the way over the couch, drawing his legs down closer to his chest. He scrambled around in effort to sit up straight.

"Daniel, I was reincarnated from a golden retriever from 1996. What's a Minecraft?"

He finally sat up, eyeing where he might need to attack to liberate the bag of chips.

Daniel seemed to have caught on, and the long hand-tongue appeared again, this time with the chip bag at the end.

"That explains a lot," he answered.

Jacob happily accepted the bag, though all four of their eyes never left the screen. Daniel began piling dirt blocks together, and put a door on it.

"Tada. I told you, I'm a genius," he mumbled as he built a staircase to the top of his earthen hut.

Meanwhile, Jacob scanned the room and its existing clutter. Present were the usual piles of clothes, a few textbooks and many more printouts, especially under stacks of dishes but, peppered in-between sat pieces of robotics, computers, and traditionally bound paper books.

A plastic Iron Man gauntlet sat on the coffee table in front of them, nearly assembled, though nestled in a pile of wires and dishes.

An English, Engineering, and Psychology major all lived in the same dormitory suite. Whoever approved that housing arrangement must have wanted to go home on a Friday evening.

"Feeding time, is it?" A bony pink hand snatched the bag of chips away over Jacob's shoulder. Then again, Martin was positively tanned compared to the man, or whatever he was, who Jacob had left at the townhouse with the bat-shaped door knocker.

In his own context, with his hair bleached a platinum blond, arranged in a not-at-all presentable haystack, Martin was more of a Ghost to Sydney's Vampire.

Jacob flopped his head backward onto the couch.

Martin stood there grimacing, as if fighting a headache just between his eyebrows. After some pondering, Jacob decided the look was probably from him having been asleep or something like it just a minute ago.

Martin's attempted re-focusing on reality was centered, through his squint, on the ingredients list of the chip bag.

Jacob stared another moment, then dragged his eye line back to Minecraft. Somehow, Daniel had built a sword, and zombies were now in the picture.

Martin stood there, silent, except for a faint crackle every few seconds.

Jacob hesitated to turn back. There was just nothing

he wanted to ask, or thought Martin would actually respond to. In two short weeks, their interactions had been limited to witty banter in an ever-messier living room and asking each other to take out the garbage. Maybe there was more on the horizon, but he wouldn't push it.

Jacob squished his nose up at a faint, unpleasant smell. He remembered he should probably take out the garbage.

"Squire Daniel seems to be feeding his brain with highly educational material." Jacob tilted his head back. "Why don't you join us?"

"Thank you, but I'm on a diet," Martin sighed. He looked up at the television screen. His eye twitched and he looked back down at the bag, then to Jacob.

"Your phone woke up. Thought you'd like to check it, seeing as you're not exactly a social butterfly."

In his free hand he lifted Jacob's cell phone, which had been abandoned in the pocket of his coat. Martin had good hearing, or slept more lightly than he let on.

That, and he wasn't above rummaging in Jacob's coat pockets.

Martin passed the phone over to his waiting hand.

Jacob turned the screen back on with the side button and sat bolt upright. He slowly stood.

"Everything cool?" Daniel asked, breaking his attention away from the screen for another rare moment.

"Yeah, why?"

Martin, resplendent in his red-purple-blue striped flannel pants and rumpled tee, shuffled back toward the bedroom. Jacob internally repeated Daniel's question, this time silently to Martin.

Everything cool?

"Just checking," Daniel said with a shrug.

Jacob texted back to Katrina.

"Hey, have you seen a kinda goth guy around school? He's like… well, tall…" Jacob trailed off. Daniel paused the game and nodded sagely.

"Shut up," Jacob said.

"I didn't say anything."

Jacob rolled his eyes.

"Like, really tall. Jack Skellington tall. Really long black coat, black hair, might be Asian–"

"*Might* be?" Daniel cut in.

"I don't know, I gue–"

"Japanese?" Daniel cut in again.

"What?"

"Chinese? Thai?" he went on. "Koreo-Philippino-Saipanese?"

"I *get* it. I know, I'm white, with star-spangled eyeballs. He looks… a little like my girlfriend, so Korean, maybe? If you'd seen him you'd understand. Also kinda looks like… undead Neo, I guess? Isn't he Asian?"

Daniel's eyes widened, then squinted in the ghost of a smile.

"Uh, no. I can give him your number, though, if I see him," he answered.

"I–*what, no, I–*" Jacob sputtered and Daniel laughed. Jacob clamped his mouth shut. He instead moved for his bedroom door.

"You know what? I'm gonna go ahead and go. I'll be back later."

"I didn't mean anything by it," Daniel said with a frown.

Jacob looked down at his text thread from Katrina.

"No, you're fine, I just…" How to explain? Should he explain? "I'm gonna be out for a while."

He quietly stepped over to the door to the right-hand bedroom and leaned in as far as he could without fully committing to entering. Martin barely stirred from under his own cover.

He leaned further in but froze as a point of white light on Martin's open laptop screen caught his eye. When he looked, there was nothing there. The room shadows seemed deeper than before.

A little, purple vinyl figure of The Cheshire Cat on Martin's side of the room grinned at him, unwavering.

Jacob tore his eyes away.

He hooked a fingertip around the pocket of his coat and yanked it toward him with a *fwip*, then gingerly closed the door behind him, almost pulling it to latch.

"Do me one more favor, okay?" Jacob said in a low tone as he shoved his arm into his sleeves, one at a time. Daniel wordlessly flopped his own head, blankets and all, backward over the couch.

"Once you decide to unearth yourself and… become a beautiful butterfly–" Jacob paused to let Daniel's sudden wide, toothy grin have a moment, "check on Martin, will you? I understand tired, but this guy sleeps every moment he's here. Could be nothing, could be something, but I'm sure you and your…"

Jacob raised an eyebrow at the tv screen.

"…archer skeletons?"

"Yeah, they're skeletons," Daniel answered.

"You and your skeletons could take a moment to make sure he's still breathing."

"Will do. Have fun." Daniel turned back toward the screen and took the game off pause.

With that, Jacob slipped out the front door and shut it gently behind him. There were too many things he was feeling all at once, he deserved to spend some time with someone he didn't have to worry about, at least not in the same way. He was there to help as a privilege.

He pictured those black-brown eyes underneath straight, cotton-candy pink bangs, and his quick walk turned into a sprint down the empty dormitory hall.

The grinning robot added to the peals of mechanical alarms and fanfare in the arcade.

Jacob looked sideways, but Katrina hopped up and down in excitement. She stopped only to lean over and ready herself at the little square panel underneath the glass box. The metal door snapped up to present her prize.

She stood and jerked the bright blue cap off the clear pod. Once she placed the red plastic ring on her finger, she held her hand out to admire it.

"That looks like every cent you paid for it," Jacob laughed in the brightly lit dark. Katrina jumped and hooked her arm around his neck, a notable effort for a woman under five feet tall.

Jacob always thought he was around average in

height, but she made him feel how he thought Sydney must feel around regular sized people. He was hit with a pang of discomfort and grimaced.

Katrina gave him a peck on the cheek and dropped her heels back to the floor. She leaned back a little, seeing his face.

"You still feel bad about it?" she asked.

He still stared into the distance, not quite there.

"Why would I feel bad about fifty cents?"

She looked up at him, silent in hesitation.

"I asked if you wanted to go do something, because you told me you had a bad feeling about… what's-his-face. Then he popped up again. As long as he's not following you around with his problems, I really don't think it's worth it to bring him along with you and ruin a perfectly good cheap date."

He looked down at the tiny woman in pink, purple, and black. Her t-shirt had been purchased from the girl's section last Halloween, displaying a glittery bat across the front.

She looked up at him with dark concern.

"Okay, so, just answer this," she pressed. "How old does he look, to you?"

The strength test deeper into the arcade rang out.

Jacob yanked his attention back.

"I don't know. Mid-twenties, maybe?" Jacob said.

"And you see him in class?"

"If he shows up again, sure," Jacob answered.

"Okay. So, he's old enough to ask for help if he needs it, and if it has to be from you then he knows one place to find you. If he doesn't ask, it's his own fault," she said.

"Yeah, I know, but—"

"When I told you to trust your instincts a bit more, I didn't mean obsess over it. You've already done a lot to make friends with a guy who doesn't even seem like he's interested in other human beings. You want waffles? I want waffles."

She whipped out her phone and he watched her open the maps. Jacob took a breath to speak, but her thumbs were faster.

"This way!" She grabbed his hand and yanked him through the glass door. She led him all the way out into the cold and they were plunged into the outer glimmering dark.

The arcade windows shone with a rainbow of stars from the inside, but Katrina pulled him further down the sidewalk by both his hand and elbow. They entered the tunnel of warm white string lights and black lampposts cast in soft gold against the black sky.

Each post was still wrapped in the fluffy faux-pine garlands from December. Though several of the red plastic bows had been spent for the season, battered and dented, there were still enough left over to remind him he hadn't been able to see family for Christmas.

"We're not going to talk about it. We're here to talk about anything else. There's a great big world out there that doesn't involve creeps using you for rides," Katrina declared, taking two steps for every one of his.

He held her hand tighter and wrapped their arms around closer, then he shoved his opposite hand deeper into his coat pocket.

"Did you ask Martin why he freaked out about the room, yet?" she asked.

They started past the bus idling at the curb. The driver watched as they approached, expectant. Once it was clear they had no interest in the open doors, she pushed her lever to close them and lurched out of the slushy gutter.

"No, I didn't want to push it," Jacob sighed. "Especially since he's being kind of weird in other ways. As long as he doesn't get weird *at* me in our room, I'll let him work it out for himself."

"Oh, side note, did you call your sister about the Air BnB thing? Myrna said no to kids staying over," she detoured in topic.

"Yeah, she said she'd get back to me. Despite her need to plan like… six months ahead for everything, I think she'll be fine," he answered. Summer break wasn't the very last thing on his mind, but was definitely further out than the sudden influx of interpersonal weirdness with Martin or anyone else.

The street wasn't completely empty, but what little

commotion present was dampened by the layer of fog. Snow began to fall again, however lightly.

"Isn't he the psychology guy? Or is he the engineering guy you told me about? Who's the name of the guy who needed space for that work table?" Katrina asked.

"What?"

"Martin," she replied.

"Oh. Yeah, psychology," he answered. She looked down and checked the map again, the glowing box illuminating her face from below.

"Well, if he refuses to talk about anything, you could always ask to borrow his books to read up on him. Use some… reverse psychology, I dunno." Katrina shrugged.

They walked for another moment or two with nothing but the sound of their boots on the pavement and traffic in the distance.

"I think all his books are digital. They can screw around with pricing more that way. But yeah, I think he might get the hint. Where's waffles, anyway? You got me hyped up."

Katrina pointed just another block down and across the street. The Waffle House sign lit the night in yellow.

Jacob's stomach rumbled, or maybe it was just his imagination. Either way, he was then distracted by the tall stretch of black wool coat facing away from them, toward the next crosswalk.

Sydney stood there with a small pack of pedestrians, off to the side with his collar turned up and arms crossed.

Jacob leaned on Katrina and guided her up to the nearest crosswalk, rather than the one further down the sidewalk.

"Wha–w-okay, then," she sputtered.

"Did you talk to your boss?"

"Which one?" she asked, abrupt diversion forgiven.

The Walk light turned green and they crossed under the enormous red lights hanging above. Much more fog, and everything would swirl together in a strange, nightmarish remnant of Christmas.

They stepped back up onto the curb.

"The one with the n–" he barely got out.

"*Oh.* She said she'd consider new hours. Since I'm actually salon certified, I think the Cheshire would understand if I took full time there, instead. But seriously, I don't know if I want to work there, anyway, with someone who freaks out like that if I call out for actual reasons. I saw some signs in another–what's wrong?" Katrina screeched to a halt and took a breath.

"Nothing. Sorry. I think you should do what makes you happiest. Money matters, but so does feeling like you're–what is it?"

Katrina leaned into him even tighter and rested her face on the side of his arm.

"This makes me happiest."

Jacob was hit with a wave of warmth from the inside, like someone had flicked the light switch on inside his chest.

"And waffles," Katrina added and patted his arm. She dragged him through the bright white Waffle House portal. That warm light in his chest did not diminish.

Sydney was tired of waiting. With a quick glance up and down the street, he crossed with long, loping strides while the light was still red, if only to avoid the strangers who had begun to gather around him.

Nobody wanted to talk to strangers on the street corner, but it wasn't just that. A curious, crackling anxiety descended upon him the closer people physically stepped. That shadow he'd seen in his bedroom window was gone, but he couldn't banish the feeling he wasn't quite alone.

After around an hour, he couldn't take that feeling anymore, and slipped his coat back on before he charged out of the house.

For another hour Sydney had pushed onward, eyes sliding over bright signs and chalk sandwich boards that had seen better weather. While some doors were closing and lights began to switch off, restaurants added the glow of their own auras.

Signs that didn't disappear into the dark marked places too loud and made him wince, or full of too many people, which tightened his shoulders with vicarious claustrophobia.

Finally, after crossing yet another street in exasperation, he found vacant windows and a quiet doorway. He pushed through a set of glass doors underneath the yellow sign and a tiny bell jangled above his head.

He was briefly blinded with a bright white, but not like the hospital. He blinked away the pain and adjusted, presented with a curved glass case housing several rows of pies and cakes.

A second long, dark reflection drifted over the surface and he flinched. His eyes darted from side to side. Only he stood in front of the counter, and he was the only distorted stretch of black.

"Hi. Anything looking good?" came a female voice from behind the bar. He was still crackling with his discomfort, but so much less than before. He didn't raise his eyes, but noted her shape in the glass, quite different from whatever, whoever, he'd seen a moment ago. Her yellow dress and dark hair were all but a smear over the curve.

He looked up from the triple-layer chocolate cake with strawberries around the edge to face the brunette waitress. *Penny Lane* played from the speakers in the ceiling, but also sounded far away. He blinked and looked away, once he caught himself staring.

"I'm fine," he managed.

The waitress paused, then smiled in a lopsided way that embarrassed him, though he couldn't place why.

"May I have a menu?" he asked, stepping toward the row of round red bar stools.

"Yep! I'll be with you in a moment." She and her uncomfortable smile moved further down the metal-edged counter. The long bar was empty but for an elderly couple further down at the end.

Sydney took a seat on the stool, letting his coat out the back. The garment was long enough to make good effort toward reaching the floor, while his feet were still firmly planted on the black and off-white checkered tile.

She reappeared just as he pulled his phone from his pocket and pulled one glove off under his arm. She held an appallingly bright menu in her hand and he could see the letters strobe even from a distance as he set his glove down to pick up his phone.

"Hey, you seem really familiar," she said. He looked up from where she placed the abomination of graphic design and found her watching him, one hand on her hip. He lowered his phone and closed the banking app.

"Are you a student?" he asked. He placed her in her twenties, and no more. She was a bit old for the typical college student, but he hesitated to assume that meant her age started with three.

"No, afraid not. And I've never seen you in h–sorry, don't mean to get nosy."

"I just have that face, I guess," Sydney said with a weak flicker of a smile. He didn't have that face. At least he had one, rather than that dark outline earlier that was shaped alarmingly like himself.

"Maybe it'll come to us," he spoke again. "However, I don't think very well when I'm hungry, so I'll have anything you suggest."

Her eyebrows met in the center for just a second, then righted themselves.

"Alrighty. Are you allergic to anything? Anything else I should know about beforehand?"

He didn't blink for a long moment. He suddenly looked back down to his phone.

"Nothing that I know of. So, if we're both surprised, I won't fault you for it."

He looked over to the menu and promptly looked back up, outrunning a wave of nausea. The vinyl-encased menu in front of him swam in its rectangular confines like a medically induced Sesame Street hallucination.

"How about breakfast number six?" She leaned in further and slid her finger down the vaguely text-shaped list in front of him.

Sydney pulled off his other glove and set it next to the first on the bar. He again looked down at where she pointed, but his eyes refused to focus. A moment more and the dancing letters congealed a bit, almost like her finger pinned them reluctantly in place. He looked up the instant he recognized the word *pancakes*.

"*Yes,*" he answered.

"Okay. Do you want coffee or te–"

"Coffee," he cut her off.

Her eyebrows shot upward this time, then settled as she took a breath.

"We don't have decaf right now, sorry. I should have said."

"That's okay. I don't intend to sleep for a while."

She didn't look anxious as before, more like amused. The look was better than the awkward smile a minute ago, but he still fought a frown.

"I'll have that out for you in a bit." She smiled the first smile that didn't make him feel like he wasn't being told everything. He also noted her name tag for the first time.

Lindsey.

"Thanks," he breathed and looked down to grab his phone. He didn't keep an eye on where she was going, but she stepped first to the register several feet to the left and disappeared into the larger seating area even further down.

Sydney pulled up his banking app again. He didn't do anything, simply stared. His unblinking gaze bored into the screen, the look of a man who didn't believe what he was seeing, and wasn't entirely sure it wouldn't go somewhere if he looked away.

In the hour it took him to admit he needed some fresh air, his exploration of the laptop had greeted him with six digits.

Lindsey appeared again in his peripheral vision, just as he backed away from banking and opened email. There was nothing there, just like when he'd checked it at the house.

She hummed quietly to herself, in time with the end of *Penny Lane* drifting from the ceiling speakers. She pulled a battered credit card through the reader, pulled it out the end, and froze.

"Something wrong?" Sydney asked. His stomach growled, a curious, distant rumble of discomfort.

She slid the credit card back into the little black book, out of sight on the other side of the register. She didn't reply.

"Declined," Sydney stated. She didn't look at him,

but stretched her eyebrows up as far as they would go and gave a vague nod. Then, almost all at once, she reached over with her free hand and grabbed a coffee pot from behind the bar.

"Oh," he said. "Is the tab for a... date, or…"

With her other hand, she lifted a full plate from the back counter and set it in front of him. His last word disappeared into the void as the plate landed. He momentarily forgot he existed, at least as anything but a stomach.

A thought trickled back into his head, but he instinctively brushed it away with a frown. All at once, the thought re-inserted itself with full force. He pushed himself up on one foot and reached back for the wallet he was sitting on.

"As long as you can inform the card holder quietly, I can take care of the bill. I mean, tell them to check the card, not who's paid."

"Are you sure?" she asked. He stopped with the wallet half-open in front of him, between him and his late dinner.

Lindsey was back again to the weird staring.

He looked down to the plate in front of him and back up.

"I wouldn't offer if it wasn't okay."

Lindsey handed him the little black book from the first order. She swiped the original card out of the top and poured him a full cup of coffee with her other hand.

He flipped open to the inside of the book and looked over the receipts. Whoever this was, he really hoped the error was just an oversight or a changing due date. The order didn't even break twenty dollars.

Sydney snatched up the pen and scrawled a signature that somewhat resembled the one on his debit card. He set his card down on top of the book and handed the whole package over with both hands.

"You said you don't intend to sleep for a while. I know we don't know each other, but hey, I'm just a waitress. If you want to talk about anything, feel free. I'm here all night." She laughed a bit, still moving with muscle memory for the reading, scanning, and typing for what he'd just handed back to her.

She looked, then looked one more time at the receipts in the black book to make sure she'd read it correctly. He'd also filled in her tip.

"Give that back to them first." Sydney waved his hand dismissively.

He picked up the coffee mug and set it back down, torn between so many places to start with the full plate in front of him.

She quickly wrote on the receipt remaining in the book, then vanished back to his left.

Time seemed to skip and took the bacon, one egg, and half the stack of pancakes with it. He took a moment to let that settle, but couldn't resist reaching toward the mug once again.

Sydney sensed her approach, but stared into the brown liquid and the reflection of the lights above. Lines of the ceiling tiles wobbled on the surface and he fell into a slight daze.

She was right. On one level, she was just a waitress. He never had to see her and her awkward smile again if he didn't want. There were plenty of other places to get pancakes.

She was, however, still a person–one who said he was familiar.

"Something happened. Something really… difficult to explain. Even to myself," he began.

"Anything you want, or don't want to explain," she replied. He took a slow, deep breath and tapped his fingers on the side of the ceramic cup.

"I can't tell if it's the best or worst thing that's ever happened to me," he continued, and watched the sound send extra ripples over the cup.

"What do you mean?" Lindsey asked, and leaned further onto her side of the counter top.

He rested his elbows on the bar and rubbed his closed eyelids with both hands. Behind him, Jacob followed Katrina out toward the glass doors.

Jacob paused in shock at the sight of the back of the

black wool coat. That coat was everywhere, unfortunately with the owner inside.

He looked back and forth a few times between Sydney and the elderly couple further down the bar. A second later, he and Katrina were gone.

"Lindsey–may I call you Lindsey? Real question. I'm sure you get people you *don't* want to talk to in here on occasion, so I can appreciate the offer." Sydney dropped his hands as the bell over the door behind him began to fade.

"If I can call you Sydney," she said with a more pleasant, amused smile. That smile dropped.

"It was on your card. Sorry."

He decided against his mug and grabbed his fork again. And paused, considering.

"No, that's fair." He slowly got to work cutting the rest of the pancakes into bite sized pieces.

"Lindsey, there's simply…" he began eating again, speaking between bursts of shoveling food into his mouth.

"Never mind. It's not so simple, who am I kidding?" he said between quick bites, and went on. "I didn't ask for any of this to happen, and was *not* properly prepared. I didn't approve *any* of this, and I don't know what I'm expected to do with it. It's just ridiculous, the whole situation."

The food was almost gone. He picked up the mug. The coffee was going to be too hot, but the allure of the painful caffeine was the grounding he needed.

He took a small sip at first, then drained half the small cup with a wince. The lava finished falling and his sore throat started to cool.

"You said it could be good, though? Gosh, are you okay?" Lindsey rushed the last few words.

He placed a full hand over his mouth, waited, then dropped his hand with a small nod.

"Fine. It's fine. I just–well," he began again. He blinked once, slowly, then took another bite and swallowed.

"Who would you be if you weren't afraid of anything? Just don't–I'm not asking you to answer that out loud. What I *mean* is… it's not something people think about. Not consciously. If they do, it's too abstract to take any real steps, mostly out of the fear they can't be rid of even if they have an answer for that."

"If you woke up tomorrow with absolutely no consequences for being who you wanted to be, no fear of what people would think–no reputation, no pressure, all the resources you might need–what kind of person would you be? Because that's who you really are."

Lindsey was silent. He had the vague, creeping feeling the elderly couple at the other end of the bar were no longer speaking only about themselves.

The restaurant was empty enough, and he didn't mind being heard. It's not as if he was shouting, though he was definitely getting some attention.

"What could get rid of that, though? What we're afraid of? That's… normal. Everyone has it," she spoke. There had been enough of a pause, enough hesitation, she was obviously thinking of specifics that he was not, and probably would never be privy to.

"That's the question," he said quietly, with a long sigh. "And is it really worth getting rid of, or worth more to power through in spite of it all? I have found myself in a… situation that's not entirely… logical. I seem to have started over, in a way I'm sure not many people are allowed to. And now I have to figure out what to do with it. I'm okay, for now, but this is all ridiculous."

She looked away, her eyebrows peaking in the middle as she lost herself in thought. Sydney caught a long, dark smear on the chrome and instinctively looked over his shoulder.

A woman in a black coat strode by outside, a child latched onto each of her hands.

"One more question, though," he said and turned back. Lindsey stood up straighter, waiting. "Can I get my own check?"

"Right. Yes. One sec." She flew through the muscle memory one more time and set the little black book in front of him. By that time, he already held a few bills in his hand–tucked into his palm, but unmistakable.

He took a glance at the receipts, then slid his card in. She slid the card out and back into the reader.

"Once you find out how that works, let me know,

okay?" she said without a laugh, but a small smile. She set the black book containing his card back in front of him. He didn't raise his eyes to meet hers, but lifted the book at an angle away from her as he wrote.

"Unfortunately, that depends on who I turn out to be," he half-mumbled, then looked up. "But, you were right. That was a good choice. The food. I *definitely* like pancakes."

Sydney closed the book and set it back down. He pushed the empty plate away an inch or so, then stood, slipped his gloves back on, and vanished out the door even while buttoning his coat. He didn't truly run, but his legs were long enough for a quick walk to qualify as a dash.

"You doing okay, dear?" the elderly woman called from the other end of the bar. The peal of the tiny bell over the door only then faded.

Lindsey watched the empty doorway. The weirdos usually came out after dark. Sydney wasn't a wholly pleasant surprise, but not as bad as she expected for that time of night. The itch of familiarity lingered, which was the worst part.

"I'm okay, Dot. Thanks, though," she answered.

"Do you know him from somewhere?" the white-haired man sitting next to her chimed in. "He looks familiar, but I can't, for the life of me–"

"*Oh*, my god," Lindsey burst and touched a hand to her mouth. "I mean, I'm fine. I'm fine, I'm fine."

The couple looked at each other, and then back to her. She closed the little black book again and looked back to the door. She looked up to the ceiling, and perhaps into the divine spaces high above. She then looked back down and opened the black book to double check what she'd seen.

The fifteen-dollar order was graced with one hundred fifty dollars in bills, and she had completely forgotten about the faint, extra set of footfalls that had followed him out.

FOUR

Warm brown wood panels. Pale yellow light streaming through the windows. The smell of baking bread.

Sydney looked down at the dented wooden table in front of him, and couldn't tear his eyes away from his hands. They were his, but not quite right, though he was embarrassed at the concern. Everything else was so... right.

Something in him was a failure.

He shouldn't be here.

Sydney held the ceramic mug of dark coffee in his right hand and looked into the inky-black reflection. Then he looked again–and into the night sky he found there.

How long he stayed looking, he wasn't sure, only that he then recognized someone sat across from him.

They held a cup of coffee in their right hand, the other laid flat on the table, just as his did.

And he still couldn't look up to see who it was. After another quiet, sunlit moment, he came to the conclusion not only did he not want to, but probably shouldn't.

All he could do was look at that person's hands, or his own coffee. Watching the stars in his cup reminded him of something he couldn't place, and grew more distressing by the moment. He looked at the hands facing him, instead.

They were his. Even more his than the one wrapped around his warm, radiating coffee full of astral bodies.

The free hand across the table reached out and grabbed his wrist. His heart leapt.

Sydney heard a yell, only at the tail end recognizing it was his own. He flailed around with one arm out from under his blanket, waiting to connect with whatever was making that awful noise.

He swatted the little black noisemaker to the floor from the side of his desk and regretted his choice upon impact. Once the sound was gone, the regret passed.

Another moment passed as he still laid there in confusion. The clock was not what had pierced his comfortable bubble of sleep. He still had a sound to kill.

The cell phone vibrated and glowed white next to where the clock had been. He searched blindly with one long arm, hoping to make contact yet again.

Once he picked it up, he sat up and the blanket fell forward off his face. The phone alarm was going off–a generic and obnoxious digital-style klaxon, eerily similar to emergency sirens.

Sydney's eyes swung around to the alarm clock on the edge of the desk. He remembered it wasn't there, and looked down to the floor. It wasn't there, either. Only the phone clock blared, but his hand still hurt.

He looked back to the phone, silenced the alarm, then turned and placed each foot on the carpet. He took a few wobbly steps after the blanket fell away, and tumbled over a stack of books he only just then remembered moving into the bedroom the night before.

From a half-sitting tangle of limbs on the floor, Sydney rolled over in effort to regain his equilibrium. The world didn't spin, but was significantly less solid than it should have been.

While he waited for reality to re-congeal, he picked up the books that had scattered under his feet, reading the spine of each one as he recreated the stack. The letters still swam a bit, as in the menu the night before, but he focused more on his search.

He stacked them one by one and, when there were no more within reach, tipped himself over again to extend his reach and capture the stragglers. He then checked the titles and authors again and tipped all the way over, face against the floor, to investigate where the one he was looking for might have gone to.

The underside of his bed was completely empty.

Existence hadn't quite returned to full solid, but he pulled himself up on the edge of the bed and then to stand before approaching his closet.

The sliding double doors revealed a grey, white, one bright blood red, and a few black button-down shirts, as well as a four-drawer black dresser nestled inside.

Sydney sighed and pulled the third black shirt from the left off its hanger and slid into it one sleeve at a time. If the world wasn't going to stop sliding back and forth like a lake ferry, he'd have to simply deal with things as they were.

However that tall, dark Ghost chose to interfere, he would take that in stride, as well. He just hoped the dream was more figurative than coffee-induced premonition, but would settle for neither.

The walk to the university didn't see much change, though the crisp air washed over him and helped Sydney stay somewhat tethered to what was in front of him. He was also thankful there weren't many reflective surfaces along the way, once he moved out of the downtown area.

Everyone around him still crackled, the closer they moved toward him. Wide, open spaces were a reprieve that unfortunately didn't do much to satiate his curiosity toward that odd feeling.

Sydney still heard the occasional footfall that sounded a little too close and averted his eyes from any particularly tall, narrow shadows that reminded him of himself, but he was left mostly alone but for occasional looks of shock from those smaller than him–which was everyone he passed.

He didn't feel much more awake than when he tripped over his own books an hour ago. Though his head was blurry, he was struck with a wave of nausea and remembered he hadn't eaten breakfast.

Sydney stopped at the highway crosswalk, a hand to his stomach. He didn't feel hungry, just wobbly, and decided not to experiment with his diet for the time being. He would eat later.

He crossed alone and quickly crossed the heavily salted parking lot.

On a mission, and with the benefit of legs far out-reaching the typical stride, the only thing that really leapt out at him on the way down the sidewalk was a passing view of a few pedestrians walking the opposite direction.

Sydney recognized Ms. Diaz from yesterday's class, only as she passed and he glanced back to get a look at the back of her head. She seemed familiar, which was just as unpleasant a feeling as Lindsey telling him he was last night.

The woman next to her wore a white knitted hat with enormous fox ears framing curly red hair and round glasses sitting atop an olive-toned nose.

The second woman struck Sydney differently–not quite familiar, but someone of note. He stopped and turned back to watch them grow smaller in the distance, then disappear through the glass doors of the lobby. He shook his head once, then turned back around toward the library at the other end of the campus.

Sydney pushed through the hydraulic doors and was greeted with a rush of warm air that made his knees weak. Though initially pleasant, he slowed and stared wide-eyed into space as his head emptied of thoughts. He floated gently above his body, like a balloon tied to the top of his spine.

It decided to stay at a manageable distance from his shoulders, so he resolved to see if the problem would improve, and pushed on, wrapped in a warm, quiet blanket.

The library's cavernous ceiling gave room to floor-to-ceiling windows. His eyes traced the staircase in front of him as it rose and switched back the opposite direction. The second floor surrounded the rest of the building as a panoramic loft.

Everything from the colored squares on the carpet to the motivational posters stretched above provoked a dangerous comfort. Through the fog of whatever was happening to his head, he felt his face soften, but only just. The side of his mouth flickered upward.

His brow hardened again, though not as intensely. He'd forgotten why he was there. He'd taken an hour to walk back to school, and now he wasn't sure why. The urgency was still present, but without the coherent thought that had gone into the planning.

Sydney walked slowly through the quiet space and barely noticed the strange glances from students around him. He sat down on one of the pale purple, gently curved sofas and blinked slowly.

Only a moment, and he'd catch his breath.

He woke to someone poking him gently in the chest.

He didn't flinch, didn't jump, but snapped his eyes open to an instant glare. Jacob's roommate Daniel jumped back and pulled his hand with him.

"Dude, you okay?" he asked in his low library voice.

"People sleep in here all the time but, dude, you don't look okay."

Sydney realized he was glaring, then discovered why.

"I–" he slowly sat up from the purple couch, "have a headache."

He sniffed and rubbed both temples with the heels of his hands, closing his eyes. His hands didn't feel right. He remembered he still wore his gloves.

"Party hard?" Daniel laughed, still hanging back. Sydney looked up, glare rekindled. He had no idea who this was, but his glare would only serve as a test of this stranger's persistence.

The throbbing in his skull intensified and black spots invaded the edges of his vision.

"I need to go home," he mumbled to himself. He started thinking about standing up. Even the thought hurt. In spite of the threat of pain, he leaned forward and his rear end lifted from the couch.

So far so good.

"Hey, so… uh, I have class. You gonna be okay?" Daniel grimaced.

Sydney stood up faster than intended and a horrible television fuzz invaded his brain as the black dust encroached even further into his eyes. He stumbled half a step forward, but caught himself and rebalanced.

"Dandy," he vaguely heard himself say. Daniel stepped back as Sydney loomed up in front of him.

"You need a ride or anything? Seriously, you don't look okay. Anyone I can ca–"

Sydney raised his eyebrows. He turned and left.

Daniel too a deep breath, as if to yell after him, but caught himself in time.

Sydney threw himself through the front doors and, much to his dismay, was followed. The cold air numbed a small part of the pain, but his abrupt stop and spin did not.

No one was there with him.

Anyone I can call? whispered his thoughts, finishing that student's interrupted sentence. There was no one to call.

The distinct presence of someone following him out

still hung there, but he saw nothing. He revisited each tall, dark shape he saw in reflections. The feeling that one more person was in the room than there actually was.

He thought of his dream, with the coffee and his own hands, then pushed the thought away lest he stay there for too much longer.

Sydney would worry in the privacy of his own home. He set aside the subject. That is, until he recognized he was at the other end of the parking lot and didn't remember the trip there. Though unsettled, he was feeling better despite himself, probably because his soul wasn't plugged firmly enough inside his own body for the reality of the situation to have taken a firmer hold.

He was being haunted. For some reason, that Ghost was himself, or chose to look like him.

Sydney wandered over the nearest white-covered lawn, populated with blurry people and annoying sounds. The air was sharp, but the sun had come out. Bright yellow light glinted starkly off a tall black rectangle in the corner of his eye.

He ignored the vending machine, a visceral revulsion flickering over his face.

Sydney suddenly found an electric lime green bottle in his hand, the battery acid sliding down his throat. He retched, then turned to the nearest snowbank and threw up.

He lifted the half-glowing bottle again. Then took another drink.

This one ended up in the snow next to the first, though more made it down his throat. He screwed the cap back on and deposited the whole package in the domed concrete and metal trash can.

Whatever had happened last night with the coffee, he had no desire to try and repeat it with a new form of caffeine. Ignoring the sharp, acrid taste in the back of his throat, he turned back to the snowy lawns and parking lot.

The library would have to wait.

Whatever DNA-rewriting chemicals that had managed to soak into his system from the soda had apparently been enough to dispel his pain. However, he'd swapped his brain on fire for a little too far the opposite.

His pain was dulled, but a new fog had descended. Every thought in his head sparked with cold, clear electricity, confusing his senses even further. He stared at himself from the outside, willing his feet to move down to the crosswalk.

They didn't.

A few seconds after he stopped trying to move his feet, he started walking down the sidewalk. The crosswalk was here somewhere, he was sure.

Sydney had to be close. He let his eyes wander down each side of the highway. Everything fought for the forefront of his attention. The flurry of sensory input sent his eyes bouncing around to irrelevant objects and sounds, overpowering that electrical crackle he felt when someone passed by too closely.

A cold, hard object hit the back of his head and shattered down the back of his neck. He spun around, staring icicles, searching for whoever had thrown the snowball.

The first person he saw was Diaz, yet again. She laughed and pointed from the bench on the other side of the lawn. That woman with curly red hair sat next to her and didn't appear amused in the slightest. The ginger friend glanced down to her phone with a frown, then back up to him.

She turned to the woman called Diaz, who was still laughing, and gave her a rough shove.

Sydney fought the angry heat in his chest. He spun around and smashed his face on the back of a stop sign.

Hello, friend.

His feet vanished from under him and he sat down hard on the sidewalk. His elbow hurt, and he remembered he had used it to break his fall and prevent his head from being smashed on the pavement.

Sydney half-sat, half-lay on the sidewalk and put a hand to his nose. When he pulled away, there was some kind of red-toned oil there on this black leather glove. He looked it over, still feeling like the scene was all on a television screen complete with VHS artifacts clouding his vision.

He sat even longer, scrambling to keep ahold of whatever had just popped into his head. Was it important?

To who?

A pair of strong hands gripped his shoulders and he looked over to a face he didn't immediately recognize.

"Oh, m–are you okay? Are you–it doesn't look broken, you just look–I mean, never mind."

Myrna's friend knelt beside him. She glared at someone at his other side, who backed away and out of any recognition Sydney might have gathered.

She pulled a small plastic package of tissues from the army green bag at her side and he stared at the keychain-sized can of mace hanging there.

The meaning of her actions finally plugged into his head and he felt heat coming to his face. There wasn't much dent in his pallor though, out of embarrassment, he didn't meet her eyes.

He took and opened the tiny rectangle of tissues, grabbing half and immediately holding them to his nose to stop the blood flow. Thankfully he'd worn a dark shirt today. He didn't need anything else to help him look like a discarded Halloween prop.

"Can you get up?" she asked, crouching even lower next to him.

All he managed was a barely audible "*Ah...*"

She tugged on his shoulders. He wasn't sure whether he'd gotten to his feet on his own or if she'd actually managed to pull him up.

"Yeah, I'm... who are you?" He pulled the tissues away and immediately replaced them. In addition to everything else, his stomach was now attempting to slide around his insides.

"I'm Skadi. A friend of Myrna." She made a vague gesture back to the bench where Diaz had been sitting. He didn't look to check.

"You should probably go to Urgent Care," Skadi spoke again. Her eyes, looking up at him, were wide and round, but still seemed to pin him down. "I can take you. I really don't think you should go on your own."

"I'm fine. I-I'm not going anywhere but home," Sydney stuttered. He pulled the tissues away one more time, hoping the flow had stopped. It had slowed, but hadn't ceased. The deep red-purple still crept through the white.

"You can't just sit around here with your blood gushing!" Skadi pled.

Struck with fear, Sydney swept the back of his hand over his forehead. There was no blood on his glove that wasn't on the leather before. She was exaggerating.

He was angry.

"I'm going home, Skadi. I feel like someone's playing hot potato with my brain," came his stifled voice through the pressure on his nose. He sensed someone approach and quickly looked over his shoulder. No one was any closer. Struck with fear she might understand what he'd just done, he turned back around and his head throbbed louder.

Skadi sighed, then rolled one shoulder.

Sydney scanned the surrounding lawn. No one was throwing snowballs anymore.

A dark-skinned man behind a comically small wall of snow pierced a hole and looked through. A tall, thin man with white hair poking out from his grey hat stepped over the wall and poured an armful of powdered snow on top of him. The first man yelled gibberish.

They didn't seem the types to have committed the hit and run.

Thankfully, they were also too involved in whatever had just happened in their own game to gawk at Sydney standing with an increasingly bloody tissue held to his nose.

"Where's your car?" Skadi finally spoke again after letting him visibly drift in his thoughts.

"My–I don't have one," Sydney confessed. "Why do people always assume I have a car?"

Skadi tensed. She gave that strange, half-amused yet concerned smile Lindsey had given him in the diner last night. Skadi's expression morphed and she shot a stern look far behind him. He turned again.

Myrna still sat there on the bench, far away. Once she knew Sydney had seen her, she stuck her tongue out. She jumped up and walked away toward the nearest glass doors.

"Fine, then. I'll take you home," Skadi declared.

Sydney was silent, but his jaw clenched.

"Do I *look* incapable?" Sydney burst. He remembered he held a wad of bloody tissues to his nose and his default skin tone was as if someone had poorly colorized a silent movie.

Keeping a hand on his nose, his eyes darted around the nearest parking lot, looking for the vehicle he might pin on the woman in front of him.

There were plenty of sedans, a couple jeeps, and a motorcycle at the other end of the lot. The Kelly-green Jeep the furthest away displayed a garland of red silk flowers hanging from the rear-view mirror.

Skadi tugged on his sleeve.

"I'll be right back. Don't go anywhere."

She darted off back toward the bench Myrna had vacated. He watched in horror as she picked up a large white motorcycle helmet from under the seat.

That was enough for him to spin back around and look to the motorcycle in the distance, sizing it up for just how worried he should be. His confidence in his safety did not increase, and he could have sworn someone nudged his side.

He looked over and Skadi approached him from behind. There was no way she had been close enough.

"Come on," she said in passing. Against his own internal screaming, he followed. Halfway there, she popped the helmet on over her red curls and he spotted a gold metallic wing on each side.

Up close, the motorcycle was more of a large bicycle with armor. A big red Suzuki *S* burned like an ember on the contrasting blue paint. The nebulous buzz of dissociation fought for dominance with the more tangible anxious backflips in his stomach.

"If Myrna wasn't being so crabby, I'd ask her to tell you about me riding to school all December, when my Jeep died," she said from inside the helmet. She then squinted at him a little strangely and didn't seem like she was fully listening to anything around her. The expression was a welcome break from her looking at him like he was helpless.

"I just don't see how–" Sydney started.

She pulled the helmet off her head and shook out her

hair.

"–this is supposed to be safer than me walking home on my own," he finished. Part of him was still preoccupied with what he'd heard upon smashing his face on the metal. It felt important, but had instantly left his head, nothing but frustration in the hole where it had been.

"Because, even going slow, it's going to be faster and safer than you walking along the highway and getting lost in the cold. Which is a possibility, yeah, after what you just did," she pressed. "What's your address?"

"I'm not going to get los–"

"You don't want to go to Urgent Care? Then you're going to humor me." Her eyes sharpened.

She held the helmet out to him.

"*Fine*," he said as he took it with his free hand.

"West Barrow Street. Number thirteen. It's yellow. If we arrive at the hos–U-urgent Care instead, I'm walking even if it's further away. And it'll be your fault."

"Deal," Skadi agreed.

He jerked the helmet roughly in an attempt to flip the visor up. He failed.

Skadi gripped it again and pulled the piece up with her other hand.

The next step was a mere matter of a small sleight of hand. He released his nose, shoved the helmet on his head, and replaced the wad. He cringed at the moist tissues, now cold.

For a moment he lamented his lack of vehicle, but a visceral repulsion swept that feeling away. His attention turned to sounds of traffic in the distance. Screeching of tires. Rumble of countless engines. He might have imagined the cascading crash, but the weight in his stomach was real.

Skadi pulled her bag open again and handed him the other half of the tissue package.

With that, Sydney turned around, shoved the soiled tissues into the nearest trash bin, then jumped on the back of her motorcycle. She had already mounted, skirt bunched up around her knees to display thick, knitted stockings.

He held his nose with one hand and gripped the pointed back of the seat with the other. The vehicle did feel more secure than expected, which had admittedly been a low standard. His knees stuck out awkwardly as he lifted them to what he hoped was the footrest, so he placed his feet back on the ground.

"You don't need one?" he asked over her shoulder.

"I'd rather loan it to the guy who could have a concussion. I know the risks of my brain decorating the highway."

She turned her key in the ignition and the bike rumbled to life, vibrating beneath him. He gripped the back of his seat and lifted his feet onto what he hoped weren't moving pieces.

"Don't be morbid," he said, his own voice echoing both in his head and the helmet. They pulled gently from her parking space and sped up. The engine rumbled louder.

"Says *Prince Evanescence*," Skadi mumbled.

"What?"

She didn't answer. They pulled confidently, but gracefully, out of the parking lot and joined the sparse traffic. From the start, she kept to the decidedly blacker stripes of road.

Behind them on the lawn, just behind the stop sign that would hold the print of Sydney's irritated face in spirit, Daniel hid inside his tiny snow fort. The grounds consisted mostly of the front wall but, if it survived the night and morning sun, he had bigger plans. He was an engineer, after all.

But it was a toss-up, particularly if Martin decided this was the best way to interact. He didn't object, but Martin's participation caught him off-guard.

Daniel laid behind the soft white barricade, covered in powdery snow, waiting for the next assault. He'd been waiting for a minute, now that he realized, and started to wonder if Martin was still there.

Daniel had thoroughly reprimanded him for cheating, but that didn't mean he had any intention to stop.

Martin wasn't exactly being social, but he wasn't ignoring him so much, either. Any excuse for a break between classes was a good excuse. Maybe he'd even get to the library later, as he hadn't been that day.

Daniel looked over the edge of the wall. Martin nailed him in the forehead with an exploding ball of snow.

"*What* have you been doing for like, five minutes?" Daniel yelled, wiping moisture off his face with his mittens.

"Not important," Martin non-answered, watching the rapidly diminishing shape of Sydney and Skadi.

He truly hadn't meant to hit Sydney, but wasn't sure what came over him. He didn't even know the name of the man he'd hit, or even mind that he hit a stranger, however familiar.

The impulse to do so was the unsettling part. It was almost as if someone else had made the decision, and he was merely the opportunity.

There was no immediate stage of waking. For how tired he'd been the last couple days, Sydney had never woken up fully rested. Except for now.

His eyes sprang open to the white ceiling of the dim room. Shadows moved across the expanse, accompanied by the airy breath of cars passing outside.

Though waking was sudden, he took another second or two to recognize where he was. He sat straight up and turned to examine the couch beneath him.

His black wool coat was spread out between his solid black wardrobe and the solid white of the furniture. He dropped one unshod foot off the edge, and then another as he turned toward the coffee table.

His hands were covered in deep red smears, as expected. His pile of bloody tissues sat on the table, along with the fallout from the open toilet paper roll. The deep red was confined to those two locations, as far as he could tell.

In the slight blue tint of the closed sheer curtains on his front window, his blood looked almost purple. He looked up from his hands and sighed into space.

Hello, friend, echoed in his head–a memory from earlier rather than a repeat. He looked back and forth anyway. His eyes told him he was alone, but the feeling someone watched was still there.

Sydney jumped up, rummaged in the kitchen for a moment, then bounded up the staircase to the second floor.

He flicked the light on in the large, greyscale bathroom.

The floor was made of tiny grey tiles in shades different enough to resemble cobblestone. A black hand towel hung neatly over the side of the long bathtub behind him, across from the back window.

He leaned forward to the medicine cabinet and pulled the towel covering it to the side with one finger. Once he confirmed his suspicion of the long smears on his face, he reached over and flicked the light back off.

The grey glow from the small window was more than enough to see what he was doing without casting things in sharp relief.

Sydney pumped the soap dispenser, turned on the faucet, and began scrubbing his hands almost before water began to fall. His face would have to come last, he decided, and glanced up as the towel slipped off the end of the mirror.

His heart stumbled. He quickly opened the cabinet door all the way, mirror away from him.

Hello, friend.

What friend? Why at collision with the stop sign?

It was almost like a voice, but there was no sound. Like a thought that wasn't his own, blossoming into his head as naturally as one meant to be there. And then it came again.

Hello, fr–

He spun around and, like a real voice, that thought was cut short. Like he expected, or rather hoped, there was nothing there.

He slowly turned back to the mirror, his body before his face, and closed the door on the empty cabinet. Its generic contents had been emptied into the cabinet under the sink. After yesterday's surprise in the mirror, he didn't want to have to pick it all up again.

This time, he knew what was coming.

There he was again, just the two of them.

The man in the back looked at him with an exasperated grimace, then crossed his arms.

"What?" Sydney said aloud. "What could you *possibly* want?"

The blurry shape of the Sydney behind him shrugged and looked out the window.

"*Fine*," Sydney said, then opened the mirror door wide again. The man behind him looked back with a glare just before he was out of sight.

Sydney's ears itched as he thought more about that *Hello, friend*. Like a radio playing in the distance, he reached for some semblance of meaning, but it never locked into place.

He scrunched up his nose and resisted the urge to pull the mirror back in place. His nose was sore, but not broken.

Sydney swept a wet hand over the lower half of his face, all but erasing the burgundy marks there. He swept once more, then scrubbed at any place that was rougher than he thought he should be.

Once the color stopped coming away, he felt his face again. He'd have to shave soon. There were no shaving supplies in the cabinet underneath or behind the mirror, and he cringed at the idea of finding a drugstore. The mouthwash and painkillers under the sink were useful in the right situation, but utterly pointless at present. He still didn't know what that goop in the little tin with the scratched label was, either, but it smelled decent.

He rinsed his hands off again for good measure, shut the faucet, and dried off on the black towel hanging from the ring before he quickly descended the stairs. Hearing no ghostly footsteps, he still paused momentarily as the ceiling creaked. Only after, he continued.

Spotting his coat, he snatched it up and reached over to switch on the floor lamp before he dropped onto the couch. Surprised by the recoil of the couch spring, he stood again and settled back down after the shock faded.

He flipped his coat around, running his hands up and down as much surface area as he could. When that completed, he closed his fingers and ran then through each seam, pressing each hem edge together.

The hem stitches were slightly raised, and he ran his fingers over them again just to be sure. He tipped his entire coat over and his wallet and phone spilled out of the pockets, but he ignored them in favor of examining that line of stitches directly under the lamp.

The stairs creaked. He looked up with only his eyes.

Nothing came of it. He looked back down.

Sydney was somewhat abnormal, in more and more ways in addition to size. If that coat fit him perfectly, there had to be a reason.

He flipped the coat back around to the collar. Light from the lamp cast a shadow across black stitching on black wool, just under the collar, between the shoulders.

M.A.D.

The coat was custom made, and signed.

There came a few knocks at the door. He dropped his coat and glared over his shoulder, staying there for another long moment.

The knock came again. He stood and stepped over the back of the couch, then opened the door.

Jacob lifted his hand away.

While Jacob jumped back, Sydney's eye line snapped down to a pink-haired girl who held up four plastic grocery bags that definitely looked too heavy for her.

"Hey! You still alive, or what?" she burst.

Sydney opened his mouth to speak, but Jacob opened his mouth at the same time. Katrina stepped under Sydney's arm and into the living room with her bags.

Jacob coughed.

"We-I thought you could use some–" he began.

"Charity?" Sydney interrupted.

"Can I call you Syd?" Katrina called from the kitchen. She had let go of all her bags and, behind his back, began stocking his fridge. Jacob's eyes widened and he made a little hop-skip before he pushed past Sydney to join her.

"No," Sydney shot.

"Why not?" Katrina complained.

She rounded the couch and discovered the highly reactive spot in the springs. She bobbed up and down on it on her knees as she talked, leaning over the back of the couch. This tipped her forward every so often. Sydney's heart jumped each time.

"Because my name is Sydney, is why," he huffed. "Who are you? And how old are you, anyway?"

Katrina stopped bobbing and threaded her fingers

together. She sat back on her heels and looked up at the colossal man, her face cold and stony.

"Katrina. Jacob's mine. Nine hundred and twenty-two," she said. Sydney stared back down at her, trying to pry open a crack–any crack–in her expression.

He took a breath, then hesitated. He took a breath again.

"Why do you look familiar?" His voice slightly cracked.

"She's *twenty-two*," came Jacob's voice from the kitchen. Empty grocery bags surrounded him. He was nearly finished emptying them into Sydney's refrigerator and cabinets, avoiding eye contact all the while.

He did, however, step into view over the kitchen bar, folding up the thick plastic bag against his chest.

"He needs groceries, not his head messed with," Jacob called out to her again.

"God knows he doesn't need it," he then muttered under his breath.

"And what, exactly, gave you that impression?" Sydney called over his shoulder with a stern look. Jacob tried to keep eye contact, but gave in and stooped out of sight again.

"When I was here yesterday, and you were rummaging in everything. As my mom would say, no wonder you're so skinny."

Sydney stepped forward to the front end of the tiny kitchen. Katrina, behind him, bounced herself incrementally around to face forward on the couch and put her feet on the floor.

Sydney drummed his fingers on the edge of the counter top. He stood halfway into the kitchen, looking back and forth from the new contents of his fridge and back to Jacob. He lingered longer on the contents of his fridge, then snapped back to the blond nerd on his kitchen floor.

Subconsciously, Sydney reached for the coffee cup Jacob had brought. The unnerving, cheerful red Cheshire cat grinned at him from the stamp on the side before his hand covered the logo.

"You really don't need to do this," Sydney said

quietly. His ears perked at the sound of a zipper, and he looked over his shoulder to find Katrina had opened up her tiny white backpack.

Sydney's volume hadn't been enough to hide what he was saying, but he felt like he should drop his tone anyway.

"You're sure trying hard to stop me, I guess I won't," Jacob said and reached for the gallon of milk. He slid it in next to the carton of eggs and pile of vegetables.

"I don't–you don't even know if I can drink that," Sydney complained, this time louder.

"And you're also not being the kind of specific of someone who cares. So, until then, you just keep your little list of things to yourself. If you don't end up wanting something, I'll take it. If it doesn't fit in my fridge at the dorm, Katrina will take it." Jacob stood back up from the lower shelf.

"Because, as creepy as you are, using privacy as an excuse for… whatever is actually going on, I do like you, and I want you to have things in your fridge. I've had people do the same for me, so I want to pass it on."

Sydney set the paper coffee cup back down and, with the same hand as a prop, leaned on the counter.

"Jacob, you don't have to bring me groceries. I'm fine. *Really* fine," Sydney attempted to clarify.

"Okay, listen. I get that you can probably afford this, but you strike me as the kind of guy who forgets to buy groceries for three weeks, then calls for delivery using a voice changer."

Sydney cocked his head. Jacob held eye contact, but his eyes had widened, as if realizing what words had left his mouth.

"If you don't want something, bring it to school and I'll take it back. No waste. Don't sweat it."

Sydney didn't get much of a chance to home in on what he saw in Jacob's face before the student stepped past him, back into the living room. The look verged on regret, but not quite. It was almost like anger.

"So, you feel any better?" Katrina looked down at the knitting in her hands, and back up even as she still clanked away softly.

"It was just a nosebleed. I'm fine," Sydney answered. He touched his nose to check for any residual deep red, but came off clean.

"I mean with all that stuff from the other day. Jacob said you were having memory issues. After hospital stuff. I didn't know about the nosebleed. Glad that's gone."

Sydney took a moment to pace his breathing. He still smelled blood coming from somewhere–the faint whiff of copper.

"I'll be right back," he fired, despite effort to calm himself. He dragged Jacob by his flannel collar, straight to the back door and outside.

The window rattled and the handle clicked shut. Katrina sat alone in the living room, staring at the door, her yarn idle in her hands.

"I'll just wait here, I guess," she said, and continued knitting.

"Okay, *we need to have a talk*," Sydney burst and let go of him.

Jacob faltered back and away, down the thin strip of snow and gravel that was only technically a yard.

"Can we do it in a temperature that at *least* starts with three? *Jeez*."

"Why are you here?" Sydney ignored his protest.

"Because your fridge is empty, and apparently so is your head," Jacob replied. "I don't care if you can afford it, because *also apparently*, it doesn't do much toward actually getting out and getting food. Now let me in, I can't feel my–"

Sydney had only to sidestep and put himself between Jacob and the warmth of the house.

"Okay, after you clarify this for me," Sydney began. Jacob glanced to the door behind Sydney and back to his face.

"*Brand* new year, I find myself in The Red Cheshire, leaving behind a nearly empty house except for wall-to-wall personal library with no rhyme or reason to the collection but I *still* feel like something is missing. Some random English major with an annoying compulsion toward curiosity in the face of stranger danger–" the sides of Jacob's mouth flicked upward, trying to hide an amused smile as he looked away for a second, "is the last person I know I talked to before going down like a ton of sticks–"

"Bricks," Jacob said.

Sydney glared.

"Bricks. When I wake up and see–from a nightmare I can't *even* explain, I have no idea where I am, why I'm here, or *even if my ID is real and if this is my house!*"

"What?" Jacob paled.

Sydney felt his shoulders had tensed up near his ears. Try as he might, he couldn't seem to unfold himself. There was also a strange ringing in his ears and that smell of blood hadn't gone away.

Jacob reached forward, hesitantly. He gently placed a hand on Sydney's shoulders and helped ease them back down.

"In the hospital," Jacob began, holding the welling panic behind his eyes, "they should have asked you all those boring questions you see in movies. Like where are you, what's your name, who's president, all that. Or they wouldn't have let you go, even if you wanted to."

"I don't remember any of that," Sydney answered. His shoulders were down but threatened to raise with his tension. Instead, he found himself looking toward the sky, trying to keep his breathing even.

Jacob let go of his shoulders.

"If you're joking, I swear, I'm gonna–I'm–"

"What, clear out my fridge and leave?" Sydney interrupted Jacob's stuttering.

"I don't *know* what I would do, but you had *better* not be screwing with me," Jacob finished. He then placed both hands over his eyes, under his glasses, and dragged them slowly down his face, stretching as he went.

"You really need to go back to the hospital," Jacob spoke again. Sydney felt every bit of his shoulders and neck tense again.

"No."

"I don't care about whatever phobia you have, or think you have, or however you're trying to rationalize not wanting to go back for some other reason–this is… this is…" Jacob trailed off as he looked away.

"I know," Sydney finished.

Jacob rubbed his eyes behind his glasses with both hands again.

"The Cat, though," Jacob blurted.

"I don't know how to find–"

"No, listen to me." Jacob clasped his hands together in the cold, trying his best to warm them up. There were more important things than getting back inside, for the moment.

"Whoever that was said you were trying to go on… well, honestly, they were making fun of you and said you were trying to go on some kind of *adventure*."

"I'm having *so* much fun," Sydney muttered and ran a bare hand through his hair.

"So, you were trying to do something during or after you went to the Cheshire. Something that another person you knew said was going to go badly. That's all I've got. Well, that and they called me a Hipster Boy."

Sydney rubbed his forehead and took a pause.

"Why would they… they know what you look like?" he spoke slowly.

"They were probably there. They're probably here somewhere. Simplest explanation. But beyond that, I got nothing."

They stood in silence. Sydney paced his breathing.

"I… I appreciate you making an effort," he started. "I really do. But I'm not asking for more help. I'll look more. Something will come up. I just–I don't have anyone… who…"

Silence fell again.

"I assume you've already looked in there, right?" Jacob pointed down to his left. Sydney jerked his head to the side and his eyes flew wide open.

He stared down the little yellow storage unit extension with the white painted door.

"Apparently not. But you're wrong. I'd like to be there to help," Jacob said with a sigh. One side of Sydney's mouth flicked more up than usual.

"At least when I don't have homework, and I am *not* on call," Jacob continued. "You *can't* get mad at me if I say no to something, all right?"

Sydney was still frozen, staring at the storage unit and perhaps into it for how long he held his gaze. Jacob's words sank in and he turned forward.

"We barely know each other, so you have full license to tell me off," Sydney answered.

Jacob crossed his arms and looked him up and down.

"Good. One more thing, though. I hope you've realized I'm obviously going to talk about this with Katrina."

Sydney pulled a sour look.

"She doesn't gossip–she doesn't tell people's secrets. And yeah, I tell her a lot of things, because I trust her. People think she's not smart, or that her brain's full of glitter or something, but I trust her and so should you, at least for this. She knows when to take things seriously. She also thinks about things differently, so that's another brain working on things. At *her* convenience, too."

Sydney cast his eyes up toward the piece of winter sky above them. The white had begun to dim, with the faint haze of sunset at one end. He didn't look down as Jacob continued.

"I swear, I have no idea what's going on either. I just tried to help out, like I've always been taught. That's it. I don't know more than you, though you look like some guy who's probably got more than a few health issues, and probably grew up reading *Sherlock Holmes Meets Dracula* or something."

Sydney's mouth flicked upward more visibly as he looked back down.

"I have an idea how you can help in the short-term," Sydney said quietly.

"Is it something I can do before my hands fall off and I can't write my next paper?"

Sydney looked back up to the darkening sky. Though the sky was still mostly white, everything on the ground seemed to have started the night without permission.

"You brought your phone with you? Out here? Sydney asked.

Jacob pulled his phone from his jeans pocket.

Sydney grabbed Jacob by both shoulders and, staring intently, switched places with him. Jacob quickly defrosted from tensing his shoulders, but it was only displaced by the heat of embarrassment. At least he was closer to the door now, if anything got weirder.

"I need you to take a picture of me. You're right. I have, well… a *look.* Take it to reverse image search. Any social media you want. Just–"

"Just don't talk about your memory, or your weird hospital phobia, or… yeah. Around anyone who doesn't know already. Right. Okay. Got it." Jacob raised his phone and opened his camera.

"Step back a little more," he directed. "And while you're at it, tell me why you can't do this yourself in the mirror?"

He accidentally took a photo at the same time Sydney stepped back. The result was a particularly eerie blur that was more shadow than human. His eyes were a little too bright, as well.

Sydney stepped back again, but there wasn't much left to go. He ran up against the faded grey wood of the slatted fence, just inside the last pale beam of sky.

Jacob raised his phone again and snapped a clearer picture of Sydney, this time head-on.

At first look, all the shadows in the photo were wrong–too deep, and split into one for each side. Sydney was also a much healthier color all-around. Jacob looked down at his phone again and the differences had vanished.

"Even if I took it in the mirror, I don't do very well with extended screen time," Sydney said. He took half a step forward.

"Wait, stay like that," Jacob commanded.

Sydney stood back up straight.

"Keep looking at the door," Jacob said. "You mean like screen fatigue, or what?"

Sydney did as he was told and Jacob stepped to either side of him to snap two more photos, one of each side of his face.

"Something like that."

"Just being thorough," Jacob explained, then locked his phone screen and moved to shove it back in his pocket. Sydney jumped forward and caught him by the elbow.

"Let me see," he mumbled and offered a hand. Jacob unlocked his screen again. Sydney swiped through, then snatched the phone out of his hand entirely.

Before Jacob could push through the surprise, Sydney had sent the photos to himself in a text message.

"You could just, you know, *ask*," Jacob complained.

Sydney only glanced up and back, then added his phone number to Jacob's contact list. He was about to hand Jacob's phone back, but pulled back to select the default icon depicting a cartoon of a human skull before he returned it to its owner.

Katrina wound up the last bit of purple yarn as they both stepped stiffly back through the door. Knitting needles were already back in the small backpack between her feet and the purple scarf was wrapped around her neck.

Once she reached the end of the yarn, she dropped the ball neatly into the mouth of her bag and yanked her hair out from under the scarf.

"You know," she began, "your back door is *really* thin, probably because of that janky cat door."

Sydney frowned but said nothing, waiting for elaboration. She had probably heard all or most of their conversation, despite his psychological need to separate himself to have it.

Jacob was adamant she was trustworthy. He was biased. Sydney would have to decide for himself.

Jacob came through to the living room from the far end of the kitchen. He looked to Sydney, then back to Katrina. Whatever Sydney had just heard gave him a look as if he'd just noticed a spider that was too close.

Sydney again laid a hand on the small, white paper coffee cup Jacob had brought him along with the other two for themselves. He absently brought it up to his mouth.

"*Don't* you look at me like I'm about to sell you to The Enquirer," Katrina spoke again. "I agree with Jacob, though. You should probably suck it up and go back to the hospital. Though, my theory is that it's kind of like drunk past you is messing with the now you, isn't it?"

Sydney erupted in a fit of coughing, alternating in gagging a moment later. He doubled over and set the coffee cup roughly back down on the counter. So roughly that the lid popped and a ring of brown liquid jumped out onto his hand.

He stumbled deeper into the kitchen and there, he found the sink. He spit out the coffee with a retching that turned the stomachs of his visitors.

Sydney's hand found the sprayer attached to the chrome basin and pulled it out with a creak. He washed his mouth out with cold water and sprayed more water on his hand. But, no matter the water pressure, he couldn't get rid of that feeling of impending doom. Exactly the same kind he felt when his grabbed his own wrists in his dream.

Katrina stared, mouth agape.

"Hey!" Jacob burst.

Surprise prompted Sydney's sudden stand. He narrowly missed the corner of the cabinet with his head. The adrenaline dampened the panic, but it was still there in the background.

"Are you okay? It says it's," Jacob said.

"I'm just–" how would Sydney explain? He couldn't bring himself to lie, but now was no time to talk about the dream, or his increasing haunting. Plus that auditory hallucination that wanted to be his friend. He wasn't even friends with himself, he didn't have the energy for the specter.

"Not in the mood," he finished.

Jacob cocked an eyebrow, watching Sydney's eyes move from Katrina's face, to his, then back.

"What mood is double espresso hot chocolate with whipped cream and a shot of cinnamon and peanut butter?" Katrina blurted.

"Is this hypothetical?" Jacob turned.

"What are you talking about?" Sydney said at the same time.

Katrina's eyes widened as they both locked onto her. She clenched her jaw under the spotlight.

"What?" She paused again. "It's what you got Sunday. Figured you… might be… interested." Her voice trailed off.

"That sounds disgusting," Sydney said with a twinge in one whole side of his face. "Is there any other room in my house you'd like to… reverse-ransack?"

Katrina snorted.

Jacob lifted his coat from the wooden table behind him. Katrina pulled the straps of her backpack up higher.

"You should really go back to the hospital if you can," Katrina said. "That or lighten up on the drama."

Both men turned toward her in surprise. Jacob's feet began to point toward the door. She froze and turned around.

"If you're not going to look into where the actual answers may be, don't complain about not finding them. I'm not trying to be harsh, I'm just trying to say what Captain America over there,"–she pointed just for a moment at Jacob–"is trying not to say because, dude, you're huge and probably a fifth cousin of Gomez Addams. There is definitely something wrong. Sometimes, you just have to bite the bullet and do something you know is good for you."

Her eyes flicked over to Jacob and back.

"Then what you thought was the worst day of your life is over and you can get *on* with having the best ones."

Sydney lifted his hands, energy pent-up to gesture as he spoke, but he felt himself shaking. He put his hand back down.

Jacob took a few more steps toward the door, looking back and reaching toward Katrina to follow him. She did, but only about halfway there.

Sydney found his voice.

"I'd like to talk to Jacob for a minute. Again, I mean."

Jacob only shrugged behind her.

Katrina noted her boot had come untied. Instead of kneeling to tie the lace, she lifted her foot and balanced on one leg.

"Alone. Not long, I promise," Sydney added. Either the room was getting warm, or he was.

Katrina finished with her boot and put her foot down.

Jacob squinted at him.

"Outside?" Sydney spoke again, a little higher–a little more forced. "Out front."

"Sure," she said, then locked eyes with him and, with one hand, pointed two fingers into her eyes and then his.

"As long as you remember I'm twenty-two."

"Deal," Sydney conceded and stepped forward.

From Jacob's vantage, Sydney's long step looked more like a lunge. Jacob jumped back and drew his hands up closer. Sydney didn't appear to notice.

Katrina escaped Sydney's rush due to her head coming well under his shoulder. She grabbed the back of the wooden chair, spun it around with assistance of her well-placed kick, and sat down to face the door.

That was just about the time it shut, Sydney casting one last, apologetic glance back inside.

Katrina didn't cross her legs this time. Instead, she planted them firmly on the linoleum and stared, waiting. Her phone sounded with a magical trill and she took it from her jacket pocket.

She didn't recognize the number, but the icon was already filled in with a black and white drawing of the Cheshire Cat.

How's it hangin'?

Her eyebrows screwed together. She tapped a message back with both thumbs.

New soul, who dis?

No answer came for a full minute. She closed her phone screen to black and shoved it back into her pocket. The room was silent.

To her dismay, the front door was better insulated than the back.

"I'm definitely going to pay you back. I'll find the receipt, if you left it," Sydney insisted, leaning into the open Mini Cooper door. He touched the back of his hand to his nose again and looked down. The smell of pennies was still there, with another wave hitting him once he stepped outside. At least there was still no blood.

Jacob faced forward, toward the windshield. He

reached up and turned the ignition, then glanced up to Sydney, to the passenger door, and turned back to the shadow over him.

"There's part of me that wants to say no, but honestly," Jacob paused just a moment as he fought the urge to look away, "I'd really love it if you did."

Sydney blinked twice a little too quickly, then his face stilled.

"What, strapped for cash?"

"More or less. There were some fees that were pulled out for something I got Katrina for Valentine's Day, and I didn't time paychecks super well. My card was kicked back last night, when the check came back. I fixed it this morning, hence me actually being able to get groceries, but it's tight."

"Double groceries," Sydney corrected him.

Jacob raised an eyebrow and one side of his mouth flipped up.

"Do you really think I got you double my groceries? No wonder you're so–"

"*Don't say skinny,*" Sydney cut him off. Jacob rocked with a low-bubbling silent laugh.

He didn't look at Sydney, but faced the passenger side window as he pushed up from his seat. Access to his back pocket then wide open, he pulled his wallet out.

In that brief moment, Sydney replayed his previous night in a manic flash of images. Lindsey looked worried. The pancakes were delicious. The coffee was perfect, but something was wrong. He focused in on the coffee a little harder, holding the door shut against replaying that dream with the table, coffee, and hands.

He failed. The hands grabbed his again.

Hello, friend, came like a poorly-tuned radio into his head.

He jerked and pulled himself out of a daze just as Jacob sat back down.

"Hey, you okay?" Jacob's voice wafted up to Sydney's ears, far too distant for just the seat below him.

"Yeah, I'm–" Sydney had fallen back into a daze.

Before Sydney's eyes was a freeze-frame of the coffee cup in his hand. The coffee was in perfect focus and, if he didn't suspect now what he didn't expect then–the innocent beverage of seeding whatever nightmare he experienced later that night and possibly even his half-awake manic reading–he might have had a craving.

The moment stretched on while Jacob stared and waited for Sydney to respond.

Sydney watched the hint of pink at the corner of his field of vision, a reflection on the chrome-edged bar at the Waffle House last night. The edges of his frame weren't blurred, as his vision in reality would have been.

The pretty pink smear instantly focused, though he knew for a fact he hadn't even looked that direction any reasonable amount of time the night before.

A figure with pink hair was getting ready to pass behind him. His face began to melt back into the frigid air of the reality in front of him.

Sydney blinked and was back.

"You date Monday nights?" Sydney asked.

"We try not to constrict a committed relationship to just socially acceptable days of the week," Jacob replied with a smirk. He dove into his blue and red leather wallet as he turned all the way to face Sydney, legs jutting out of the warming bubble of the car. The Captain America shield was stuffed with receipts and cards of every kind.

Sydney took a breath as Jacob pulled something out. It was a small white business card, which he held out. Sydney let out his breath and took it.

"George Lorem," Sydney read aloud.

The car was heating up despite the door sitting open. Jacob reached over and turned the engine off.

"Yeah."

Sydney looked it over for a few more seconds. An ink drawing of a tree was printed next to the text, at the left. It reminded him of something he might see on an inspirational poster in the school library.

"*Clinical psychiatrist.*"

"Yeah," Jacob said again.

"You don't believe me?" Sydney looked up from the card. He tried to look angry, and tried to pull his eyebrows down, but wrestled with the real contender.

His eyes glazed over slightly and he felt the corners of his mouth try and drag his whole jaw downward. His shoulders began to follow suit.

"No, I *do*. I believe you. There's no reason not to. He teaches at school, but he's also open to talk. Kinda free appointments, and I know he's referred people to some other places. I just think…" Jacob trailed off and looked away for a second.

"I just think if you're not going to go back to the hospital, you may as well talk to *someone*. Maybe to help you get over why you *really* won't go back, or why your brain's on the fritz, at least if it's not medical. And as much as I like you so far, that *ain't* me. At least right n–"

"For an English major, your grammar can be atrocious at times," Sydney muttered under his breath, looking back at the card.

He turned the card over, then back, and looked back up from it.

"Fine," Sydney spoke again, fighting the congealing awkwardness with a grimace and glance away.

Jacob turned back to face the steering wheel.

"Great. Tell Katrina to get out here, so we can stop hassling you."

"Are you going to let me say what I came out here to say?" Sydney asked quietly, still holding the card out in front of him.

Jacob glanced behind Sydney, and Sydney turned to see Katrina, bent over with her nose pressed up against the house window. She grimaced. Once she knew she'd been spotted, she stood back up and threw her hands up.

"Never mind. I'll save it for later," Sydney said and moved to turn all the way around. Jacob jumped up and caught him by the sleeve.

"No, just make it quick."

Sydney tried to put his hands in his coat pockets, only to realize he wasn't wearing it. He didn't feel cold. He surreptitiously threaded his fingers together to see if he felt cold there. His skin was cold, much colder than he felt.

There would be time to figure that out later. He instead sighed and his shoulders fell from sudden anxiety to resignation.

"Depends on if you like Sherlock jokes."

Jacob blinked a few times in confusion. He sat down.

"Only if they're funny, I guess," he answered.

Sydney checked over his shoulder and found the front window vacant. He leaned closer to the car door and swallowed, looking across the street to the glowing windows instead of down at the man in the car.

"I can't think of any way to make this shorter, so please, don't interrupt," Sydney asked.

Jacob stared a moment, then shrugged in answer.

"You're a college student working at a used bookstore, typically on the weekends, which means your best date night is during the week," Sydney began. Jacob's eyebrow raised, but Sydney went on after a pause.

"You have far more keys on your key ring than I'd expect for someone of your age and part-time work, which is a book store called *The Iliad*, judging by your employee key tag, which, yes, is the name I looked up. Paychecks like that can't be what are keeping you at the University, so you must have help from somewhere else.

"That could be anything from loans, to scholarship, to particularly invested parents," here he noted an additional flicker in Jacob's eye, but pressed on, "but none of those, except maybe parents, cover enough to keep you with a haircut like that, or allow you to buy things for your girlfriend that would put you over your balance or credit limit without realizing, but have you fix it the day after. But you're still working, so you at least know the value of not relying solely on someone else's money even if you accept their generosity, as the case may be."

"Therefore, you're either supported by your parents, have a scholarship or some type of loan, or a combination. Regardless, you still work more than necessary and don't want to settle for the bare minimum for your own input, which would be easy for someone in your situation."

Sydney chanced a glance down. Jacob's eyebrows had lowered, but he didn't seem upset.

Sydney looked away again.

"You know what you're doing, even if you're

nervous about it, and you work harder on top of that to get more of what you want instead of just asking other people to give it to you. But that still doesn't mean you're totally extravagant. Except for the car, maybe, which is totally inappropriate for Colorado Springs, which I'm thinking means you're from further south in Colorado, if not New Mexico."

Sydney caught his eyes drifting to rest on the back wheel of the car. The Mini Cooper had snow tires, but the whole vehicle was ridiculously small for the kind of snow drifts he'd seen in a few short days.

"I think if you were the kind of person to complain about the consequences of your own choices, you would have by now. When I'm not looking directly at her, Katrina *does* look like she's fourteen, but you've obviously been good to her and allowed–supported her being, um..." Sydney glanced over his shoulder to the window. It was still vacant. "–the way that she is."

He turned back.

"I don't like people on the whole. I do remember that part. But, whatever's going on, whether I knew what was going to happen or not, I'm glad you're... here. And tell whoever taught you to care about people, to help out when you can, I'm saying thanks. I don't know what you saved me from, but I have the feeling you did. Just by, you know..." Sydney looked further into the sky without moving his head, searching for the end of his sentence.

"... not...seeing... me like... other people do."

A small but distinct smile blossomed on Jacob's face, replacing a ghost of sadness.

"Did Katrina's ex like the whole–" Sydney's eyes widened, as if just realizing he was still speaking, "Magical Girl look, or did that come out when she met you?"

Jacob's eyebrows arched high, reaching even further for his hairline.

"I don't even know what that means–is that an old kids show or something? How old *are* you, anyway?"

Sydney's gaze bumped just above the top of the car, his brows low. He reached back and pulled his wallet out of his pocket and bent the front fold back toward the street lamp above.

"Twenty-six," he answered.

Sydney was saved from the exponential growth of Jacob's laughter as Katrina yanked the front door open.

"You guys done with your bro time so we can all go home?" she called from the doorway.

"Is that what that was?" Sydney rushed in conclusion. He finally looked back down to Jacob, but once again deflected his eye line to something inconsequential across the street.

Katrina appeared at his side, right under his arm. He lifted his arm further and stepped back across the sidewalk.

"Yeah, we're fine," Jacob said. "That was weird, but we're fine," he said quieter, only within Sydney's hearing.

Katrina looked from him, to Sydney, then back again. She rounded the front of the car and jumped inside the passenger seat. Jacob shut the door.

Sydney's shoulders relaxed and, just in a few steps, he was back at his front door.

He turned back around upon hearing the buzz of the car window rolling down.

"Sydney?" Jacob called. Sydney clenched his jaw.

"Get some sleep," Jacob said. "I'll see you later."

The little car closed back up and pulled away into the deepening night. After a moment, the buzz of the window came back.

The last thing Sydney heard was Jacob shout "*And eat some food, gosh dangit!*" with an arm pointed out the driver's side window. He pulled it back in before the car turned and he and Katrina fully disappeared into the dark.

After that, Sydney was left alone on his own doorstep. He looked both ways down the street, then turned the handle before he pushed the door back open.

The overhead lighting burned his eyes. He flipped the switch off and, in the shades of deep blue-black, reached over and turned the floor lamp on and glanced over to where his coat sat draped over the back of the couch.

He started to feel a little cold again, but there was still no explaining why not earlier. The coat wasn't that special, only that it was wool and actually fit him.

You lied.

The silent intrusion sparked his jump. He smelled the faint scent of blood again and checked his nose on the back of his hand. Nothing new.

He looked out across the living room, long shadows cast across the carpet radiating out from the floor lamp.

"No, I didn't," he muttered to himself, crossing the living room with long strides. He opened the back door and stepped out.

By omission.

The two words stuck to him like invisible mud. He fought a shudder, only partly from the cold, and resisted the urge to look back into the dark house. He instead stepped up to the attached storage unit.

The space wasn't very large, but the closed door made it look positively enormous. He tried to turn the handle, but it wouldn't budge.

Sydney folded himself up in a crouch to get a better look at the underside. There was no keyhole.

He stood back up and took a better grip. Even through extra force, it didn't give way.

He ran back inside, holding his breath involuntarily, then reappeared as he let it go. He slid each black leather glove onto his hands and hoped they weren't particularly special, because he was about to–it still didn't budge.

Temper flared. He planted a swift, hard kick next to the doorknob on the wall. The mechanism rattled deep inside.

Sydney reached forward again and opened the door toward him. He forced it open even further, against the gravel and snow drift at the bottom edge.

Inside hung a giant black bicycle with deeply treaded tires and dramatically curved handlebars. Though gigantic by usual standards, the bike was probably about his size.

The rest of the space was empty, uninsulated walls with a concrete floor. There wasn't so much as a cobweb.

He shut the door firmly and stalked back inside, the ember of his anger still glowing.

His stomach growled and he growled, himself. There was nothing more immediate than giving in to its demands for food.

Though he was definitely in favor of exploring the kitchen, he was a little wary of diving deeper into whatever Jacob and Katrina had left him. The threat of low blood sugar far overshadowed his concern regarding any lurking allergies or religious predisposition.

The coffee at the end of the counter was off-limits, sadly. He eyed it, sizing up the risks to benefits.

Drink me.

"Shut up," he hissed.

The potential for another escalation to his hallucinations, and any potential nightmares, tipped the scale to negative.

Even before his decision fully solidified, he reached forward to the tall paper cup. He would banish it to the depths of the sink drain, where it belonged.

A presence wafted through the living room from nowhere, and he resisted the urge to turn around. He'd see nothing through the kitchen cutout or, worse, he'd see something.

His plan for the *Red Cheshire* cup changed once he lifted. The cup was empty.

Instead, he threw the whole thing in the trash can under the sink, with his blood-tainted tissues. If Katrina wanted his coffee, he'd have to come to an arrangement for her to take the ghost, as well.

FIVE

Sydney didn't know what he–or rather his body–was used to, but liked to think waking up before 10AM was out of the question. That is, as long as the thought gave him an excuse to roll over as soon as he realized he was staring at the light through the bedroom window facing the street.

He started turning over, but a strange disturbance pulled at him, like something he'd forgotten but hadn't quite made it into the deep, dark hole inside his head. He reached over and lifted his phone to look at the screen.

8:00 AM.

He unfortunately jolted awake.

In one last effort, fueled purely by denial, Sydney rolled back over anyway. Not as awake as he might have been, he rolled the wrong direction and crashed onto the floor, tangled in his blanket. The padding muffled a few pointed, shortly-spelled words regarding the situation.

There was no going back after that.

After ten minutes of exploring the kitchen, interspersed with several attempts at reading labels and feeding his anxiety with a good portion of them, he gave up entirely. How did normal people make these decisions?

There was something his breakfast distinctly lacked. Dedicating himself to what that might be, he scarfed down a single banana and bowl of instant ramen.

He wasn't full, but set the dish in the sink and ran the water. He watched the crystal-clear stream in the indirect light, letting his mind wander.

The Ghost was still there, but thankfully silent.

A hint of bitter displeasure lurked in that dark space further back in his head. The place where that second man came from, grimacing over his shoulder in every reflection and shooting silent quips.

Sydney turned around to where the coffee cup had sat the previous night. A ring of brown was all that was left outside the trash can. If his theory was correct, he had been moments away from another dream of that comfortably warm coffee shop and uncomfortably cold hands.

Still, the incomplete breakfast nagged at him.

He rummaged the cabinets again, shuffling cans and

boxes. Once he started to suspect the search would still not yield anything remotely satisfying, he started loading the groceries from the cabinets and fridge back on the counter.

His head was starting to get fuzzy, so he wasn't entirely sure why he was wasting his time. The shelves were quickly bare and he gave in to disappointment.

The last of the tea had been used when Jacob brought him home. He didn't remember throwing the box out, but it was nowhere to be found.

Sydney threw his hands up and surveyed the kitchen. Ideas were popping into his head more and more, but no big revelations about what was missing. At least this one, he could control.

He pondered over the word while pulling up the maps on his phone, searching for what Jacob had called The Red Cheshire. Control was often a matter of perspective. If he could regain enough perspective and therefore control, maybe he could even repeat whatever he'd done with his memory last night and rewind far enough to–

Sydney dropped his fork. Metal rang out against the linoleum as it bounced, echoing through the open floor plan.

He shook pins and needles from his hands as he bent over to retrieve it, only then remembering he hadn't been holding a fork a moment ago. He had lost his train of thought, especially as he spotted the bent reflection of two of him on the stainless steel.

He rinsed out the bowl that had also appeared, and set it in the sink next to the first. He then rounded the counter top and ascended the staircase, four steps at a time.

Whatever was happening, something was reaching out for attention. Like that hand in the dream with the starry coffee, he heard sounds in the dark, coming from something that wanted to be found. That Ghost looked like him, moved like him, but didn't quite sound like him. He could go even crazier pondering all the potential explanations for his long string of quiet horrors.

The best place for that was in an empty house with not much else going on. He would, therefore, have to change that.

If he was going back out into the world, especially

back to the hospital, something aside from his black t-shirt and skull-polka-dot-shorts would be in order.

Martin rubbed his eyes with one hand and saw fluorescent stars. The lights in the library weren't normally so bright. Everything had been turned up past the end of the dial–sounds, smells, and even the weight of his own shirt collar.

He stood alone in the quiet, grey-carpeted aisle and waited to see if the throbbing pain at the back of his head would dull if he kept his eyes shut. It didn't, and he was forced to open them again.

There were things to do. He'd had worse.

He hefted the textbook higher under his arm, then squinted through his fingers as he unlocked his phone with the other hand.

Martin moved down the row, not bothering to look at the titles as he passed.

He stopped and took his list from his pocket again, looking it over. The letters swam and he looked up, directly into a red and white spine.

Hesitantly, he pulled. The front cover was disappointing and he pushed it back in, only to pull out another book just a foot or so to his left.

Thinking In Pictures.

Martin looked it over, shrugged, then added it to the books pinned under his arm. Sometimes, he just couldn't get the right words out of his head, and keep inside what he wanted to stay there. If there was a way to blurt out his pictures instead of having to get into complicated language, things could be much easier.

He looked back into the vacant space and found the shelf also vacant on the other side. That enormous man with the black coat was there, sitting at one of the double-sided desks. His eyebrows sat low in one hard line and, though his mouth was mostly the same, it turned down just a little bit at each end.

Martin fought an amused smile. It wasn't funny, but it was, really. That spark was the same little piece of glowing mischief that told him to throw the snowball. Try as he might, he still couldn't feel guilty. Which made him feel guilty.

Such was life.

Sydney made the mistake of pulling the hospital forms out of his pocket before taking his time looking through shelves. That gnawing, hollow feeling expanded as he stared at the Social Security Number field.

He couldn't bring himself to check himself back in, so he requested his records instead. There had to be something useful in there. Unfortunately, though he was amply supplied with the printing fees, there was no information for him to use for the request.

Tingling, fuzzy creatures were nearly gone from where they had crept up his arms as he'd stood in front of the receptionist's desk. His mouth was still cold, but the quiet of the library had dispelled all but the last traces of his welling panic.

Now it was just the usual, which he'd experienced as long as he could remember. He hated himself for leaving behind the discharge paperwork he was sure he must have been given. There wasn't much to remember from Monday morning, except the panic as he woke up, his rush from the hospital and then, later, his deep, bubbling anger at his phone alarm and the relief of cold air on his face as he walked to school.

That is, other than the vague impression he was seeing something in the mirror that wasn't supposed to be there. Maybe that was the initial drive to check himself out, now that he had a little clearer perspective on what he might have seen.

He held up his insurance card next to the forms, scraping up the nerve to give the company a call. What would he say, though? He couldn't remember any of his information, so please give it to him?

On a hair-thin hope that he might come upon the information later, he accepted the hospital forms and made his way to the university. One disappointment might have a chance of negation in remembering why he was so obsessed with visiting the library yesterday.

Sydney sat frozen there at the double-sided desk, the form suspended between his hands, his insurance card on the surface and his face squashed into a grimace.

A white blur planted itself at the opposite desk, like a seagull on a railing. Sydney wouldn't have been so alarmed, had it not spoken a second later.

"Havin' a problem?" Martin burst.

Sydney yanked his hands back, nearly crumpling the paper completely. Though quiet, both the words and paper were still almost above the polite noise threshold for the library.

"No, I..." Sydney un-crumpled the form, spreading the paper down on the desktop. He slid back toward the grimace, but unwrinkled his face once he realized the skinny, white-haired student was still staring. Unblinking.

"Sorry, have we met?" Sydney asked. The fuzzy, tingling sensation began creeping back, this time into his eyes. He had a little trouble focusing on the person in front of him. There was no crackle, but he wanted desperately for him to go away, like bad news might spill from his mouth any moment.

Martin blinked. His phone buzzed and he pulled it from his pocket to check the message. His face fell.

"Nah, sorry," he said and rose again. Before Sydney could say anything else to him, he strode away and back into the sea of aisles. The blurriness in Sydney's eyes was gone.

Sydney still watched the spot where Martin disappeared into the psychology books. His brain ticked a few times, waiting for something to make sense. The forward student was a distraction from the hospital forms, but a welcome one despite discomfort.

Left alone, Sydney reluctantly looked back to the paper, but didn't really see what was printed there.

That thin man was slightly familiar, but not in any way that excited him. He left a bad taste in Sydney's head. Maybe it was the way his voice didn't quite match up with who he was.

Sydney jumped up and wandered in the opposite direction of whoever that was he almost met. If he was going to remember what he absolutely had to find here, he would probably benefit in actually taking a look.

Other than the suspicious sense of ease being surrounded by so many books gave him, it was a library. Just a library. Nothing in particular jumped out at him, at least on the second floor.

He quickly descended the staircase and strode over to the help desk. He lied that he'd forgotten his password.

The elderly librarian with enormous glasses nodded silently from behind the service desk. His stunned, owlish expression was particularly due to his thick glasses lenses.

"Can I see your ID?" the bow-tied man asked.

Sydney produced his license after a moment of fumbling with his wallet. The old man typed on the computer.

If there was an account in his name, there could still be nothing. Or there could be a lot of things. That, or an infuriating mix of potentially invaluable, yet possibly completely worthless things.

Sydney's head hurt again.

He stopped drumming his fingers, once he identified where the sound was coming from.

The librarian wrote slowly on a sticky note. There was definitely at least something.

He handed the paper to Sydney, who took a deep breath. Whether the situation was intentional or not, he felt his pre-Monday self laughing at him, just as Katrina had suggested. That would account for the double he had been seeing, though he seemed perfectly sober, and then some. And there was something much more complicated than simply being drunk going on.

ColoradoDracula

Password reset: 1111

Sydney thanked, then walked away from the staff.

Halfway to the purple couches, his senses twinged with the faint, anxious thought that he was being looked at. He fought the urge to turn around, unsure of what he would find there, if anything, as usual.

Instead, he hooked his hand around the post at the bottom of the stairs and swung around to the rows underneath the loft deck.

He was rewarded with 813-843–general fiction. Where he kept looking didn't matter, only that he did.

He swung around the corner again and pulled the first interesting-looking book he saw. The volume was little, yellow, and he bent the soft cover back and forth in his hands. The letters on the cover still wobbled a bit in his eyes, but calmed down the longer he looked.

Anthem.

It wasn't what he was looking for, but wasn't in his collection at home. He'd keep it with him for a while.

He spun the book around in both hands and was hit with another pang of recognition. His attention jumped to a wide, black spine on the lower shelf, right down around his ankles.

He hesitated.

Sydney bobbed a couple times, then forced himself down. His scarecrow frame folded into a sudden crouch he wasn't looking forward to undoing.

He pulled the book from the bottom shelf.

Sadly, his attention was commandeered once more. Myrna's black boots were there on the other side of the shelf. Sydney froze, holding his breath.

The boots moved. Sydney moved.

He stood straight quicker than he should have and saw spots. Visual distraction was the only thing that turned internal expletives into external sputter as he turned around.

Myrna stood there.

He held the big black book between them, along with *Anthem*.

"Heya!" she said loudly. Brightly. Unlike he expected from all experience with her from a distance.

She kept her hands clasped behind her back and looked up at him. She said nothing, but rocked back and forth heel to toe.

He let his eyes lower slowly, but barely met her eyes before he grimaced and spun away on his heel. Her boots were heavy enough for him to hear her as she followed.

"So, I've been meaning to ask you," she started, pushing her strides to get in front of him. She took three steps for every one of his but, even then, didn't seem to get the hint he was trying to outrun her without running.

"What is it you *do*, nowadays?" Myrna finished. The question pierced Sydney so sharply, he stopped in his tracks, silent. He took a breath, then let it out.

He then turned to her.

"What, *exactly*, makes me look so different from you people? What do *you* do, Myrna? Other than laugh when people you've never met get hurt, and constantly look like you're about to slash your ex-boyfriend's tires?"

That cheerful spark in her eye was doused.

"It'd be my ex-girlfriend, if anyone."

"*Oh*," was all he said.

They stood there for an empty moment.

Sydney turned again and left her without further word. Something felt *off*, and he looked down to where he carried three books–*Anthem*, *Octavian Nothing*, and *The Little Prince*, a thin, blue hardcover children's book.

He looked it over, front and back.

There were those distinct footfalls again, and Sydney turned to her.

"*Why* are you talking to me?" He threw his hands up, a book in each. *The Little Prince* was gone, the same yet opposite problem of the second bowl of instant ramen appearing this morning.

He hadn't yelled, but had still blasted her at a volume not at all suitable for the middle of a library. He looked back and forth at his hands, instinctively looking for the third book though knowing he wouldn't find it.

The Ghost still screamed for attention, and was getting cleverer about it. He'd have to read *The Little Prince* sometime soon.

Myrna glanced to either side of him, this time wider, taken aback by his outburst. A little pink had risen to her tan face.

"Well, a pretty good person asked me to go ahead and give you a chance. *Sorry*," she said with a cock of her head and a hand propped on her hip. Her brow fell to one hard line, then bounced back up as she gave him a mocking smile.

Sydney tried to speak, but there wasn't enough there

to even make him stutter. He wanted to look anywhere else, but his hearing wandered in place of his eyes like an octopus reaching out for anything it could find.

Somewhere in the loft, sketchbook pages rustled.

Four people rummaged in bags, one nylon.

A woman back near the periodicals giggled.

He dropped his volume and, within the first words watched Myrna subtly lean forward toward him to listen.

"You needed Skadi to ask you to be nice before you actually thought about it?" he said more than asked.

Her face fell and she crossed her arms.

He turned to leave, but her words reached out and tethered him.

"You don't remember me, do you?"

Sydney took a breath before he turned all the way back. He could have ignored her, and definitely entertained the thought.

Instead, he poured all the panic, fury, and confusion he could into that black hole where his memories should have been, and hoped it could at least convert into a more useful response. With all the self-control he could muster, he turned to face her again.

"No, I don't. I've been a bit busy."

"You've been busy for *two years*?" Myrna burst. She clamped a hand over her mouth and looked back and forth, surprised by her own volume.

Sydney's hands began to shake. He transferred *Anthem* to his other hand and stuck the hand now freed into his coat pocket. His death grip on the books would hopefully hide the rest.

"I've had a *hectic two years*, and you're *obviously not an ex*," he said quietly but forcefully, wondering if he was lying.

"Welp," she started and stepped alarmingly close. Sydney held up the books between them again, but the barrier didn't seem to faze her.

"Just remember," she said, getting even closer. She reached up for a hard poke with one finger into his lapel, then slowly traced the lines of stitching up and down.

"When it dips below ten again–y'know, dips below

zero–and you get *real* cold… you owe me, with interest."

She patted him on the shoulder, forced a grin, then strode away behind him.

Sydney stayed there, unsure of what had just happened. He heard the words, but there were no appropriately shaped keyholes to plug them into.

He frantically tested each lock, sure he would find an opening. Yet there was something working faster than he was, locking them back up just before he tested. Parts of him that wanted to remember were denied by parts that didn't.

Finally, a single lock clicked open and he remembered the stitching at the back of his coat collar.

M.A.D.

"Are you doin' alright?"

Sydney's vision focused and he looked down to the elderly librarian in the bow tie and glasses. Myrna was gone.

"I'm…" Sydney coughed. He remembered he still held onto the books, both the huge black hardback and the tiny yellow pocket-sized paperback.

"I'm… I'll be fine. Can you take these, though?" Sydney asked. The librarian held out his wrinkled hands and took the weights.

"Thank you," Sydney concluded. "I'll be fine."

He started back toward the front doors in more of a wander, but quickly shifted to long strides away.

The librarian watched him leave and, after a moment, shook his head gently. He then retreated toward the nearest cart of books to deposit his charges.

"Sure, sure," he mumbled to himself.

Sydney could have sworn to his phone buzzing in his pocket, but his attention was wrenched away.

"*Sydney!*"

Skadi darted from the glass-enclosed entry to the building he had already passed, and in a flash stood behind him, bundled up in her faux-fur bomber jacket. She slid around and skidded to a halt in front of him.

He grimaced, but lifted a hand in the bare minimum of acknowledgement.

She moved to cross her arms, but forced them back

down.

"About yesterday," she started, "I'm really sorry about the attitude.

Sydney looked past her, down to the crosswalk he hoped he would have taken by now. He looked back to the redhead.

He knew he had seen her yesterday and rode home with her, but the rest was warped almost beyond recognition.

"The… attitude?" he asked. He busied himself with putting both hands back in his gloves.

"Ah, yeah. My boyfriend is kind of being an idiot lately, and I… kind of let that bleed into other things," she explained.

Sydney tensed at the word *bleed.* He forced his cold, locked shoulders to relax before he spoke. It was still too late, and he caught the faint scent of blood from nowhere and brushed his nose with the back of his hand.

"I'm sorry, Skadi, but I'm not sure what you're talking about." Sydney recalled being somewhat annoyed at her, but had assumed it was all because he didn't want to be on her motorcycle.

Her expression fell.

"Well, that's fine, I guess." She paused. "I'm sorry anyway."

"Uh… it's fine."

He strode past her, still aiming for the crosswalk. She let him go, but after a few steps he spun on his heel, caught himself from tripping over himself, and took a couple steps back.

"In case you can't tell, I *kinda hate people*."

He paused to cope with his own confession.

"It's nothing personal, and I don't hate you, I just… it…" His brow lowered and he squinted, looking into space for some way to salvage the sentence.

Skadi held one eyebrow raised.

"I'm working on a lot of things right now," he concluded. Skadi was silent.

She blinked and most of the skepticism vanished. She smiled, but ran her tongue along the side of her teeth.

"She talked to you, didn't she?"

"Yes, she *did*, but there's a lot more going on than owing Myrna *hundreds of dollars and some stupid glamor shots*. I'll *get* to it."

Sydney's eyes widened at the sound of his own voice and the information it contained. He only added to the spike in his volume, otherwise Skadi may have attributed his worry to something else entirely.

Skadi put her hands up.

"Jeez, I get it. But since you're technically both talking again, I just think you should share what that is, or she'll haunt you."

She shrugged, but Sydney had already turned back on his heel.

Liar, came his own voice in his own head, but not fueled by any thought of his own. He blinked widely, shook his head, and kept on toward the highway.

"*Full sentences would be nice,*" he hissed to himself along the way.

Skadi sighed heavily, then reached into her coat pocket for her phone.

She jumped with an outburst as Martin looped an arm around her shoulders.

"Sorry," he said, but kept his arm there, restraining her. "I see you made a new friend. Care to share?"

She glared.

"Don't touch me unless you're here to say sorry, for the nine hundred and ninety ninth–" she ducked out of his arm. He didn't reach for her.

He only dropped his arm and a cloud passed over his face.

"Look, what if I gave you a time limit?" Martin pled. He stepped forward, one arm stretching out.

She quickly took half a step back–not enough to avoid his reach, but enough for him to catch sight of his own long arm, frown, and drop it to his side.

"Explain." Skadi crossed her arms. She drilled into his eyes with her own.

"You're right, I'm worried about some… stuff. I'd just like to tell you once it goes through, ah, Saturday. I'm–I'm fine. If I don't, then I, I mean, you–"

"It's not like I want a hundred percent of your attention a hundred percent of the time," she interrupted. "I can actually do pretty well on my own, *if you haven't guessed by now*."

"I know," he replied. He crossed his arms and looked away down the sidewalk, across to where Sydney had vanished.

"I just can't be with someone who doesn't want to be there, wherever *there* is."

He looked back to her.

"I know. That's why I, I-i-i--"

"If it's something that you can tell me, then I accept. Tell me about it Saturday. Because if you don't, I can't–"

Martin jumped forward and put one finger over her lips. She looked down at his hand and then back up with an eye roll.

"Saturday. Until then, who's the corpse?" Martin lifted his hand from her lips and gestured vaguely toward the crosswalk a hundred feet away.

She grabbed his wrist and yanked it around her neck. He jumped closer and happily obliged. Her same-side hand reached up to hold his.

"Myrna says he's an old online customer, from before she started school. Skipped out on the portfolio photos he promised, and the other half of payment. Black wool's *not* cheap and if you want to keep your sanity, don't ask her how–"

"Didn't she move from Oregon?" Martin blurted.

"Yeah, then from Boulder."

"Why would he be here? Did she send it to Colorado, or—"

"I don't *know*, why don't you ask him?" Skadi turned under his arm and raised an eyebrow with a sideways smile of disbelief.

"Seems kind of stalkery. Where are you going?"

Skadi let go of his arm and strode away down the sidewalk, but turned.

"I got a ride for my cello!" she called back. "You coming with, or?"

Martin's eyes sparked and he jogged to catch up with

her. She held out her hand and he threaded his fingers into hers, following as she started walking again.

"Like we've established, having something going on doesn't mean you should expect everyone to give you a free pass," Skadi said.

"Ah, I–"

"Works for Sydney, too, I mean," she explained. "Seems nice enough, though, provided he's actually as self-aware as he says."

"What's '*nice enough*'?" He held the glass door open for her.

"He hasn't called me a really tan white girl yet, so there's that."

She crossed the door and took his hand again.

"He doesn't look like he'd have much trouble spelling *Vargas*, so you may be in the clear for that one."

Katrina's head jerked up as the tiny bell over the door sounded.

Sydney stepped up to the counter with an unusual look on his face. He looked almost, but not quite, like he was… *smiling?*

"Why do you do that?" he asked, that smile barely there. It did reach his eyes, but still didn't look right. His brow had relaxed and looked less like he was constantly preoccupied with some obscure math theory, but there was something else in the look she couldn't place. He looked tired, in that vacant way.

"What, knit?" Katrina shoved the mass of black wool and long metal spikes behind the rack of chips to her right.

"No, try to multitask when you don't need to."

"I don't really multitask," she started. "I just switch tabs *really* fast. Not great for brain power but, then again, no one really cares, most of the… time."

She had started to trail off, looking down and away, then pushed through to the end of her sentence.

"Hey, you okay?" she asked and looked up.

"Hm?"

"Are you okay? You seem a little… I don't know, you just seem kinda–" she began.

"You did hear me talking to Jacob last night, right?"

Sydney didn't look up at her, but into his wallet, for no apparent reason but not to look at her.

"Yeah. Did you go to the hospital yet?"

"No. But it–hasn't gotten worse," he said, looking up from his wallet, though he still held onto it.

Liar, came his own voice in his head again. He ignored it but hoped she didn't see the flinch on his face that he felt inside.

She didn't look like she believed him.

"What can I get you?" she said after a deep breath. "You want what you had last time?"

"That cinnamon abomination?"

"Yeah," she brightly answered.

"No. Medium London Fog, thanks." That slight downturn at either side of his mouth was coming back. He hoped that dream was prompted by coffee, rather than caffeine, giving him a loophole. He was too tired to avoid caffeine entirely.

He shoved his wallet back in his coat pocket, unable to pull the bills inside apart while wearing his leather gloves. He began pulling them off.

His skin buzzed. He could barely feel his face. He wasn't physically numb, but something else. It wasn't as if he'd done much in the last few days, but he deserved a short break and to pretend like everything was normal.

Despite the increasing thoughts in his head that weren't his own. Things were definitely developing, but also on the verge of getting out of hand.

"Alrighty." Katrina fed the order into the register.

The bell above the door behind him rang out. Sounds of traffic bled into the quiet space and with it came the faint scent of blood. Both silenced as the door shut.

Relief washed over him, expelling the panic. His fear of Myrna's appearance was only semi-rational. He heard no leather jacket, and there were no heavy, booted footfalls. The customer was a stranger.

The glass front refrigerator near the door opened and closed with a pop of the gasket. The man stepped up to the counter and set down a plastic-wrapped sandwich.

Sydney looked to the sandwich, then to the person who stood next to him.

He looked like an older, stretched-out version of Jacob, except for the hair, which was a much lighter, ashen blond, almost grey. He was also closer to Sydney's eye level than he'd seen anyone yet achieve, though not quite as thin.

Even through a solid black hooded coat, the man was still built like a lightweight boxer. Mostly the dog, but Sydney wondered why he felt a pang of fear that he might be within punching range.

Sydney deflected the thought and glanced down at the stranger's shoes. From there, he was simply more conflicted.

He wore a pair of grey wingtip boots, a sharp contrast with the casual jacket and Sydney's violent first impression.

His scan couldn't have taken more than a second or two but, when Sydney looked back up, the new customer gave a lopsided grin.

"Sorry," Sydney said under his breath and turned his eyes back toward the menu. The letters still wobbled and hurt to focus on, but it was more comfortable than eye contact.

"No problem," said the other customer. He then looked Sydney up and down. A ghost of a smile remained.

Sydney resisted the urge to stare dead center back into the stranger's face, if only out of spite. An unnerving familiarity coated his every thought since he'd walked in, even worse than that white-haired student an hour before, or anyone else. It was different from the crackle of crowds.

Much more of this, and anxiety would do much more than make his face numb and give him a persistent sense of déjà vu. He was already missing small pieces of time every so often, and didn't like to think about what that might mean, particularly if he was being haunted by anything from his own head.

Katrina returned with Sydney's tea, a little paper cup capped off with white plastic inside a cardboard ring with that grinning cat logo stamped onto it. He pulled out his wallet again.

She trusted him well enough to get him the order

before payment, and he wouldn't disappoint.

"Haven't I seen you around somewhere?" the man with the fancy shoes asked, that same annoying amusement hovering over his face.

"No, I don't think so," Sydney half-mumbled and handed Katrina his card, rather than bills. Best to be over with this quickly.

Katrina gingerly took his payment and glanced between the two men. She raised her eyebrows and looked down and away at her scanner.

"No, I think I really–" the man in wingtips started again. Sydney's resolve broke and he turned.

"You really think you'd see someone like *this*," he waved his hands up and down his long stretch of self, "and you'd have to ask yourself if you'd seen him somewhere?"

They stared at each other just long enough for Sydney to regret speaking. Katrina drummed her short nails on the counter.

The other customer frowned in concession and looked away with eyes that didn't match the surrender. He pondered the concept Sydney presented. Then he looked back, thankfully only briefly.

"That's fair," was all he said, a hint of that smile again playing at the corners of his mouth.

Sydney took his tea and decided the next best step was to hide in the tower for a while. He strode away toward the staircase and swiftly ascended.

A wave of recognition crashed into him. For a brief moment, he was almost convinced there were many more people on the first floor than he had seen.

He turned around on impulse. The man was still there on the ground floor, but held his phone in his hands, tapping away with both thumbs.

The background of the text screen was a neon-colored cat face, unless Sydney was mistaken. He wasn't, but cringed a little, wishing he was.

He pushed the feeling away, as well as the sickening sensation that the weather outside had bestowed upon the *Red Cheshire* the shortest blizzard known to mankind. He'd been there, but in much different weather. The memory was vivid, but without any useful context.

The rest of the *Red Cheshire* was vaguely run-down, in a time-worn way from the deposits of others memories in the form of various dings, scrapes, and footprints.

The construction was profoundly solid but, though the plaster may not have been completely smooth, a few signs and frames were nailed up over what he suspected were portals to electric wiring. The rafters were untouched and wide windows shone onto real plants that complained about the season but were still very much alive.

Sydney kept going until he ran out of stairs.

The top level featured a tall loft and windows that encircled the entire space. An upright piano sat at the back wall, the lid sitting open.

After a mental shudder, imagining the task of planting the piano on the third floor, he walked up to it, tea in hand. The order was warm through his glove.

A brown-skinned teenage boy sat in the corner closest to the stairs, typing away on the black laptop in front of him. He wore a set of enormous headphones over his dark, tightly-curled hair and the brown argyle hoodie hung off his shoulders a few sizes too big.

Sydney hoped those headphones were noise canceling.

The piano shone out with an invisible neon arrow. It was the only way he could describe the feeling. He was drawn to it, but there was nothing overt, nothing in explanation, only that he *wanted* it.

That little voice inside him that was technically his own was still quiet, and he quietly crept over to the piano, hoping he wasn't tempting it to surface again.

The faded blue paint was scraped up on the sides, probably from moving in. One of the black keys had been repainted to a black that didn't match the rest. There was nothing particularly shocking about the instrument, except for it being on the third floor, up two flights of stairs with more than one landing before the end.

He pulled the bench out with one hand. The low rumble of the bench didn't disturb the other patron, so Sydney didn't hesitate to sit down, though the seat rattled and creaked.

He set his drink on the ledge above the keyboard and felt eyes on him.

"You probably don't want to put it there," came the boy's voice. He was older than Sydney took him for.

Sydney didn't turn to look. He just took a moment to keep from snapping back, especially because he was right. He instead pulled one of his gloves off and set it on the bench. He picked up the tea and set it on the floor next to his foot.

The typing behind him resumed.

Sydney kept his eyes on the keyboard, but took off his other glove and set it next to the first. He then dragged one hand over the slightly uneven keys.

One lit up with that same invisible neon that had drawn him there. There was a light he couldn't see with his eyes but was easily felt, like sound that didn't reach his ears but he could feel through a surface. The correct key was *that one*, though nothing had changed.

Sydney struck the white key. He struck another that lit up, and then another. The chain of notes grew slowly, but swelled to a web of high, low, and comforting, familiar melody. The third-floor vaulted ceiling became a giant music box, filling every corner, crease, and dent.

Everything melted away, and he was only dimly aware of his body. His hands floated at the end of his arms, somewhere in the distance. Between here and there, only the song played.

It was the sound of what was missing–so close, and ever-present, but without words or explanation. The space between the thunder and lightning, anticipating epiphany but none promised. A quiet river he couldn't locate, a windowless attic with a draft, the smell of baking, a country drive, starry sky, and

This is your fault.

Sydney fumbled and pulled his hands back. His last crash of the piano keys left panic in the air.

"Why'd you stop?" the boy with the computer asked.

Someone sat down next to him. When he looked, the teenage boy was still at the table with his laptop. He had only turned to face Sydney's back.

"That was pretty good, though," the boy added.

Sydney's attention wrenched away from the disturbingly realistic feeling not only of someone else sitting there, but the sound of his own voice in his head. It wasn't just a thought from somewhere else–he'd heard his own voice with his ears.

He was about to mutter a thanks, but was cut off.

"Self-taught?"

Sydney hesitated.

"Sort of."

"Cool, cool. Any favorites?"

Sydney snatched up his gloves and turned around on the bench as he put them on.

This is your fault echoed in his head. Echoes without original sounds started rising from the dark.

"Listen, I shouldn't even be here," he said. He started to stand, but was overcome with a wave of panic and sat back down. The echoes were louder, but he couldn't quite hear what was being said.

"I know that feel, but we do what we can" the boy laughed.

"Shouldn't you be in school?" Sydney bit back with a scowl.

"I am," he replied.

Sydney must have made a face, because the boy grabbed the base of his laptop and turned the entire thing to give Sydney a better view.

Sydney didn't know what the image was, initially. Once the red and yellow and white of hospital machinery, as well as everything inside it clicked into focus, his stomach turned.

"American organ transplant procedures. Though, it's more of a lead in to transfusions and some of the metaphys–you okay?"

Sydney looked up to the ceiling as far as he could without tilting his head, to get away from viewing the screen. His bones still jittered from an inconvenient panic and he wasn't sure if he should stand. The echoes didn't grow louder, but he was having trouble focusing. It was almost like he was remembering several things at once, all of them tasks overdue, yet not being able to focus on a single one before recalling the next.

"I–sorry, no. I have things to do."

Sydney kicked off, headed toward the stairs. Something splashed and he turned around with equal panic.

Tea ran from the overturned cup under the piano bench, across the wood slats of the floor.

The worst part was, he still felt like three people were in the room. Holding onto what he saw, or rather didn't see, he pushed through the quick-seeping chill and reached down for the cup.

Around half the tea survived, so he set the open container on the bench, as well as the plastic lid. His hands shook as he popped it back on. He grabbed both his gloves with the other hand, hesitated, then shoved his gloves in his pocket and strode away toward the head of the stairs.

He was already gone from sight when the boy in argyle called after him.

"Nice to meet you, too!"

Katrina leaned forward across the counter as Sydney fell back to earth. That not-quite-a-grimace was back. Though he looked like his usual self, she frowned in disappointment.

He half-fell, half-lunged toward the paper napkin dispenser, next to the milk and cream pitchers around the corner from her counter-top.

"I'm sorry, I–yes, sorry. I spilled. On the floor." His old expression was back, but his usual voice had all but gone. He set his half-empty cup on the counter.

Katrina barely opened her mouth. Sydney's sudden, vacant eyes wiped out whatever she was going to say. He turned to the stairs again, simply looking, this time with a fist full of napkins.

She watched his face for any change, but none came.

He slowly dropped the napkins back to the counter. They left his hand one by one as a few of the echoing sounds in his head congealed.

What do you want for your birthday? came a

woman's voice through static.

It'll be okay, came the voice of a little girl, clearer, but from a hollow space.

Sydney? then came the voice of a man, who sounded just like him, but wasn't quite.

He blinked and his shoulders tensed. He yanked out his wallet, shoved something she didn't count into the tip jar, and vanished out the front door on fast forward.

"*Sorry,*" she thought she heard, barely above the bell over the door. He was already gone.

Katrina rummaged through her head to find any real explanation for what she just saw.

She kicked back on her bar stool and leaned further back, holding onto the inner edge of her counter.

"*Leroy! Checkin' a spill! Be right back!*" she called back to the netherworld of the back room.

Without pause she let the legs of her stool back down to the floor and locked her screen with the tap of a few buttons. She slid under the gap in the counter without lifting the gate and darted up the staircase two at a time.

Katrina stood at the entry, surveying the room.

There was nothing there particularly worrisome–not even a spill. Which worried her.

Outside air didn't help much, only crystallized what had just happened. He took the steps almost all at once and took off in no special direction. The enormous metal sign watched him go, a giant red striped cat wrapped around a coffee cup with a wide grin almost too big for its own face.

He kept walking.

His feet carried him for quite a while.

It began to get dark.

Moving didn't help keep him from thinking, but it slowed him down just a little. He staved off the scene in the *Red Cheshire*, but it merely replayed in his head over and over and over and over and…

This is your fault.

Memory didn't just leave the human brain on its own. There had to be a catalyst. Some kind of event. One method was injury, but he seemed relatively healthy and there was nothing left over from the hospital to suggest otherwise.

The only other method he knew of was an issue of mental health. With what he'd been seeing for the last few days that was decidedly beyond the scope of how normal people interacted with the world.

Why normal? came his own voice in his head.

"*Shut up*," he hissed quietly through gritted teeth.

What do you want for your birthday?

It'll be okay.

Sydney?

It was this, or the mirror. His double didn't speak in reflection, but was becoming significantly chattier. What he could have brushed off, with enough denial, as an intrusive thought before, he heard as clearly as his own voice, played back to him with no memory of speaking in the first place.

The street lamps glowed high above, points of pale-yellow bulbs scattered throughout the darkness above like stars almost within reach.

He looked behind him and didn't recognize where he'd been. He looked down, then up to find he stood on the street corner with a handful of other people crackling around him. He looked up and down the street and wasn't sure where he was.

For good measure, he looked up and down each street one more time, holding his breath to fight off the panic.

He stood back from the group of strangers, who dispersed as the walk light changed. Then he pulled his phone out and called Jacob.

"No, *no*. I'm fine. Can you give me a ride, though?"

He glanced up to another group of people approaching his corner, and cut across the walkway to stand in the overhang of the building instead.

"What do you mean, no? I have no idea where I am."

"*I mean a friend from work had an emergency. I'm bringing him home, then giving him a ride tomorrow. Can't you just pull up the map app or something?*"

Jacob spoke into his phone, held up to his ear by the man in his passenger seat.

"Never mind," Sydney said, his shoulders fallen. "It's fine. Good night."

"*Sorry. But hey, call me back in like fifteen minutes, if you can't–*"

Sydney hung up. A woman at the back of the group had hung back, and had since turned to face him.

He stared back at her.

She didn't crackle, but he smelled blood.

Jacob's passenger pulled the phone away at the cue from Jacob's frown. The boxer-shaped man from The *Red Cheshire* looked at the screen, then dropped the phone into the cup holder.

"I don't see why I couldn't have put him on speaker," he said.

"Levi, I told you about him. He's a little particular about some things, is all," Jacob answered.

She continued to stare at Sydney, and wasn't exactly unpleasant to stare back at. He simply noted that his own voice in his head was conspicuously silent, and wasn't sure what he was really looking at. If he heard the woman, the girl, and the man who wasn't quite him, what was this?

Still a few yards away from him, she smiled gently. He tentatively lifted a hand and gave a weak wave.

She waved back, then swung her arm around to point down across the street. He looked.

The neon purple glow of the signs in the occult shop window shone out through the yellow-tinted early night. He rolled his eyes. He wasn't going to buy a Ouija board, not even as a last resort.

"*Go play in traffic*," Sydney hissed, welling up from a deeper, darker place inside him.

The woman's smile dropped. She turned and stepped into the road. Sydney's heart leapt. In two long strides he reached out to grab her shoulder.

He clawed down to pull her back and found air. There was nothing but the pale reflections on the road in front of him.

He stared at his leather gloved hand. Blaring car horn

pulled him back to attention.

Sydney jumped forward, out of the path of the large black truck and into the path of a little silver station wagon. He jumped forward in the sea of lights and horns until he found the curb again. There, he took a moment to catch his breath, and leaned forward onto his knees between the lamppost and trash can.

The neon purple caught his eye again. That occult shop was only a few doors down. He stood back up and started walking toward the door. He was done fighting.

His attention was captured.

"That was uncalled-for," he muttered to himself.

Says you, himself replied.

The cold seeped into his bones, and was a part of them, now. The dark space inside of him laughed, even as he slipped his coat off and hung it on the peg inside his house.

Sydney didn't believe in magic, and was sure he never had. He didn't believe anyone could make him do anything he didn't firmly want to do, no could, or should, he be too preoccupied with getting others to do what he wanted.

However, stage magic was based on illusion and perception. That could be done without such theatrics, but drama did help with distraction from how things really worked.

Whatever was going on inside his head, there was obviously an explanation. However, that explanation was currently held by whatever part of him thought it necessary to lead him into the middle of traffic to get him to do what it wanted.

If the second man he saw in the mirror had anything to do with the one he looked like, then maybe the answers weren't so far away. All he had to do was dig in a different place, perhaps with a different shovel.

After climbing to his bedroom, Sydney pulled the desk chair up closer behind him. He pulled a black velvet bag out of his pocket and, with his long fingers, pulled the deck of tarot cards out and fanned them out in front of him in one hand. He threw the receipt from last night back somewhere toward the door.

He pulled a card from the center and pushed back in the chair, before he pivoted and threw it down face up on his bed. He was seeing himself, and hearing himself, in his conscious thoughts, so maybe he could find the back door into wherever the rest of his memory was stored.

Tarot was built around archetypes and symbols, so there was a good chance he could trigger a memory and pull on yet more threads from there. He didn't know how he was supposed to read them, but that wasn't really the point, was it?

Ten of Wands. The man in the illustration on the card carried entirely too many long sticks, and looked on the verge of dropping at least a few, if not all.

Sydney's life had been relatively short so far, but there were so many things to keep track of. What would he do if he missed something? What would happen if he made a mess, despite his best efforts? There was no one to help him pick up the pieces, except maybe Jacob.

Who he'd known for less than a week. He swept the thought away.

Sydney gathered and shuffled the remaining cards. He spread the deck with one hand and pulled another card from the middle.

He turned *Ten of Cups* right-side up and threw it down on the bed, next to *Ten of Wands*. The card landed upside-down, as he'd first pulled it.

The illustration wasn't as distinguishable inverted, and looked more like someone had scattered several golden goblets all over the floor. It was a mess.

He was a mess. A sharply-dressed, reticent mess.

Then again, Sydney thought best when everything was out in front of him. What looked like a mess to others could simply be more interesting to him. Provided it didn't involve too many people talking to him at once, real or imaginary.

He may have been in over his head, but everything the double inside his head had said so far gave him the impression that he had done something to put himself in this mess. He just wasn't sure if things had gone according to plan, or if that deeper, angrier part of him was so angry because it hadn't.

Was he working out a successful plan, or was he correcting something that had gone horribly wrong? What did success mean, anyway?

He waited for his own voice to come back to him, to tell him that he had ruined everything. That everything was all his fault. He sat there in silence, holding the fan of cards out in front of him. No answer came.

Sydney shuffled the deck again, pushed everything together, and threw the top card down to the bed.

The Devil.

He was glad he didn't believe in magic, and didn't even know what the cards were intended to mean, because he might have been frightened at that point. He just read the names on the illustrations.

He thought of Martin for a moment, with the deep red horns from the man on the card. The pale-haired illustration was cast in a red light that tinted his hair, as well.

Actually, the more Sydney looked, the horns on the figure looked a little like cat ears. He rolled his eyes.

Sure, it was all the fault of someone called *The Cat.* He laughed to himself, then felt a pang of something he didn't recognize. The Ghost had been quiet since Sydney's near-death experience in the street, but other sensations had been surfacing.

Whatever was his fault, he felt the guilt.

He picked up *The Devil* and stared into it.

If the devil was in the details, his every effort was raising Hell.

Without shuffling, Sydney threw another card down from the top of the deck.

The Devil.

His brows knit together. He threw another card from the top. *The Devil.*

Sydney threw another card.

The Devil.

And another.

The Devil.

Sydney threw cards faster and faster, all from the top of the deck, his hand spitting them down to the top of the pile forming on his bedspread. He was sure he should have run out of cards by now, but they still came out of the deck in his left hand.

He yelped and kicked back even harder as he dropped the deck. The last card that fell on the bed also read *The Devil*, but showed a black-haired man in a dark coat on a background of red snowflakes. The eyes glowed like hot embers over a knowing smile.

Hello, friend, he heard clearly in his own voice.

The rest of the night was a blur. Not even when he cracked his eyes open to the morning light was he sure if he was awake or not.

He slogged through forcing himself out of bed, limbs heavy and floor not entirely solid.

He didn't remember going to bed, but the distinct lack of tarot cards on his desk jarred him roughly awake. His head hurt, as if he'd had one too many drinks last night, which was his only saving grace against panicking over the onset of whatever he was feeling. Other people dealt with hangovers, so could he.

Bracing himself on the walls and anything else within arm's reach, he stumbled out his bedroom door and made his way downstairs, one enormous stair at a time.

He turned the corner at the landing and spotted the pile of tarot cards down on the glass coffee table. The day had started very *wrong*, but he couldn't articulate his own thoughts clearly enough to see about fixing it.

All he knew was that he felt like he was being watched, and closely, as if someone else was behind him, watching him stumble like a drunk into the kitchen. He wasn't even alarmed, at this point, just more annoyed. And angry.

If they were so close by, why wouldn't they help?

If part of him knew how to fix things, why wouldn't he just let himself do so? What was so awful, what had he done that was so terrible, that he would punish himself like this?

He pulled out the tea box and rummaged in the cabinet for a particular mug. Not sure which one, but he needed one in particular.

He pulled down the black teacup rimmed in silver and set it down on the counter, next to where he'd left Jacob's card.

Dr. George Lorem's card.

The little rectangle of paper pinned down Sydney's meandering, wordless thoughts. He stared at it, unblinking.

Clinical Psychiatrist.

He skipped tea, somewhat regretfully, and rocketed through dressing himself. He double-checked his grey-button-down collar and combed his hair with his fingers, but left the house with a suspicion he'd missed something and still looked a bit disheveled.

He resigned himself to catching the bus, people around him at the stop dispersing like he was a stone dropped in a sandy puddle. He didn't mind, and didn't think much of it, until he wished they would get further away. Each of them did, until he was standing in a nearly perfect circle with only a dim sense of the crackle at the back of his thoughts.

He promptly forgot about the happening as the bus approached and he boarded, dropping a few coins onto the floor but finding new ones without issue, ignoring the fact that he didn't carry coins.

Sydney held onto the rails hung from the ceiling as he walked himself all the way back. Fearing he might not get up again if he let himself sit, he looped one hand into the nearest fabric strap on the rail and held on as the bus pulled itself from the gutter.

He glanced to the nearest seat, but it was empty. He expected someone to be there, looking up at him. That feeling swung around behind him, and he looked over his shoulder. That seat was empty, too, though the feeling had moved to a third location.

He rubbed his eyes with his free hand, then kept them closed, only opening them when he felt the bus begin to slow.

The ride was long.

The folding doors eventually opened one more time and he quickly stepped down into the frigid air. The moment his boot hit the pavement, panic seized him. He stood at the bus stop, back toward the road, unable to move.

He told himself to move, but nothing connected with movement. He heard traffic, and faintly crackling people pass by around him, but he still couldn't force himself to turn.

He was going to a psychiatrist's office, and he couldn't press the right button in his own head to turn around and keep walking.

Let me, said his own voice in his head. His will reignited and he promptly spun around as if a key in his back had turned a too many times.

Sydney stepped off the curb and was flattened by the next bus.

He screamed from the bottom of everything he had and flailed so hard he fell off the long, white couch, onto his face.

He stayed there for a minute, face against the short carpet. His heart seized as the house creaked, but he didn't relax once he decided he'd heard nothing consequential.

He heard a footstep through the floor and this time jumped up, propelled by his racing heart. He pulled himself back up on the couch and looked both ways, expecting someone there. He was alone, but alive.

Sydney, sitting up from the floor, looked over to the coffee table. The tarot deck was strewn across it, with a few cards on the floor. The laptop sat there, screen dark.

From his vantage, Sydney watched a version of himself, fully dressed in his white button-up shirt and black coat, sitting on the couch behind him.

He pushed himself up off the floor and strode over to the floor lamp near the long dining table.

"Alright, I'll play," he muttered to himself. "You want my attention? You have my attention. Say what you want to say, dammit!"

He ripped the cord out of the wall, dragged it to the side of the coffee table, then plugged it back in on the long, white wall between the fireplace and the front window.

He sat back down to a crisp but dark reflection of himself on the long white couch. Unfortunately, he sat there alone with nothing but the fading scent of blood.

SIX

Jacob's jaw set and his eyes widened as his phone buzzed again in his pocket. Katrina sat back on the blue vinyl booth seat, but tapped her fingers on both hands.

"So, uh, anyway–I think the book idea is fine, you should probably just–" Katrina continued. "Don't tell me that's him again."

Jacob rubbed one eye behind his glasses.

"Don't know, don't care. What were you saying?"

"Uh, I think it's a good idea. But like, it's kinda hard to explain. I just think that you, as a guy, should probably be prepared for some… um, negative feedback, if the main character is sixteen," Katrina explained.

The two sat across from each other in an enormous vinyl booth. Chrome encircling the edge of the table was a bit scuffed and dented, which was the general tone for the rest of the pizza parlor.

Heavy rafters remained bare, made of a dark, burnished metal but shone from string lights and innumerable dots of phosphorescent paint spread throughout the ceiling. The vertical space was populated with stuffed carnival prizes, strange models of bicycles, and enormous metal stars and gears.

Their booth was near the front window, where a giant, cursive *Gizmo's Pizza* cast a backward shadow across their faces and table from the lampposts outside. The late morning was overcast and threatened to sleet more than snow.

Plastic-sleeved menus sat between them, barely moved from where they fell once accepted from the waiter.

"I still don't follow," Jacob confessed.

"I just think that you, as a *guy*, should be aware some people will see you writing a teenage *girl*, and be, ah, less than thrilled.

Her deep brown eyes drilled into Jacob's blue.

"Why, if I'm not doing anything… you know, weird?"

Katrina hit herself in the face with the plastic menu.

Jacob's pocket buzzed again.

"*Why* is he texting you this much? It's like he's *trying*

to ruin breakfast," she complained, wagging a finger.

Jacob sat up straighter and reached into his pocket.

"How should I know? But I haven't set any text tones, so maybe it's just Martin, wherever he's gone t–" his face fell.

"Go out there, give him a call, maybe tell him what you found with those photos he made you take."

Jacob's eyes widened.

"Okay, then tell him to shut up for a bit, then come back here and eat your pizza before work." She threw up her hands, then stabbed the air to her left. The glass-enclosed entryway stretched out the window back behind Jacob and to the left.

"That, or just turn off your phone, like I *said*."

"I told you, I have a bad feeling about Martin. And I'm waiting for my sister to get back to me, I can't just–"

"Then *call the needy gothy dude*. Make a choice!"

Jacob sucked in a breath like he was about to speak, but Katrina held up one index finger. He let it out, then kicked off out of the booth seat and rounded the corner.

He pushed into the entryway, a glass door in front and behind him. His phone rang in his hand and he turned it over, hoping for happy coincidence, but found Sydney's name there instead.

"You really need to stop and take silence as a cue," Jacob sighed into the receiver.

Sydney laid face up on the white couch with his feet hanging over one arm. He stared languidly up at the ceiling, cell phone pressed up against his ear.

The fireplace didn't quite roar, but was alive enough to have warmed the room up comfortably. The heat was just enough for Sydney to have resigned himself to the only shirt he owned without sleeves, with the side benefit of feeling his limbs start to thaw, which he didn't know before now was needed.

The ghostly presence played at the edges of his awareness, sometimes back in the laundry room, sometimes on the staircase or sitting in the black striped chair. It never moved as close as before, more like an animal hesitantly watching him from the fringes.

"I just wanted to get ahold of you before you went to work. I wasn't sure when that would be, so I just kept… checking. You're doing something else, aren't you?"

"Yes, Sydney. I am," Jacob shot. He sighed again and massaged one temple, taking a pause to go over the words that had popped into his head.

He committed.

"What is it? What's worth fifteen texts with nothing but '*call me*'?"

"What are you doing, though?" Sydney pressed.

"*Sydney!*"

"I just don't want to be the reason you're preoccupied with anything else. For all I know, you could be having breakfast with Katrina," Sydney spat out, with hardly a space between words. He found the will to sit up, but did so too fast and saw a flurry of deep-colored spots.

"Okay, you need to stop that."

The entryway was getting colder the more he stood there. An elderly man held the door open for an equally elderly woman in a pink waffle-weave scarf and floral half-mask looped around her ears.

He stood to the side and gave in to the pull of the waiting bench.

"Stop what?" Sydney pulled him back to the phone call.

"Stop playing Sherlock. I don't care how you knew, just *please* stop. And just tell me why you called. I'm preoccupied enough as it is, I don't care about anything else, as long as you stop texting me for the weekend."

A long silence followed.

"There are just a few things I've discovered–a few theories I have, and I want to bounce this off someone that's not… myself," Sydney said, a bit haltingly. "One big one is that I probably didn't expect this to happen."

"Yeah, no kidding," Jacob replied.

Sydney took a seat in the black striped chair. His head swam. He was upright, but at what cost?

"No, I mean, I've started to remember and connect a few things. Nothing massive, but I used to be into some weird… psychological stuff. I'm here because of something

I did. Specifically."

"Yeah, that fits," Jacob said with a sigh. He breathed on the glass wall and drew a cat face and a pair of ears.

"What do you mean?" Sydney stared into the gas fireplace.

"Those texts I told you about, with whoever you called The Cat–she was telling you that whatever you were about to do wouldn't work. And said something about you talking to me? I don't know, but leave me out of it if you can."

Jacob wiped away the cat face from the window.

"She?" Sydney pressed.

"I dunno, by the way it was written I just assumed an ex or something. She or he, or…you know, *they*, it's not my business."

Another long pause came.

"Thanks for being clear on that, but I don't… think… that's really my thing. Any of those."

"Wait, what are we talking about?" Jacob shifted on his bench.

"Me calling you later so I can actually gauge how insane the rest of my theory sounds," Sydney answered.

Katrina drummed her fingers along the tabletop. If she leaned to her left, just enough, she could see Jacob sitting on the bench in the entryway.

She held back from leaning over too often, because then her impatience might turn into annoyance, and in her annoyance she might forget that she herself suggested he go make the call.

To aid in her own self-control, she pulled out her own phone.

Annabel said you came by the Cheshire, she typed out with both thumbs, right underneath her last message. She was happy to pick up Skadi's cello from time to time, not only due to the mutual friend.

Myrna was instantly there in the animated ellipsis at the bottom of the screen.

Yeah theres a tonne o yarn at the theater that was supposed to be historic reenactment smthn smthn but some idiot ruined it. its super tangled.

Katrina looked up to what had been Jacob's seat across from her. She leaned to the left and Jacob still sat outside on the bench. Hopefully the annoying lengths the conversation was getting to meant it was going good places.

She looked back down to her phone.

Ok, you want me to help? She added a smiling emoji in the shape of a cat. Myrna typed for another moment.

No u can have it if you want it

Nice light purple wool. Nobody wants 2 fix but I didn't want them to trash it without asking u

All yours

Katrina's head snapped up as she sensed the waiter approach. The wide, dark-haired man balanced an enormous round tray on one hand, and landed it gracefully in the center of the table.

Katrina, starry-eyed, set her phone down on the wide windowsill to her left, just before it buzzed again. Myrna could wait. Unfortunately, the icon instead depicted a Cheshire Cat face in neon lights.

Sydney thought again about standing up. He thought about it a little longer, and wondered what color the spots might be when he actually brought himself to do it.

He dropped off the chair to his knees. The command to stand up had misfired. He hooked a hand over the arm of the armchair and, planting a foot, managed to begin his ascent.

"What happened?" Jacob heard a loud *thump*.

"Nothing. I'm fine. Just fell off the–not important. I'm just not feeling well."

Sydney finally stabbed both feet firmly into the floor beneath, but leaned heavily on the back of the chair. He carefully let go, then slowly turned and transferred his support to the arm of the couch.

"Oh… kay. I'm happy to listen to your insane theory later, but don't call me okay? I'll call you later."

"When?" Sydney asked. He finally had the confidence in his ability to stand up straight without the universe dissolving around him. Not one to let a triumph of any size go to waste, he resolved to make a cup of tea and turned his attention toward the kitchen.

"Today. Don't worry about it. I'm serious, though. Don't call me, I'm–"

"Waiting for another call?" Sydney cut him off.

"*You really need to stop–*"

"That's part of what I wanted to talk to you about. But, I'll let you call me later. I have the agony of disease to get back to."

He ended the call and set the phone down on the counter. He scared himself with unintentional enthusiasm and a loud slap of the gadget on the stone, then stared into space for a minute, fighting nausea.

He reached for the tea on the top shelf, then pulled it down to a new notification on the screen. He tapped the little red flag.

This is Katrina. Jacob says you're sick?

Sydney ignored her, as well as the obvious conclusion Jacob had shared his phone number.

He stood there in the silence but for the hum of his refrigerator and the quiet bubbling of the electric kettle. The anticipation of tea was almost as comforting as the thought of going back to sleep.

The only downside would be what new dream or nightmare crept up on him.

Chamomile and lavender tea dropped a stream of gentle, deep gold, falling like an underwater plume of smoke.

He sat back down on the couch and placed the mug with the trailing tag from the tea bag to the right of the open laptop.

He picked his phone up off the deck of cards he cleaned up and put back inside the bag and tossed to the other end of the table. He then picked up the bag itself. Without much of a second thought, he pulled the string open and, without looking, pulled a card out of the middle.

The Fool, it said, and showed him a gangly man with a bag on a stick over his shoulder, swaggering confidently off the edge of a cliff.

"*Funny*," Sydney said to himself. He perked up and

turned over his shoulder.

He sensed, rather than heard, faint laughter.

Sydney turned back and put the card back into the bag, but the shape didn't comply. He tapped the bottom edge of the deck a few more times, adjusting his hold from the outside. The tap did help but, once the first card slid in, he fumbled and several more exploded out of the bag and onto the table.

One in particular slid further than the rest. He glared, regretting his attempt at dexterity in his state.

There was nothing supernatural to the deck, he told himself. He purchased it for a scientific experiment.

Maybe it was enough to push him past whatever made him feel like someone else. Help him remember whatever his original intention was in the situation.

Maybe he'd remember where he was from.

Maybe he'd remember family.

Maybe he'd completely lose grip and go insane.

Sydney pushed the thought away. He picked up that card that had slid further than the rest, and flipped it over.

The Hermit, that card said. The man in the picture wore an enormous black, billowy cloak with a hood that hid his face.

"Funny!" Sydney said as if to himself. "You are *so* funny."

I try, said his own voice, distinctly in his left ear.

The cards exploded out of his grasp and rained down on top of him. He didn't think he'd been holding on as tightly as necessary for that, but wasn't surprised the stress channeled there.

He glanced up to the screen on the laptop, then shut it. Only one reflection there.

He brushed away the cards that managed to land on the couch cushions, set the remainder of the deck down, and pulled his feet back up from the floor.

He then rolled over to face the back of the couch, read resting on his elbow. Maybe, sleeping during the day, he would avoid the sense of impending doom that had descended upon him, giving him only minutes of sleep in fits and starts for all of yesterday.

Maybe with a quick nap, he would feel better, and think clearer.

Once he realized what he heard, he thought probably not.

It whispered like the wind in the trees. That's all there was–nothing to see, or feel. There was, however, a taste. An airy bitterness, like something long since burned had been caught in a gust, running across vague, grumbling vocal cords.

Wind picked up and he felt almost as though he was caught in the open. His heart sped and his bones shook beneath and inside him. The voices were louder, but somehow still not words, not like before at The Red Cheshire.

They weren't angry, or particularly sad, but he couldn't hear what they wanted him to know. The urgency pulled and scraped at his everything, and he shook inside, looking for somewhere to go.

Sydney's hand shot out above him and smashed into the edge of the coffee table on the way down. He woke with a yell, tried to sit up, but ended up spinning all the way around and fell onto the floor.

The resulting tremor jarred a couple more tarot cards from the table onto his head.

Smooth, came his own voice from inside.

"If you're not gonna show up, *shut up*," Sydney said into the floor.

There came a series of quick, enthusiastic–almost manic–knocks at the door.

He lifted his head and waited. To his disdain, whoever stood there knocked the unrecognized knock again, this time slightly slower.

"One *minute*," Sydney called in his exhaustion. The dream, or whatever just happened, had given him a bit of an adrenaline rush, which only made him more tired. His hands shook.

He peeled himself reluctantly off the floor, joints protesting and the helium-filled balloon of his head swaying.

Curiosity overshadowed the temptation to ignore the knock and see if whoever this was would simply go away.

Stepping barefoot, one foot in front of the other, he finally reached the patch of linoleum just inside the front door.

Sydney slouched to get his eye closer to the peephole. Then he ducked a little more.

Someone tall and light skinned stood there. He wasn't sure, in the bright white of the street, if that person was platinum blond or just elderly. They were thin enough even through the army green coat that they might have been the latter.

Sydney looked over his shoulder and scanned the empty room for the presence he knew he wouldn't see. He felt the space was empty, then that feeling popped up again and he turned all the way around to the end of the kitchen.

"*Play nice*," he whispered, then turned back.

Sydney reached down and turned the doorknob, bracing himself against the inevitable rush of cold air. He popped the door open just enough to see his visitor's face.

His face paled.

Martin stood there holding a yellow plastic shopping bag full of odd shapes, forcing a smile.

Levi shoveled waffles into his face, alone in the red vinyl booth. He ate quickly, but with a bounce of subtle merriment. That bounce vanished as his phone buzzed.

If only he could turn it off from time to time.

The middle-aged man pulled his phone from his coat pocket and unlocked it with the password.

That issue with Sydney, The Cat began, followed by an irritatingly long moment waiting for the rest of the sentence as the ellipses animated below.

The recent or ongoing one? Levi tapped back, swiping across letters rather than deign to lift the phone and use both thumbs. He used his other hand to take half a sausage off into his mouth.

The problem of his not updating.

Levi rested his fork and lifted his coffee.

I've enlisted another agent to assist, at least in this case.

Levi raised an eyebrow high, everything else frozen.

He lifted his phone with both hands and tapped away with both thumbs.

There's someone else in town? I mean, apart from the usual?

There was no activity on the screen for entirely too long for comfort. Sights and sounds of the *Waffle House* trickled back in, from the checkered tile to the dingy edges of the ceiling speakers.

Paul McCartney played to him somewhere in the distance.

Not important. I just wanted to let you know I'm placing you on another task, provided this one goes according to intent.

"Are you going to say something, or what?"

"*How* do you know where I live?" Sydney obliged.

Martin looked away and gave a heavy sigh. The fog of his breath faded up into the sky.

"See, I *told* her that you'd be freaked out. Skadi's at orchestra. She heard you were sick, so she wanted me to come by with, ah, stuff."

He held up the yellow plastic bag.

"How does *Skadi* know where I live?" Sydney accused. Martin was silent for a moment.

"Do you want what she asked me to bring, or not?

Sydney looked down at the bag, then back up to Martin's progressively reddening nose.

Whether out of boredom or threat of what more time alone might contain, Sydney didn't know, but he stepped aside and pulled the door open wider.

Martin half-hopped and stepped inside, getting the last few shivers out of his system.

"Who told Skadi I'm sick?" Sydney asked, closing the door against the cold.

"I don't know," Martin started, eyes roaming the room. "Who did you tell you were sick?"

The only person Sydney could think of was Jacob, and he wasn't sure how to trace that all the way into the current conversation. It didn't help that he had no idea why Jacob would have mentioned it to anyone other than Katrina, in the first place.

Unless Katrina was much more connected than he expected.

Sydney's eyes also roamed the room, this time for where he left his phone. The best person to ask about the curious case of having visitors was Jacob.

His eyes fell onto his phone at the end of the coffee table. He strode over and snatched it up.

"Bit of a minimalist, are we?" Martin said, standing awkwardly in the center of the room. He held the bag away from his body.

Martin watched him messing with his phone, but Sydney noted him double-glance somewhere else and looked up, himself. Martin still watched him fiddling with his phone, as if nothing had happened.

Did Katrina tell anyone I'm sick? Sydney typed out.

"I suppose," Sydney mumbled aloud. There was no indication Jacob had seen the text, so he set his phone down on the glass table to force himself into patience.

"You're either *really* not feeling well, or… you don't like me, do you?" Martin raised the bag up and set it on the thin dining table.

Sydney's head snapped back up at the distinctive *clink* of a storage tin.

"I'm just…" Sydney began, and then the rest of Martin's sentence came back to him. He glanced toward the kitchen and decided on another approach, rounding the couch toward the linoleum.

"I'm not a people person. Sick doesn't help anything, as I'm sure you can imagine," he corrected.

Upon discovery he'd taken his phone with him, instead of set it down as intended, he typed furiously with both thumbs, hoping auto-correct would pick up the slack without too much embarrassment.

Because what the only thing that makes sense is Katrina told someone, probably Myrna, Myrna told Skadi, Skadi told Martin, and now he's in my living room and I would like him to leave. Call me when you get this.

Martin promptly sat on the arm of the black striped chair, much to Sydney's discomfort.

Sydney tossed his phone onto the counter and flipped the electric kettle on.

"I'm just being…" Martin trailed off, half-looking over his shoulder toward the laundry room alcove. "Silly."

"There's some loose tea in there, in the tin. Skadi had some left over from a bad cold about a month ago. Bottle of Nyquil, if it's good for anything. And she thought you might like the movies. I've never seen either."

Sydney stepped over and pulled the handles of the bag aside. Inside sat a round, obnoxiously floral tin. He lifted it and the unnaturally blue bottle of liquid to reveal the face of a preteen boy with glasses under *The Pagemaster* in golden gothic font. He set down the tin and bottle and lifted the DVD case to another one underneath.

The Crow.

Whatever she thought about his tastes, he approved.

Sydney's heart jumped. He spun around to see Martin quietly stacking the mess of tarot cards in his hand.

Was Sydney's house really all that strange, or had Martin noticed something he hadn't yet?

Martin stooped down even further to pick up a few more cards up off the floor.

"Do you… want some tea? Or something else?" Sydney croaked.

Martin didn't reply, or even appear to have heard him for a moment.

He's anxious, came Sydney's voice in his own head. Martin stood up straight with wide eyes.

By now, Sydney barely flinched whenever that happened. His visitor, however, coincidentally appeared as if he had heard what Sydney knew he couldn't have.

Could he?

"What?" Martin answered.

"Tea before you head out?"

"Oh. Well, yeah. Sure. Obviously save Skadi's tin for yourself and all that, but… sure," he answered.

Much to Sydney's alarm, which threatened the return of his not-quite-beaten nausea, Martin fell back into the arm of the chair. He crossed an ankle over his knee.

Sydney stared at the side of his face as he looked

down to check his phone, taking a few seconds to keep hold on his composure. Also, to see if Martin looked around anymore at things that weren't technically there.

Sydney managed to tether his irritation to a thin leash and turned back to the kitchen to choose mugs.

"Are you from around here, or out of state?" Martin turned and called into the kitchen.

Before Sydney could process why Martin's voice sounded a bit *off*, Martin went on.

"Went home for the holiday?"

"No, I'm… working here. New job, don't want to–jinx it," he lied. "I hope you understand. What about you? What with the… the–the–" Sydney's words left.

He stepped up to the end of the counter, waiting to perhaps be saved by the click of the electric kettle. He gestured vaguely with one hand, circling his mouth, hoping the right words to describe his question would come, though he wasn't actually sure what he was asking.

Recognition sparked in Martin's eye.

Though his color had somewhat returned to normal since stepping inside, he flushed faintly pink.

"Not sure what you mean," he said and looked away, but forced himself to look back.

"I don't know what it is, but you sound a little… Actually, to be honest, I don't even know how to–what I'm hearing."

Martin was silent for a long moment. Over that moment, his face began to relax.

Finally, he sighed.

The voice that came out next was the same, but in a completely different shape.

"Strangers think they mean well, but don't understand they may be the fiftieth in a week to tell me how wonderful I sound. Or weird," Martin confessed, all his letters standing stock upright, but a few key ones dropped out.

"Grew up in Brighton, came over with my dad when he got a job in Austin I won't bore you with."

The shape of his words fluctuated the longer his sentences stretched, the flicker of anxiety mirrored in his eyes before he put it back in its place.

"You and I can probably agree that's not really the best environment for people like us, so I moved out on my eighteenth birthday." He turned a little away from the kitchen cutout.

"People like us?" Sydney asked. The electric kettle turned off.

"You and me. A bit more long black coat and, ah… tarot cards than cowboy boots and ninety-four Fahrenheit summers," he answered, turning away even more. His voice fluctuated less and less, though shifting more back toward Austin, less of Brighton every word.

"Ah, yeah," Sydney agreed. He turned back to the kettle and pulled it off.

"What about you?" Martin called into the kitchen again.

The tea might have gotten Martin to stay longer than Sydney would have liked, but the separation of the bar gave him an excuse not to look him in the eye while he probed for answers. The problem was, he wasn't sure what he should be asking.

He's lying.

Repeatedly raising his voice didn't do much for his own comfort level, either. He sensed a sore throat coming on, in addition to his wobbly limbs.

"Huh?" Sydney said with a cough.

Martin glanced around the room again.

"Except for no boxes, it looks like you just moved in. Recent job, or…" Martin trailed off. His head turned, but only slightly and back, as if he'd heard something but didn't want to look at where the sound came from.

"Yeah, fairly recent. That, and I just don't like distractions."

The answer wasn't *really* a lie, Sydney told himself. Then and there, checking his phone again for Jacob's answer, he decided it might have been best not to hide his dislike of him so much when they had met in the library.

Sydney inhaled to speak over the bar, but the universe was having none of it. Something hit the back of his throat and he bent over in a violent coughing fit, nearly disappearing from Martin's view.

Each time he hoped the fit was over and inhaled, the whole rough mess started all over. By the time he was done, the aches were back, and instead of dark spots he saw bright stars all around the edge of his vision.

He took a tentative breath.

"You good?" Martin asked, eyes wide and round from where he stood at the edge of the linoleum. Whatever Sydney sensed that made him want to keep Martin far, far away was nearly gone in that moment–still flickering beneath, but briefly irrelevant under overt concern.

"Fine. Thanks," he rasped.

Sydney stood up straighter and grabbed the cardboard tea box out of the cabinet. He breathed deeply to make up for lost time.

"Okay. Well, wherever you work, I hope you like it. Or it likes you," Martin finished with a nervous chuckle.

Sydney tore open each tea bag and dropped them in.

"Either way, it's something new. Sometimes you just have to make a choice and work with it," Sydney said.

He wasn't sure where the words were coming from, but the conversation had already gone on far too long.

Martin still looked him in the eye, but was slightly vacant, as if he was thinking of something else.

"Yeah, I guess so," he replied, more hesitantly than any of his words before. Suddenly, Martin's eyebrows turned upward, and he looked like he was about to cry.

As quickly as the look surfaced, it was gone.

"Thanks for the tea," Sydney blurted.

Martin said nothing.

"And the movie. Movies," Sydney added.

Martin was still silent. Sydney was, as well.

Finally, Martin quirked his eyebrows toward the center.

"No rush on the return. Hope you feel better," he said, and vanished out the front door with a short gust of cold air, but not another word.

Outside, he pulled his phone from his pocket and called Skadi. He stepped all the way to the curb, and wobbled forward and back on the edge, between the cars.

"Hey, uh, *yeah*. You're still at the theater?"

He paused as her voice came over.

"Okay. Then where can I find you? No, nothing's wrong, just wanted to meet up instead of later. Yeah, Sydney's fine."

Sydney broke away from staring at the closed door. He strode over and locked it again.

"*Why* is he lying? How do y-*we* know?"

Drink your tea, came the reply.

At the tiny metal click of the doorknob, a different idea planted itself. The implications spider-webbed out from the origin like a crack in a windshield.

Even if it made the hallucinations, or whatever they were, any worse, there would still be more to work with than his tarot deck. He was looking at the issue through a straw, too afraid of what might happen if the blinders were removed.

He turned back to the blue bottle on the table, then wondered where that old bag of instant coffee he'd seen earlier had gone to. It was time to open his eyes wider.

"You're doing it *again!*" Skadi's voice pierced Martin's daze, a lightning bolt through the winter fog.

For a terrifying second, he wasn't sure what she had said. More terrifying than that, he wasn't sure what he had been thinking about. He just looked over at her and blinked, letting the haze melt away to see what he might discover.

The cafeteria came back to him, as well as the buzz all around them. He remembered the sandwich in front of him and looked down.

He raised his eyes and jerked back.

"No, *don't* you act like that," she said. "I *told* you what that's like, and you *told* me you understood. I know you said you'd explain this week, but I just can't keep–"

Martin held her gaze, boring into Skadi's dark eyes, though she didn't appear to notice immediately.

Her fire flickered, but she kept on.

"I just can't keep assuming it's a fluke. Either tell me what you're so preoccupied with, or I'm going to have to just fill in the gap. That's how it works. I can't just–*Martin!*"

He ripped his gaze away and dropped his eyes to the battered grey backpack sitting slumped against the leg of his chair. Pulling the zipper with one hand wasn't practical, so he reached down with both and turned completely away from her.

Skadi waited, staring daggers with her jaw clenched. She started turning pinkish, but he didn't seem perturbed.

That is, until he sat up again and faced her. He gently set a small orange bottle with a white cap down in the center of the table, his face bloodless and glassy eyed.

She wanted to keep staring into him, but the neon orange was a powerful force. She fought the draw, but gave up and let her eyes fall to the prescription bottle.

Skadi snatched it up with a faint rattle. She looked back up at him. Martin hadn't moved. She looked back down.

"I don't know what this is," she said with a shrug.

"It's an anti-psychotic."

Skadi looked down again. She rolled it over in her hand, reading the long word around the bend of the bottle.

"What am I supposed to do with this?"

"You could give it back, for starters. That's my last–I pick up more later," he said.

Skadi set the bottle back down in the center of the table. She grabbed her backpack, pushed her chair out, and left her seat.

Martin didn't watch her go, but slowly reached out toward his bottle.

He jumped as Skadi fell into the plastic chair to his left. He had accepted her leaving, but only realized that's what he had braced for after she sat back down.

She grabbed the seat with both hands and slid herself closer to him as he grabbed the prescription bottle.

"I know you *know* we should talk about it. Is that okay right now?" she asked. She was so close, and radiated heat. His icy shell began to melt, though his core stayed solid, just like it had been for a while.

"N-not just now. I'm still going to cope with the fact I actually showed you this part."

"Okay. I'll ask again later." Skadi stared out across the sea of chairs with him.

Martin looked back down to his room-temperature sandwich, and she reached across the table for her own tray. They ate without words for a minute.

His mind began to drift into the fog again.

"Movie, by the way," she finally spoke. He blinked and sat up straighter.

"What?"

"I asked you if you wanted to see any of the movies at Cinemark tonight, even though it might be crowded. I know you don't like crowds, but you said you wanted to see something–I just don't remember which one," she explained and leaned into him further.

"Oh."

He handed her a potato chip from his plate.

"Remind me which ones are there?"

Skadi took the chip from him, then pulled her phone from her sweater pocket to pull up a list.

Sydney felt the silent phone vibrate in his coat pocket.

"I can't say anyone's really asked me that before. Without being facetious, I should add," said the man behind the desk.

"Are you sure you're okay?" he added.

He was a fairly narrow man, at least in face, accentuated by the cut of his grey suit. He wasn't much older than Sydney at first glance but, upon a second look carried faint lines in the corners of his dark eyes.

The rimless glasses perched on his brown face tipped the whole package over into an overt declaration of academia. If not psychology professor, he still carried an air of English, but not quite Philosophy.

Dr. Lorem had also recently shaved. Sydney ran a hand over his chin in thought, both in how to reply and wondering if he might need to do the same soon. The prickle was there, but he'd been too uncomfortable with every other aspect of existing to notice most of the time.

"I'm fine," Sydney lied.

He sat there in the cozy office arm chair, reluctant to move. The last twenty-four hours or so had been filled with nightmare, tarot, and a rekindled suspicion regarding everyone he met. His memory was trying to come back, but had taken the worst possible form–translating to hallucinations of near-death experiences and a fairly evil-ish twin.

His only choice was to wait around until his other self began talking to him more enthusiastically, or take the next logical step.

To get out of the house, he had to do something about how he felt. Physically, at the very least.

He therefore chugged a potion of apple cider vinegar, orange juice, chamomile tea, and liquid cold medicine to see if he felt any better. He did, right after he threw it back up in the kitchen sink.

After eight ounces of instant coffee, he found himself impulsive enough to run out and catch the bus. Everything was so bright. So loud. He had to keep moving to outrun it all.

"If you say so," Lorem said from behind the desk. He leaned forward onto his elbows and threaded his fingers together.

"But, I can spot an exhausted student a mile away. You want some coffee?"

"Nope," Sydney answered quickly.

Lorem had an odd twinkle in his eye that only shone brighter with curiosity at Sydney's immediate reply.

If Sydney could write and edit his own memory as well as rewind it, such as in that conversation with Jacob about Monday night, he might have been tempted to incorporate Dr. Lorem as an odd, academic uncle who gave him a beat-up paperback copy of *Lord of the Flies*, once.

He toyed a moment with the idea of coming to Lorem for a real therapy session one day, rather than dancing around the topic. Rather than using him for what Jacob was not convenient to be earlier.

"No, I'm fine. I don't like coffee," Sydney answered.

"That's unfortunate for a student, but suit yourself," he said with a chuckle.

The professor's original statement sank in. *An exhausted student a mile away.*

Sydney paused, looking over the six-foot gap between the desk and where he sat. The chair was the first comfortable looking place he saw, and he had trapped himself there, it seemed.

Sydney lifted his foot and gingerly placed his ankle on his opposite knee. Still aching, he did all he could to stifle a wince.

Lorem chuckled and leaned back.

Sydney held his gaze, then let his eyes drop to the spotless, perfectly arranged desk. Everything at right angles, not a speck of dust or item out of place.

It looked fake.

Lorem sat up straight again and continued.

"When I got the message that someone had called ahead, I thought it was a joke. I'll be totally honest, there."

He spread his hands and shrugged.

"'*Why should I take Psychology?*' you asked? Well, due to the… interesting circumstances of the question, I'd ask you to ask yourself a different question first. Why shouldn't you? You've already said you're not interested in a degree, you're just taking classes you want. If you're taking single courses, why shouldn't you take this one, as well?"

Sydney wasn't fully listening.

The office was larger than expected, leaving ample space not only for a set of armchairs, but a few small file cabinets and tall book shelves. Lorem sat with his back to the wide windows, outlined by stark winter light.

The blue metal cane rested against the far end of his desk.

"Precisely," Sydney curtly replied.

"Well, Mr. West–you said West, yes?"

"Yes."

Lorem leaned forward and out of his chair with a flurry of crackles. Sydney didn't want to know where the sounds came from if not the furniture.

The Professor grabbed his cane and made his way over to the chair in front of Sydney. Once he rounded the end of the desk, Sydney looked and looked again at the teacher's footwear, grimacing slightly in distaste.

The black and bright white saddle shoes struck a chord. A mixture of comfortable déjà vu and disgust washed over him.

Lorem, apparently ignoring Sydney's reaction, pulled the rolling armchair closer and turned it around to face Sydney. He sat and placed the cane between his legs, resting on one knee.

Leaning forward on the cane handle, he smiled.

"So, why are you really here? You seem like someone who likes to make your own decisions. Why ask anyone else?" This did not go as planned.

Sydney twitched a single eyebrow. He also wasn't sure what Lorem saw in him to prompt such a comment.

The only thing he was concerned about was getting into a conversation regarding something outlandish and entirely too specific, either in oversharing details or getting off on a tangent of self-diagnosis. He wasn't interested in getting paperwork that pretended to encapsulate what was wrong.

Then again, in the hands of the right person, maybe it could put him into a space to talk more freely. As long as he could still leave things alone if someone broke out the white coats.

"There are a lot of things going on," Sydney began. Lorem leaned forward a little more. "It's something I've wanted to do for a while, but–"

"*But*," Lorem interjected.

"–though now seems the best opportunity, I just don't want it to be some kind of…" he searched for the word a moment. "Decoy."

Lorem blinked.

"Decoy?" the Professor asked.

"I mean, I have plenty of time. Money doesn't matter right now. It looks too perfect, so I suppose I'm just–"

"Okay, wait, wait, wait," Lorem interrupted. He leaned back into his chair.

"I don't think I've ever heard that sentence come out of any student's mouth," he added, laughing more openly.

"I don't want to get into it."

All amusement dropped off Lorem's face. He sat back up straight and pushed his glasses up further on his nose.

"Okay. But, if I might make a suggestion," he started again. Sydney perked up.

"Try a different approach. What's the worst that could happen?"

Sydney's brows lowered.

"What approach is that?"

"No, I mean that literally," Lorem corrected. "What is the absolute worst-case scenario you can think of, if you do go ahead and take the class you're interested in, for the mere sake of that interest? If cost doesn't matter, what's still making you hesitate? Obviously, I'm somewhat of a… biased respondent."

They sat in silence.

Lorem waited patiently as Sydney cycled through a variety of scenarios. His face might have shown the cycle, but he tried to focus more on working it out on his own rather than the professor's waiting face.

At realistic best, Sydney would learn more about people, as well as why he was the way that he was. Even if what he learned didn't explain away seeing two of himself in the mirror, one of which was trying desperately to communicate and only irritating him, he might have a few new tools to work things out on his own.

He was sure there were plenty of people who took Psychology for parallel, but slightly saner reasons, in addition to the occasional burning desire to justify getting judgmental.

But he figured, at about five days old by the most technical sense, he had some license to judge. People around him did it all the time, but there was nothing in his head to consciously sway him like others had.

Remnants of the life before still trickled in, wordless feelings and gravitations, but he wasn't afraid of looking at things how they were.

Worst case scenario, he'd discover The Cat was a handler from a remnant of MK Ultra, and he'd eventually be caught and sent back for reprogramming and everything would start all over again. This time, in Texas.

Sydney's mouth flicked up at one side.

There was a lot in-between the best and worst, though.

He came back to the room in front of him. Lorem still stared, waiting, and Sydney's mouth dropped back to the usual hard line.

"Did you get an answer?"

Sydney didn't respond for a moment.

"Maybe. I suppose I'm just… afraid to get answers."

He forced out the words, the confession. Lorem paused yet again, looked away, then drummed his fingers on the side of his cane as he looked back.

"Hey, listen–" he began, "you don't have to tell me your life story. You don't even have to tell me what you're really afraid of–I get it. But, I'm here to talk, even if you don't take my classes. Sometimes we need to bounce things off other people so we can trick ourselves into feeling like it comes from somewhere else, so it's easier to look at."

Sydney slowly raised an eyebrow.

The ease at which Lorem sat was disturbing. Nothing he was saying was particularly suspicious, but something unnerving had sprouted.

"Hard things make us who we are, but that doesn't mean we should be sticking our faces into it all day every day," Lorem went on. "As long as you don't forget where you put that box, and it starts to smell later."

"I have a… hypothetical, then." Sydney's sentence started as a burst, but caught in the middle and he had to force out the rest. He glanced down at Lorem's odd shoes and back up.

"Okay, shoot."

"If there was a way to… take out the hard things, you'd agree that we'd no longer be the same?" Sydney asked, more slowly than he was used to speaking.

"Yes, I agree," Lorem answered.

"So, I–what if there was a way, psychologically, or medically–I don't know–to remove some event that makes someone most who they are?"

The Professor paused.

"I'm afraid I don't follow," he said.

"Like, a way to remove a memory that's pivotal to making someone who they are–would they really be a different person, or just act like they're different?"

Lorem's mouth twinged upward slightly.

"You said your other class is English?"

"Ah, yes," Sydney answered. He pulled his sore leg off his knee and set it on the floor, battling the pins and needles.

Lorem was nice enough, but something about him felt *empty*. Like when Sydney looked himself in the mirror. He was a gentlemanly cardboard cutout with a voice from somewhere else.

"If we're talking sci-fi, I'm afraid that's not really my area of expertise. But, as for the real world, you can't really, definitively remove an event from someone's past, even if they don't consciously remember it.

"There's more to memory than just literal, reel-tape style playback. You can take out the reel, but it's already taught everything else in a person how to react, even if it's not there, so it might just as well be. That tends to be what we in *the business* call Post-Traumatic Stress Disorder. Something tells you that to protect yourself, you have to let go of certain things, but you can't so easily let go of the effects."

"Sorry, I just realized I'm late. I have to get to class," Sydney burst.

He jumped up, swept his line of sight across as much of the office as he could, and disappeared from the room without turning back. He quietly closed the door behind him.

Dr. Lorem sat for another moment in the naturally lit room. He tapped his fingers on the arm of his chair, a lopsided grimace on his face.

"Sydney…" he said to himself. "You're making this harder than it has to be."

He propped himself back up on his cane and began making his way back to his desk.

A low black Mustang pulled up in front of the

pharmacy. Its blazing red brake lights cast a sinister glow against the dark pavement, deepened by the overcast sky and remnant of the early evening sunset.

The lights of the strip mall had already begun to cut through the approaching night.

Martin stepped out of his car and slammed the door behind him.

He flinched.

Neon flashed behind his eyes, the image of the grinning cat forcing its way into his thoughts. He shook his head and banished the picture, but his distaste was more from its persistence.

Though there were definitely more pressing issues than a light-up *Cheshire*. Images popped into his head all the time. He'd learned to move on. However, this one in particular came with an unnerving, familiar tone, like a ringing in his ears.

Regardless of whether or not it was relevant, in a way that should be managed or otherwise, there were other things to attend to first. He'd ride out the smaller bumps, whatever they left him with in the end.

He locked his car with the press of a button and a comically light beep that didn't match the intimidating silhouette. With a hop over the curb, he then disappeared into the drugstore's light.

A few minutes later he returned, not running, but not quite walking. He opened the driver's side door and threw the white paper pharmacy bag inside. The hair on the back of his neck stood up.

He yelled and shrank back as a human shape loomed up.

"Hey! Sorry," Levi said and spread his bare hands, palm up. "I didn't mean to scare you. You okay?"

Martin's eyes weren't as wide and round as they were in Sydney's house earlier, but his brows had fallen to one hard line just above them. He didn't reply.

"I just wanted to ask if you had some spare change. I'm short for the bus, and–"

"Oh, *don't start*," Martin hissed, his artificial voice completely dropped. He drifted further to his right, putting more of the car door between him and Levi.

"I'm sorry, do we know each other?" the older man asked. He reached forward and wrapped a hand around the top of the door.

Martin looked down at his grip and back up.

"If you people don't leave me be, I swear I *will* shoot you."

The edges of Levi's eyes flicked vaguely upward, like he was trying not to smile. He kept his hold on the door and slowly added his second hand.

Martin snatched his pistol from inside the driver's door and stood again, leaning further back.

Levi's almost-smile fell and he pulled his hands back. That is, until he realized the gun shape was mostly clear plastic with a bright orange tip. There were more black, plastic-looking pieces inside, in addition to the grip under Martin's hand.

"You're joking, right?" Levi said, that ghost of a smile blossoming full and with bemused disbelief. He leaned forward and wrapped both bare hands around the top of Martin's door.

"You think that works on me, you twink? Of *all people?*"

Martin fired off four shots, two into each hand. The fire-cracker *pop* of each was almost drowned by Levi's outburst before he pulled his hands out of danger.

Martin huffed, stepped into his car, and shut the door. He pulled out from the parking space and drove away even while Levi shook his hands out, trying to rid himself of the pain.

He stood there, arms crossed and hands under each arm, not against the cold but to see if he could encourage the throbbing to subside any quicker.

Once he resigned himself to the fact the pain would take its course, he stiffly pulled his phone from his coat pocket, examining the deep pink welts on his hands.

He selected his contact simply labelled *The Cat*, with an ink drawing of The Cheshire Cat from Alice In Wonderland as its photo.

"Yeah. Me. Texting is a bit of an issue right now,

yeah. No, no, no. I'm fine. Found Martin, though, like you'd asked. And tried to, you know, check up on how that earlier thing went. Like you'd asked."

There came an odd, tinny voice from the other end of the line. The tone spoke quickly, like a tiny, angry sewing machine.

"How well do you *think* it went, huh?" Levi answered. "Does he still think he's schizo?"

The garbled machinery spoke from the other side.

"No, I *know* he is, but does he still think all this is from that? He switched meds again, he has to be catching ont–"

One more word slipped through from the other side.

Levi clamped his jaw shut and sighed through his nose.

"If you tried to use him to deprogram our favorite scarecrow, I don't know that it's worked properly. There may be some feedback. Sydney's smarter than most give him credit for, you said yourself."

A small squelch came through.

"But yeah. Martin. He half-remembers me, and he *definitely* has some idea what he can do. Even if that thing with Sydney worked, he just tried to pull that image switch thing he can do, and shot me with some stupid toy gun."

Sydney reached his front door an hour later. The walk had helped him keep from slipping into a total fog, but his mental energy was still straining to keep a charge.

Lorem was familiar.

Colorado Springs was becoming too crowded.

He slammed the door behind him and looked for a distraction that didn't involve tarot. He wasn't sure if it was working, or simply giving himself an avenue to make things worse.

The movies Martin had dropped off were out of the question at the moment. He might as well have gone back to the deck of cards if he wanted to wheedle more disturbing images out of his subconscious.

Instead of continuing to focus on Lorem, it was time to see what he could dig up on other topics. He simply wasn't wired for time-wasting of traditional distraction.

Sydney opened the laptop computer on the coffee table and hit the power button. The computer wasn't slow by any means, but he took the short wait as an excuse to get up and rummage in the kitchen.

He liked faces more than names, because while names could change, or be even outright deception, faces were more trustworthy. Unfortunately, they typically came with someone behind them who expected conversation.

Over the last few days, faces had grown more familiar. The ones that weren't, were still surrounded by odd little details that made him feel like people weren't telling the whole truth. Some people were empty, while others were facades hiding something more important inside.

Lorem and his saddle shoes would have to wait. Sydney would first test his theory in a few smaller ways, once he made it back into the living room.

He opened the tea tin Martin had brought from Skadi and found a wire tea strainer. The mesh ball was laughably small, but the only one he had.

He pinched and dropped some of the dry, loose tea into the ball on the tiny chain, guessing at what it actually contained. It smelled disgusting, and something of grass clippings with a hint of dirt. But he didn't care. It was something new.

He smelled it again with a grimace, putting his nose inside. For a moment, he smelled the metallic blood again–but only for a moment. The scent of the metal tin replaced it.

He popped the electric kettle on and strode back into the living room. He sat down on the couch and leaned over the laptop like a giant humanoid question mark.

Then hesitated.

He typed *George Lorem Psychology* into the web search and stared at the words.

He backspaced several times, then held the key. He then typed *MK Ultra Colorado State* into the box, instead, then leaned back and crossed his arms.

That search might be slightly less regrettable, and warm him up for the hard truth.

The electric kettle turned off and he stood to finish

his tea. He jumped as the house creaked above him.

He wasn't sure whether the sound was a footfall, but weighed the cost of deciding either way. The house was nearly empty, except for the library upstairs. He didn't mind if someone stole his toothpaste, whether that person wore his own face or not.

With the way things were going, if someone really had broken into the house, he wasn't sure if he could react in any meaningful way. The hallucinations, if they were really technically unreal, were growing more pronounced.

Despite his attempted attention given to them, it seemed the other half of his brain was determined to continue acting out in more outlandish ways.

Sydney glanced under the wooden table and caught a shape out of the corner of his eye even as he stepped forward. He nearly tangled his legs turning back too quickly.

Bracing himself on the arm of the sofa, he stooped over and picked up a tarot card from off the carpet.

The Magician, with an illustration of a black-haired man in a black robe. He wasn't sure what it supposedly meant, but noted this card was a bit heavier than the rest. He rocked it back and forth in one hand and found it had a holographic layer, switching the blacks to white and then back again.

He sighed and threw it behind him, somewhere in the vicinity of the coffee table before he entered the kitchen again. He pulled the tea strainer from the cup on the counter-top and threw the mesh ball in the sink.

Sydney froze. He'd grown used to the occasional feeling there was someone else in the room, but this time his hair stood up even more. Not only was there a presence on the other side of the kitchen cutout, but it was staring.

He wanted to remember what was going on, but another part of himself was the issue. The rest of his life was so close, he could have reached out and taken it back if not for someone else holding his wrist down -- that part afraid of what would happen if he was whole again.

He kept his eyes down but turned to squarely face the bar. He slowly raised his eyes to the counter as he stirred his tea, then raised them a little more. Once he saw the chair and carpet, he finally looked all the way up to the empty living room.

The stairs creaked and his whole body flinched, spilling hot tea over his hand. He set down the mug and turned the faucet on.

Cold water ran over the pain. He wasn't burned, but it made him more comfortable. Maybe he should get a travel cup, he thought. Something with a lid.

That presence congealed right in front of him, as if someone stood on the other side of the bar. His head snapped up and he saw nothing, but the feeling didn't leave.

He stood there, staring wide-eyed out into his own house.

The moment was like seeing a new face, without the face. Every time he met someone new, there was a voice that spoke to him out of nowhere, though not so explicitly as hearing his own from the same place.

The whisper begged for him to listen, to understand what laid beneath. Sometimes he could, when prompted, such as something in how that person walked, the way they cut their hair, or how they held a cup.

Here, it was just that wordless voice, nagging.

Pleading?

He tried to prepare himself for some momentous discovery that he was really just insane. If he was, how would he know? There was no one in his life he would dare check himself against, not explicitly.

Though he mildly amused himself in the worst-case scenario exercise earlier, another came to mind. The idea was another in a long line of possibilities, but only one of a few that gathered enough evidence to itself.

Was this what being dead was like?

Or was he dying somewhere, pestering himself to come back to himself out of necessity?

Sydney took a sip of his tea, still staring–waiting for whatever he was looking at to blink. It was, again, likely some aspect of himself trying to force its way into his senses. A twisted sense of déjà vu as two shards drifted almost close enough to touch.

What was so horrible that he'd risk doing whatever

he'd done, and put himself in this mess? What was in his brain's recycle bin, trying to claw its way out?

And, while he was at it, would Martin still be looking at things that weren't there, if Sydney was having a normal time of things? *Folie a deux* was the name for a shared delusion, but Sydney hadn't actually shared anything about the situation. There was no reason for Martin to see or believe anything Sydney had never talked about.

The tea was still scalding hot, but somehow satisfying over his sore throat. It burned not only in temperature, but with a medicinal quality he couldn't place. He liked it.

That is, until he realized his fingertips were numb.

Whatever he'd stashed in his recycle bin would have to wait, regardless of how irritated that part turned out to be. Martin saw something, and Martin was also lying, if the voice of the ghost was ever to be believed. The ghost was more tangible than Sydney thought at first, or everything was an unfortunate coincidence.

He couldn't count on coincidence. Not now.

Sydney stopped drinking the tea, then tore his eyes away from the Nothing across from where he stood. He stared into his cup, tracking the progress of the strangely pleasant Nothing creeping up his arms.

He turned to the opposite counter where he'd left the round tin, but lost his footing on the linoleum–just as his phone buzzed from the dining table.

He finally lost all feeling in his hands and dropped the mug. It smashed on the floor.

Adrenaline spiked. He hooked what he thought might be his arms around the back of the wooden chair.

It didn't help.

Sydney fell to the floor and shuffled on his hands and knees, through spilled tea and shards of ceramic before he collapsed on the carpet, facing the drafty back door.

The room was silent for another long moment.

The phone buzzed again, a text message pushing its way past his lock screen. The icon was a softly glowing cat face made from neon lights. And it read,

Have you learned your lesson yet?

SEVEN

Something was wrong with Martin, Jacob was convinced. He sat in front of Jacob, talking to him outside the dorm. On a Saturday.

Maybe they both had the same level of social life–none.

The cafeteria wasn't very full, but Martin had made the obviously conscious decision to sit in the next seat over from him. He practically fell from space, almost skidding the chair across the linoleum floor.

Jacob didn't hear what he was saying at first, but caught on in time to pretend he'd heard all the words.

"–bit of a panic, turns out I left it in class. Don't know why they bother with physical books anymore, especially since the last one I got had all the answers in it. Thanks for looking, though. Are you going to eat that or stare at it?"

Jacob planted a hand on the entire top of his sandwich.

"Sorry, licked it. Means it's mine," he said. "You couldn't find your books?"

"Yeah, like I told you. On the phone," Martin answered and pulled his backpack onto his lap.

"You never called me about any books, though."

Martin's eyes slipped vacant, then snapped back.

"Ah, never mind, then," he finally spoke. "I'll be right back."

Martin jumped up again. The chair jumped a few inches across the floor as he launched himself from his seat. He slid across a patch of wet footprints left from other students, right into line at the cafeteria.

Jacob sensed a new presence and turned to find Skadi standing there. She silently looked across to where Martin stood.

Her eyes fell to Jacob, and she raised one eyebrow.

"Is he doing okay?" he asked, removing his hand from his sandwich. He'd squashed it a little, and pulled the bread up at the corner to inspect the state of his lettuce.

"What do you mean?" Skadi took a seat in the chair Martin had just vacated.

"I don't know. He just seems a bit… I don't want to say '*off*,' since I barely know the guy, I just don't… never mind," Jacob finished, half-mumbling. In the distance, Martin fast-walked back in their direction, tray suspended between his hands.

"I didn't know he was headed over here, by the way. But I realized I could probably ask you about something else." She pulled her bag into her lap and pulled out a big, round glass container of green and popped the clamps off each side, one-by-one.

An idea wormed itself into Jacob's head, and he wasn't sure if he should encourage it to worm its way right back out again.

"I'm not exactly an English nerd," Skadi started, "but the more we get into the Hamlet score at Theatreworks, the more I keep wondering about actual stage play formatting. I don't know anyone in the production this time, otherwise I'd just swipe a script. In a friendly, non-threatening manner," she finished with a laugh, wiggling her eyebrows.

"Why don't you just download a–" Jacob stopped as Martin made a cutting motion across his own neck with one hand.

"You prefer hard copy, I take it?" Jacob corrected.

He was still a little stunned at the sudden overturn in his immediate social group. He wasn't necessarily unpopular, but people didn't tend to stick around or move him to the top of invitation lists.

He got to know a lot of people just a little, but never thought he'd find Martin and his girlfriend in that rotation.

Martin pulled out his chair and took a seat across from Jacob. His tray landed hard and his soda bottle fell over, but he righted it without missing a beat.

Jacob's idea was still there, beginning to grow roots.

"Sorry, scripts aren't really my favorite, either," he explained. "It's not exactly the same, but if you can't ask someone in the production, maybe you can ask around in the film department."

Skadi slapped both hands down, open-palmed, on either side of her salad.

"No, don't worry. That's the idea face," Martin

offered through a mouth full of pizza.

"I need movie scripts," Skadi said, eyes bright yet distant.

"Yeah, that could be a good start," Jacob spoke more quietly.

"Uh, personal question, though," he continued.

Martin tensed and tried his best to keep his eyes from widening too much.

"Where'd you guys meet, exactly?"

Jacob noted Martin's subtle worry didn't disappear. He'd also stopped chewing.

"Theater," Skadi didn't quite burst, but the rush of the single word was apparent.

"Last Spring, before he swapped out, a bunch of History majors came to see The Importance of Being Earnest, and I knew one of them, so."

Martin glanced back at her, then jumped back up toward the drinks fountain.

"No, seriously. What's wrong with him?" Jacob asked under his breath.

Skadi's head fell almost between her shoulders, and she looked at him sideways.

"Can you just leave it alone, *please*? It's personal, so if he hasn't told you, he doesn't want to. He's trying to be more social. What more do you want?"

"I'm sorry, it's just…" Jacob hesitated and looked into space, as if he might find the right order of his words there. He looked back and didn't find her much changed.

"This week has been *really* odd. Some weird stuff going on."

"With Martin? What do you–" she started.

"Well, I'd hope not," Jacob rushed. "Just when someone I live with starts being a particular kind of weird, even if it's, you know, all fine, I'd just feel better knowing what's going on."

Skadi only stared.

"Why don't you just ask him?" she calmly offered.

"Ask who what?" Martin also asked. Jacob and Skadi jumped.

He stood behind the two of them, holding another

hard plastic tray. There were another two slices of pizza sitting there on a second paper plate and, from the look on his face, the question seemed genuine. He waited patiently.

Jacob glanced to Skadi and back.

"I just wanted to see if you guys would be cool with a double date at some point," Jacob said, trying to smile.

"Oh." Martin folded one slice of pizza in one hand. "I guess if Skadi, you'd like to, that sounds… fine."

He didn't seem fully convinced, but tore his eyes away from Jacob and looked to Skadi. That anxiety from a minute ago was still there, his eyes a little too wide and pupils a bit too large.

Martin looked back to Jacob, but didn't say anything for a few seconds. He softened, but was still very much on edge.

"You like pizza?" Martin blurted. "I know a place downtown that's nice."

Sun high in the sky, an old, beat-up white truck pulled up on front of 13 West Barrow Street. The faded vehicle gave a cold groan as a hand in a thin black work glove pulled the parking brake to engage.

Levi pushed the driver's side door open, pushed it harder when it wouldn't move, then shut it before he stepped up to the door of the yellow house.

He shoved his hands in his black coat and looked over the doorway, lingering with an amused smile on Sydney's black iron bat knocker.

Enough of that. Down to business.

He raised his hand wide, as if he intended to bang on the door, but stopped short. Instead, he daintily took the knocker between two fingers and let it fall three times.

He stepped back and waited.

The wait was too long. He pulled his phone from his pocket, pulled one glove off under his arm, and hit only two buttons before he held it to his ear.

"It's the yellow one, right? Well, yeah, I see the bat. I just wanted to be sure."

He waited as that same tinny voice from his call in the pharmacy parking lot spoke from the other end. A cartoon cat voice forced its way through a barely functional ham radio.

"You really thought Martin was the best choice for this guy? No, I'm not questioning your judgment, I'm just– well, no, I'm questioning your j- no, of course not. I'm saying regardless of what Martin can do, he's still an idiot and I don't know why you didn't just–"

The Cat vented over the receiver.

"All I'm *saying*, is that if he's not answering the door, there may be a different problem than it not working. Well, unless he's seen me before, like *really* seen, in which case I'd understand."

Levi side-stepped to Sydney's front window.

"Never mind who you sent, then. Either it worked or it didn't, and I'll let you know if it's somewhere in the middle. Though, you're sure it's been long enough?"

Levi glanced up and down the street before he looked closer in through the window. The curtains were drawn, but a floor lamp was on inside and let him see through once he put his nose closer to the glass.

He could also see the kitchen light at the far end of the room. He tilted his head and took another step to the side. Changing perspective, he spotted Sydney's hand laying on the floor near the back entrance of the kitchen.

"And you're sure you got past his defense? Your new little pawn didn't bounce off, as usual?"

Fargo let his eyes wander up further left, up to the back door and the boarded-shut cat door. Satisfied, he stood up straight from leaning suspiciously in toward the window.

"Speaking of defense–" Levi spoke again. The tinny cat interrupted before he finished.

"Because you supposedly know everything, that's why."

He stepped to the left side even further and stood squarely in front of the dark, narrow alleyway.

"I think I see him, so I'm going in. I just don't want to get stabbed, or shot, or… aneurism'd, or something. Yeah, I have my gloves."

Levi sized up the entry, tilting his head to the side like a dog confronted with a strange bug. He then spun completely around on one foot and leaned against the wall just outside the mouth of the alley, instead.

"Okay, never mind about that. I think I have an idea," he said. "Yep. Good idea. Foolproof. See you in a bit, hopefully with your poster-boy."

He closed the call, but didn't put his phone away. He walked slowly to the curb, eyes on his phone screen. Once there, he cast a glance up the street, then down, and then one more time in the first direction.

Satisfied he was alone, Levi spun on his heel and strode quickly down the alley, along the way stashing his phone and putting his glove back on.

Sydney registered a creak from the direction of the back yard, muffled through a cloudy consciousness.

Attempting and failing to lift heavy eyelids, he acknowledged a curious texture at his temple. Carpet?

There came more creaks, then a loud, wooden *crack*. The crash was almost enough to jolt Sydney fully awake but, though his brain lit up, he didn't physically move.

His internal gears were starting to tick again, but he was still wrapped in a heavy, warm blanket. The creeping, icy air brushed the fingertips of his outstretched hand.

Why's the door... open... came the sound of his own voice in his own head.

Sydney sensed a presence and dismissed it as the usual haunting, until he heard a footfall through the floor. He stirred slightly, pushing harder through the heaviness with the help of sharp, outdoor air.

Levi froze in the back end of the living room. Sydney had stirred but didn't wake up.

He stepped in a little further.

Sydney was still breathing, at least.

An open laptop computer rested on the coffee table, and the phone sat over to the left of the front door. It still showed the image of the neon cat, but disappeared into the black as he took another step.

Levi's gaze lingered on where he'd seen the icon from a distance.

"Well, *you're* sure of yourself," he mumbled.

Martin's job was to get Sydney thinking about what

he didn't want to think about. The pawn should have pulled enough to unravel this ridiculous thing Sydney West had become.

Levi screamed–half howled.

"*Don't!*" he burst. He jumped back and wrenched his ankle out of Sydney's hand.

"Who the *hell* are *you*?" Sydney said, forcing each word out into reality one at a time. The fog had all but lifted, but left him feeling a bit like he'd just stepped outside with wet hair. He was also heavier, but not sure why.

"Jacob sent me. Had to get to work and you weren't answering your phone. But, more importantly, what are you doing on the floor?" Levi asked as he bent over, forcing a casual tone back to the surface. Hopefully he'd buried the embarrassing scream for good.

Sydney rolled over to face the ceiling and dragged the inside of his elbow over his eyes. He groaned.

"Okay. No problem. Can I help you up?" Levi offered, still leaning over him.

"No, don't–" Sydney rolled over again and planted one hand on the floor. "Don't touch me. I can–"

He stopped after rising to all fours, staring at the ground, then quickly looked up to Levi.

Levi stood straight and gave a lopsided smile, hands in his coat pockets.

Sydney didn't flinch, but his total freeze for a second was enough for Levi to take note.

He rose to his knees, then grabbed onto the edge of the counter to turn himself around before he attempted to stand. His socks slid on the linoleum, but he was able to grab onto the other counter-top to help himself up and forward at the same time.

Away from the intruder.

"Where'd you say you know Jacob from?" Sydney asked. He looked around for where he'd left his mug, then realized it was at his feet in pieces. That also explained his damp socks.

He grimaced and moved forward again, through the debris.

"From work. I had some car trouble yesterday.

Vintage does *not* mean reliable, turns out."

Sydney looked over his shoulder and began the slow process of turning around. He felt more and more stable, but there was something distinctly unsetting in how he felt in his head. Everything was so vivid in the dimness. The quiet, so loud.

"He gave me a ride," Levi went on, "so he asked if I'd return the favor and check up on you. Are you sure you're okay?"

Levi looked Sydney up and down as he finally turned to squarely face him. He held onto the end of the countertops, heels on the carpet, like he might suddenly collapse into a pile of bones.

"Do I *look* okay?" Sydney bit back. There was also the part about Jacob checking up on him. Jacob being worried. It was all a bit too out of character.

Oddly concerned for Sydney's well-being, yes. The first to reach out, especially when Sydney was told not to message him so much, no.

Levi crossed his arms, considering.

"I mean, I'll be okay," Sydney corrected with a cough. The cough echoed in his head.

"What's your name, anyway?"

"Ah, it's Levi," he replied.

"Levi what?" Sydney pressed.

"Levi Novak. Friends call me Levi. Enemies call me *That One Motherf–*"

"*Nnnnn*-okay. Levi Novak." Sydney paused, and took a breath. Though he was upright, something was distinctly amiss, aside from the damp socks. His skeleton shook inside him.

"I would like–" Sydney began.

Levi's eyes widened as he straightened up even more, like a puppy in front of someone holding a treat. He waited a moment in anticipation.

"–you to leave my house. Tell Jacob I'm fine. He can call any time."

Levi's face fell, but only to the same vague, polite amusement Sydney had seen in The Red Cheshire. He turned and took a few steps toward the back door.

The boards blocking up the cat door had been loosened on both sides and created a gap just large enough for someone to reach through to the door knob, provided that arm was also just large enough.

Levi laid a hand on the door knob and popped the exit open a few inches.

Sydney cleared his throat.

The half-stranger turned back, expectant yet again.

"Front door," Sydney commanded.

Levi closed the door, turned back, and grinned brightly. He walked quickly through the kitchen, side-stepping shards of ceramic on the floor, and then past Sydney, shrinking his posture in careful effort not to touch him.

From there, Sydney stepped behind him, past the kitchen-end of the couch, and pointed sternly to the patch of linoleum at the front door.

In a moment and one more burst of cold air, the unwanted visitor was gone.

Sydney locked the door, then leaned right to look out the window. Levi stood there with his phone to his ear, saying something quietly Sydney couldn't make out, though everything else was so loud.

"*No, but it's a start. Looks like he shut down to avoid reboot–he's fine. But I recommend keeping an eye on him. Something else is going on,*" he would have heard, otherwise.

Sydney pulled away from the window and, in a moment, listened to the low rumble as Levi drove away. He looked back through the translucent curtains. The truck was really gone.

That man, however, probably wouldn't be.

Sydney turned around and scanned the room for wherever his phone had gotten to.

He wasn't really sure if the tea had truly put him out cold, but the effect was slowly wearing off. He hadn't yet located his phone, but was stable enough to ascend the staircase without holding onto the rail, even if he did list to the side the longer he refused to hold it.

Sydney descended the staircase again almost before

he stepped foot in the upstairs hallway. He stood at the foot of the steps, listening to the cacophony of the empty house.

The refrigerator buzzed. The wind blew.

The tree outside scraped while Sydney's shirt rustled on his skin, his socks squeezing his feet just enough to make him anxious. The faucet upstairs dripped and traffic in the distance screeched and honked. The ghost of a collision echoed in the back of his brain and he clapped both hands over his ears, screwing his face up toward the center.

He found himself hunched over the kitchen counter again, everything tensed. He slowly removed his hands from his ears and opened his eyes.

Sydney was alone.

He really, truly felt alone in the house.

His eyes wandered to the broken gap in his back door, where the white noise of ambient air filtered through. The entire door would need replaced not only because of the gap, but because that space was now within arm's length of the doorknob.

He stepped over to the wood panel to find it wasn't broken. He lifted it and set it back on the nail Levi had pushed it away from. Still cold, but would do for now.

And still, he felt alone in the house.

He spotted his phone on the end of the dining table and strode through the kitchen.

Then came a whisper, and he jumped and looked back across the living room. Still alone, he grabbed his phone and retreated to the kitchen, leaning back on the countertop, facing the bar. He glanced into the reflection of himself on the microwave door and raised an eyebrow.

There was only one of him in that reflection. He looked back down to his phone, and only one text from Jacob, and no calls.

Levi was lying.

You still want me to call or something? Jacob's last text read, which was delivered at about 9:00 PM last night. Nothing else came after that.

Who's Levi? Sydney texted back, and waited. He glanced up at the computer on the coffee table, then back down. Still no reply.

He glanced back up and a chill went down his back. It may have been from the hole in the back door, but not likely, given his general immunity to the cold.

Sydney stepped forward and over the back of the couch, where he sat down, shuddering against the sensation of his own clothes against his skin. Phone in one hand, he tapped the track pad on the laptop with the other.

Every muscle in his body tensed. He snapped out of it as Jacob's reply buzzed in his hand. Though, he still felt a bit electrified and not in any desirable way.

Friend from work. Why?

Broke into my house and said hi, Sydney replied.

wtf are you talking about?

He said you asked him to check on me, since I wasn't answering my phone, he shot straight back.

The ellipses animated far too long for his comfort. Sydney glanced up at his laptop screen and then back to find Jacob had finally replied.

I might have mentioned something about you not liking to talk to a lot of people, but I never would have sent him over there.

That's what I thought, Sydney answered. *If he's working today, I'll come over.*

I don't think he is, but I'll keep a look out. That's really weird. He's not someone I'd guess would do that and I'm sorry.

I'll come by anyway, Sydney replied.

You don't need to do that, I'll keep a lookout and talk to him, Jacob's rushed.

No, I mean I still want to talk to you about some stuff I've been thinking about, Sydney shot back in equal enthusiasm.

I'm off at 6, I'll come by, Jacob offered.

Sydney's phone read 12:07 PM. He sighed.

Sounds good, he answered, then closed his screen and set the black rectangle down next to him on the white.

He still felt alone in the house, which he supposed should have been the default, considering he was the only person consistently there since Monday. However, with his current expectations, a pattern had clearly been broken. His senses had shattered, and reached out for each and every distraction that presented itself. The whole world shook not in monumentous tremors, but thousands of little crackles like walking over miles of eggshells.

He almost wished for his haunting to return, rather than staring across to his open laptop screen, nothing but the black in front of him.

Levi tapped his wingtip shoes under the table, in time with the music from the ceiling he wasn't consciously listening to. With bare hands, he shoveled a slice of his waffles into his mouth, then checked the watch on his left wrist.

He looked up to Lindsey standing at the end of the table. Down to the little rainbow striped heart pin, then back up to her face.

"You still doing okay? Anything else I can get you?"

"Eeeuh…" he looked out across the table, where the decimated remains of multiple orders littered the surface.

"More coffee would be great. And maybe Search and Rescue for the person who actually asked me here, but I'll settle for coffee."

He smiled, then let it drop.

"Right up!" Lindsey replied before she disappeared again.

The bell over the door jangled, and Levi leaned out to his left, coffee cup tipped up toward his mouth. With a jolt, he sat back up straight and frantically arranged his plates in a neat stack and shoved them to the side.

Dr. Lorem slid into the bench seat across from him. He leaned his cane on the space at his side.

"Don't you get fed during the week?" Lorem asked, looking over the stack of plates with distain.

"On a good day," Levi answered with a grin. "Today, I'm calling it a work expense."

"That's… great," Dr. Lorem started, not making eye contact. He leaned forward and threaded his fingers together on the table.

"I'd like the update, and to be on my way, if you please."

A small, amused smile bled out onto Levi's face. He took his time reaching for his coffee cup again, lifting, and then frowning down into it once he discovered it was empty.

George Lorem coughed.

"Okay. Alright. Turns out, our mutual interest has set up a few more road blocks to… repatriation. My, ah, *manager* seems to think we need to go in heavier, rather than let the half-assed job of the last agent run its course."

Lorem rubbed one temple, then laid his hand back down.

"I get that we're *technically* working on the same thing, but if you could just say things simply, I'd be much obliged."

Levi paused, then took a deep breath. He leaned forward and threaded his fingers together in front of him.

Lorem pulled his hands back from Levi's.

Levi smiled.

"Boss sent another agent who was supposed to help bring out the Sydney we both know and loathe. They didn't do their job, apparently, though they got a few things started by tipping his internal alarms."

"Like?" Lorem cut in.

"Well, when I checked on him, he was passed out on the kitchen floor. All that sensory stuff is starting to come back, which means he'll be reaching out even more, widening his radar, whether he likes it or not."

Lorem looked away and frowned, then looked back.

"How long would it take if things develop on their own?"

"How long was he in your program?" Levi asked.

"It can't take that long. He's not starting from zero, and we're on a timeline." Lorem's eyes drilled across the table.

Levi swallowed.

"Like I said, we may be going heavier. He'll have to go heavier to match, which will break through whatever he's done to his head," he offered.

Lorem sat up straighter.

"How heavy is *heavy?*" the Professor asked.

Levi stared, unblinking.

He then leaned forward on the table, propped up on each elbow. Lorem drew his hands back even further.

"You want to talk to our feline friend yourself, or continue working as things are?" Levi asked quietly.

Lorem leaned forward a little, though shoved his hands under the table.

"I'd just like to be sure you don't go so hard that you forget who's looking the other way, Mr. Novak."

Levi leaned back and grabbed his empty coffee cup to move it closer. He looked away with a slow, deep breath, but Lorem spoke first.

"If you push him, he *will* do worse than kill you. Which I wouldn't mind, except we'd have to start over, and he'd be ahead now. Call me when you have a *full* update."

Lorem turned to leave the booth.

"*No*, no, no, no. Wait."

Levi reached out, which only made Lorem push himself out even faster, his eyes wide. He sat there on the end of the bench, just beyond the reach of Levi's bare hand.

Levi pulled his arm back and placed it under the table.

"Sorry. That wasn't on purpose. Just hold up a minute."

Lorem turned back. He slowly slid back into the seat, holding himself from blinking.

"You'll get this guy back," Levi said. Lorem didn't place his hands on the tabletop again.

"My people, your people, you know, we want the same thing in the end." Levi tapped absently on the table a few times. Lorem looked at his hand without moving his head.

Levi stopped tapping. He pulled his hand under the table with the first.

"You want Sydney back. We want Sydney back, *with you*. Just because my boss hates your guts, that doesn't mean I'm not gonna be honest with you guys."

Lorem sighed.

"Okay, listen," he began. "We've been at this for months. You and your furry friend have made barely any progress except for tracking this guy, and still can't tell us why *we* can't do that.

"If you want us to keep letting you do… whatever it is that you do, you're going to have to give us real, tangible proof we're getting somewhere. We've filled in the gaps for you, and you're not returning the favor. Without that, there's no reason for us to continue this relationship."

Levi leaned all the way back, then crossed his arms.

"Yeah, that's fair."

He uncrossed his arms and sat up straighter.

"Going into this, we ran on the assumption he's unstable, based on… well, you know the story. But, there are a few patterns that suggest he's planned further ahead than we thought." Levi cleared his throat.

"Honestly, I think he *wants* to be found. The break was always a possibility, but he's set himself up to make sure he can get back what he loses. Just not sure if he knew he'd lose this much. We're also not sure what abilities he's set up Sydney version two with. I don't want to go in heavy and find he has a bomb strapped to his brain or something. It'll take some time to see if he deprograms this little *fugue* thing, himself."

"As we've established–how *much* time?" Lorem insisted. "Not all of us can afford to spend our time waiting around in diners. Creepin' on the waitresses."

Liam hesitated. He rolled his empty coffee cup around on the lower edge.

"Not my type."

He dropped the cup flat again.

"I'll have a better idea on timeline next time I see him, I think. I just do what I'm told." Levi looked into the ceiling and back.

"Mostly. But what I can tell you for certain, that last agent is probably gonna get replaced. If that helps."

Sydney felt a few taps to the back of his head. He wiped his hand over his hair to see if anything was there–there wasn't–then took a few more seconds looking up to the ceiling, pondering why the feeling was so *wrong*.

Those taps were a sound. That sound was a series of knocks at the door. He'd been so lost in thought that the interruption was felt more than heard.

Sydney turned back to the wall after passing acknowledgement of his front door. He placed the yellow sticky note in his hand next to a clipping from a magazine, which was pinned down with a clear thumbtack.

He picked up another square from the yellow block sitting on the coffee table and pulled the pen from behind his ear as he turned back to face the project.

The knock came again, more deliberately this time.

He held the blank yellow box mid-air, then turned and glared at the door at the dark end of the room. It was only then he noted that the room, in fact, was mostly dark. He looked out the window, and so was the sky.

Sydney adjusted his uncomfortable shirt collar, then grabbed his phone from off the table to check the time. He was definitely due to open the door.

He turned his back to the mosaic of pictures, clippings, and sticky notes on the wall, then pushed his long strides even longer once the sound of clicking metal joined the whistling wind outside on the street.

He unlocked the door and swung it wide open.

Jacob hopped up from a crouch, multi-tool in hand.

Sydney's eyes dropped to the spiky metal gadget, then came back up to Jacob.

Jacob hurriedly folded the tool together with both hands and hid the entire thing in a pocket.

"I could have you arrested," Sydney said, standing in the cold doorway, and getting colder. He watched a spectrum of decisions flash behind Jacob's eyes.

He had apparently settled on one, and stepped into the slightly warmer house without additional invitation.

"But you won't," Jacob countered.

"Oh, won't I?" Sydney said under his breath. He closed the door.

Jacob spotted the mess on the wall, hesitated, then threw his messenger bag onto the couch. He started sliding his jacket off, one sleeve at a time, continuing to stare at the wall.

Sydney's laptop sat on the coffee table, plugged into the outlet near the fireplace, screen dark. Conversely, the whole side of the room Jacob had entered through was oddly dark. Whatever was happening on the living room wall was lit only by Sydney's floor lamp.

The rest of the space was indirectly lit from the cold light of the overhead fluorescence from the kitchen.

Street lamps outside did give some light through the venetian blinds, but was more of a glow–nothing to read by. Or maybe that was just Jacob's preference.

Sydney may have simply preferred the high contrast and long shadows, to match his shape.

Jacob fell down back into the couch, face sluggish. He dropped his jacket next to him, then took off his glasses and tried his best to clean them with the edge of his flannel shirt.

"Is this what you wanted to talk about? Your detective wall over there?" he asked.

"No." Sydney dropped the pen on the kitchen counter as he entered. Still avoiding Jacob's eyes, he began searching the cabinets.

Jacob waited for any further explanation. He craned his neck over his shoulder, and then some more.

Sydney still didn't look at him. He found a light sage grey mug with a chip in the handle.

"Aaalrighty. Can I at least ask when you got a cork board?" Jacob conceded and turned back to the wall, giving his neck a rest.

"I didn't," Sydney said. He flipped the tap open.

Jacob put his glasses back on.

He squinted at the messy rectangle on the wall and heard the mug fill somewhere in the background and the water tap turn off.

He threw his head backward so he could see the kitchen a little better, however upturned.

"So, you're just sticking things to the wall?"

"It's *my* wall to stick things to," Sydney declared. "Did you see Levi at all, or did you just come by because you like my sofa?"

Sydney hit the switch on the electric kettle. His upside-down figure then loomed up in front of Jacob's reddening face.

He pulled his head back upright, blood rushing back into place.

"Uh, neither. But it's a nice couch, don't get me wrong." Jacob ran a hand over the cushion.

"You wanted me to come over and hear some crazy or not-crazy theory of yours and place it on the spectrum for you. Or did you forget, since I apparently had to pick your lock?"

Jacob still looked for a pattern–any pattern–to the display of cheaply printed photos, magazine clippings, text blocks, and hand-written notes that littered the wall. All that was missing was a web of red yarn to connect it all.

Sydney stood behind the couch, staring along with Jacob. He crossed his arms and clicked the pen, picked up off the counter. And then he clicked it again. A moment later, he punctuated the air yet again.

"So, anyway–I have twenty minutes until Katrina is off work. I'd appreciate getting on with it."

The kettle turned off and he heard Sydney retreat into the kitchen, footsteps however faint.

"I feel like I knew this was going to happen," he called from the bar.

"What are you talking about?"

Jacob's eyes wandered the mess, willing himself not to try so hard to make sense of it. After all, Sydney's method seemed to come more naturally. There was no forcing understanding. There was no forcing connections.

His eyes rested on a small red circle on a printed map. He squinted and read the shape was marked *Doyle Memorial Hospital*.

"What I mean is, we both understand that The Cat, whoever that is, talked about me doing something. And it going wrong. But I don't think it went wrong, entirely."

"Can we establish what, exactly, '*it*' is, first?" Jacob complained.

He continued absorbing the swarm of information in front of him. Though he was starting to recognize individual pieces, the connections still eluded him. Most of them had to do with Colorado Springs, but that was only at the center. The more he looked into it, the more it branched out into other towns, and even other states.

He spotted a photo of a donut place in Oregon. That same feeling from Sunday crept back in. Maybe what he was doing was a mistake, but it was a mistake he hoped he was making for good reasons.

"Broke my brain," Sydney interrupted.

Jacob stepped back and bashed his calves into the coffee table. He lost whatever he was thinking about behind a clenched jaw and spike of pain.

"Are you alright?" Sydney asked.

Jacob rubbed his legs and looked over his shoulder.

Sydney stood behind the couch, calmly stirring his tea. He struck an eerie silhouette against stark kitchen light.

"Yeah, fine," Jacob replied. "You broke your brain, then what?"

Sydney hesitated.

"You're sure you haven't seen Levi?"

Jacob rounded the assaulting table and fell heavily into the couch again. Sydney stepped back with a grimace as the whole thing shook.

"Yes, I'm sure. And I'm prepared to ask him why he broke into your house, in front of our manager, to get a real reaction to me asking."

"I've taught you well!" Sydney smiled and pointed his teaspoon.

"You've taught me exactly nothing except I'm too nice. Broke your brain, then what?" Jacob rested an ankle on his knee.

"No, no, I mean–I tried to shut something down, or take it out–some fact, or memory, and it was connected to too much. You obviously can't remove a part of someone. Not entirely. "

"Okay, I'm going to stop you there," Jacob forced his way in. A high clang of metal rang out.

Sydney picked the second spoon back up off the floor and set it in the sink.

"What?" he called.

"I said I'm gonna have to stop you there. What do you mean, took out your own memory?" Jacob asked. "This isn't some kind of sci-fi, so you're going to have to elaborate on that one."

"You want some tea? You seem tired. And irritable."

The idea appealed to him, but he fought with distaste for Sydney's obvious attempt at changing the subject. Though, that subject was the whole reason he was here, listening to a madman, so he wasn't too angry. Things would come back around.

"No, I'm f–"

Jacob turned to a white ceramic mug held about a foot from the tip of his nose. Sydney set the hot tea down in Jacob's hand and he quickly transferred it to the opposite one, holding the handle more securely.

With his free hand, he rubbed an eye behind his glasses. Cleaning them didn't do much good–the blur was merely exhaustion.

"I can frame it in more typical terms, if you like," Sydney offered.

"Is that even possible?"

Toast popped from somewhere on the other side of the kitchen, and Jacob knew Sydney was right. Caffeine was a good idea. He was no detective, but his focus on the note wall had only been a diversion from taking Sydney's words too seriously.

"Something… happened… to me, or I found something out that I didn't… want… to know," Sydney started.

"Well, you don't have to go *that* slow."

"Something happened to me at some point, or I discovered some information that changed how… changed everything. Whatever I was doing before changed enough where I had to take other actions. So, I decided to block it out, or… *let* it get blocked out, if anyone else has anything to do with this.

"But, it wasn't like taking one card out of a deck–more like prying a piece out of a stone arch. The rest came down after, and… well, here I am, I suppose. I'm just not sure what I hoped to gain from the pile of whatever's left."

Jacob pulled his foot down from his ankle, which was beginning to feel pins and needles.

"Do you want the sane person's interpretation of

what you just said to me, or the English Major?" he called behind him.

A silence fell.

"Both?" Sydney answered.

"I think..." Jacob took a breath, coping with what was about to leave his mouth in any semblance of serious discussion.

"Assuming that's possible, that makes sense. If this was a normal, everyday thing that someone told me they were going to do, I'd definitely recommend against it. Then again, who knows what would be possible, assuming that's possible in the first place?"

"*However*, that is *not* possible, unless you went to some kind of hypnotist to help you block out half your brain. And even then, you can't get rid of it entirely. It's like–I'm not in psychology, so don't quote me on this–but I'd think it's like dementia. It's not that everything just gets dumped, but it's still there, you just can't get to it. It gets rearranged, I guess?"

"Except for the... other implications of your word choice, that's my point, though," Sydney said, this time from the closer end of the kitchen.

"There's a point to this?"

Sydney moved to smack Jacob's head with the spoon, but thought better of it and hung back.

"I've been..." Sydney swung the spoon back and forth in one hand, glancing up at the wall of paper. "Remembering a few things."

Jacob perked up. He turned completely toward the kitchen, lifting his heels onto the couch.

"Like what?"

"Nothing really profound. It's more like... well, I remember something about coffee," Sydney explained.

"You have solved the case, sir," Jacob mocked, running a hand across his forehead.

Sydney sighed heavily, and his shoulders fell.

"It's hard to explain. I just feel like... pieces of me are filling in, I suppose? No facts, no figures, just... I remember coffee. And rain. I like rain. And I have some ideas why I have seven button-down shirts and two t-shirts."

Sydney tugged at the collar of his white button-down. The sleeveless shirt was better than the tee, but both threatened to subtly choke him over the course of the last day. His button-down had one less button fastened than usual.

"Any luck with the photos, by the way?"

"Nope," Jacob answered quickly. Too quickly.

"I've checked all the main search engines, then specifically all the main social media sites. Nothing's popped up yet. Anything actually *useful* you remember? Or is this performance art?" Jacob waved a hand over to the wall.

"I remember coffee, rain, and… flying saucer. Have you checked any dating sites?" Sydney asked.

"Flying saucer?"

"I… don't know. I just remember I didn't like it." Sydney retreated back to the kitchen.

"And why dating sites? I thought you said you're Ace?"

Sydney's head popped up over the kitchen bar.

"What's Ace?"

"Asexual," Jacob explained. Sydney reached for something on top of the refrigerator.

"Oh. Yeah, I guess. But that doesn't mean I wouldn't be there, necessarily."

The black laptop screen, opposite where Jacob sat, reflected his exhausted eyes over the cup in a dark mirror. He watched himself, then tore his eyes away.

He started to nod off. In direct denial, he jumped off the couch and yelled as the hot tea jumped with him and out onto his hand. Sips were one thing, a ring of lava was another.

"What happened?" Sydney leaned over into view through the bar.

"Nothing. I'm–I'm fine. Speaking of dating, though, you're invited to a date turned general lunch… thing. Tomorrow. You like pizza?"

"Slow down. A what?" Sydney leaned heaver onto the ledge.

"We arranged this double date thing at a pizza place

for tomorrow, but Martin's a little…" Jacob wobbled his hand back and forth. Sydney watched it and began to nod with each direction.

"More than just Martin there, then?"

"Well, yeah. Me, and Katrina, and Martin's girlfriend, a couple of our friends," Jacob explained, his words slowing the more he used.

"I could stop by, sure," Sydney answered.

"Sounds… good. I'll… send you the address, or just the name, I dunno. If that's everything you wanted me to listen to, I think I'll go ahead and go." Jacob rushed all the rest of his words almost into one. He leaned down to set the cup on the coffee table.

Sydney tensed.

"No, wait," he rushed, coming around the counter. "Have you ever taken a Greyhound from here to Denver?" Sydney asked, no hint of pretense on his face.

Jacob took a deep breath and one long, exaggerated blink.

"What?" was all he said.

Sydney waved a hand toward the wall with all his notes. He pointed at something in particular, but Jacob, through his blurry eyes, wasn't sure which part that was.

"Because things are getting more familiar, I started branching out into outside Colorado Springs. Just because I'm here now doesn't mean I'm originally from here, particularly since it doesn't seem anyone's looking for me.

"But, even if I'm originally from here, that doesn't mean I'm *immediately* from here. By now we can both agree I'm probably not the most social, but there has to be other locations for me to test out my theory, and see if anything comes back.

"But, I'm thinking I moved here for some reason–a specific, important reason, because even if I removed all personal items from this house, it's still set up not to look like there's much activity here. And this house is fairly new, except for that ridiculous cat door."

"There's also the coat from Myrna, and the fact I was out in public just before I did… whatever I did.

Jacob let the words catch up with his processing.

"I guess that–what do you mean, coat from Myrna?" Jacob took a sharp turn in his sentence.

Sydney shrugged.

"I found out… the other day," he began, unsure what day it was, "Myrna made my coat. I don't think I ever paid her properly for it, either. I feel badly enough about that, I think that part survived."

He planted one index finger on the side of his temple.

"Pre-Monday you sounds like a great guy," Jacob shot.

"Yeah, don't remind me," Sydney muttered. And yet, the voice he'd started growing accustomed to hearing, particularly in irritation, was silent. The world had gotten so much louder, but he felt it had always been that way–he'd just recently remembered.

Sydney looped around the couch and sat next to Jacob. The length of his legs allowed him to sit back and place his feet well underneath the table.

He threaded his fingers together and popped each knuckle, one at a time. His knee started to bounce up and down.

Jacob could barely see the words from where he sat, so he wasn't sure what to say next.

Sydney spun around on his seat. His legs hooked over the back of the couch and he pulled himself up to place his feet back on the floor and stand.

Jacob leaned forward to grab his tea, unfazed.

He half-turned again, in effort to see who he was actually talking to. After a moment of listening to Sydney rummage in the cabinets, he turned forward again and set the mug back down.

He pulled his phone from his pocket and pulled up the search engine. With both thumbs, he typed *Identification Regulations In Colorado*, and tapped the magnifying glass icon.

The kitchen had begun to look lived-in. The trash bin under the sink was now weighed down with packaging, and there were dishes in the sink. It wasn't dirty, but *felt* dirty.

He pulled a paper towel off the free-standing roll and started sweeping for crumbs that may or may not have been there.

"So, you have two choices, I guess," Jacob called over his shoulder.

"And what are those?" Sydney's voice came out more sarcastic than he meant it, but hoped Jacob would overlook the mistake.

"If this thing is really possible–someone doing this on purpose, or something like it on purpose, even if this went sideways–either you did it, or someone did it to you."

Sydney stopped sweeping.

"I thought about that," he said quietly and threw the paper towel into the trash under the sink. He took a breath to speak, but Jacob beat him to the punch.

"You don't do well on caffeine, do you?" Jacob called from the living room.

"Why do you say that?"

"You're just… kinda jumpy, is all," Jacob answered.

"I'm no such thing," he objected.

"Maybe not for the average person, but dude–you're practically a corpse. It's weird seeing you move this much. *Talk* this much." Jacob drank more tea. If he squinted, the wall mess looked kind of like a double-decker bus.

He shook his head to bring himself more awake.

"Yes, well, consider it my effort toward acting more alive. Even through fits and starts. What time is it?"

Sydney opened the overhead cabinet doors and grabbed another box of tea.

"You don't have it on the stove?" Jacob called.

Sydney clenched his jaw and forced air from his nose. Luckily, he found himself venting his tension into gripping the edge of the counter rather than Jacob's neck.

"Yes. I just wanted to point it out without being rude," Sydney said. "It's not that I *want* you to leave, it's just that if all you're going to do is humor me, I think we're fine leaving things off there."

Jacob held the warm, half-empty cup close to his chest, mustering the courage and energy for a reply.

"Hey, I offered what I thought. No need to get snippy."

Sydney realized his mistake in the middle of Jacob's

sentence. He replied without much of a pause.

"Eleven, by the way," Sydney said. He sounded closer but, as Jacob turned again, he found him still at the end of the linoleum.

Sydney held his sage grey cup in a death grip.

"I've had eleven cups. And yes, I feel it. Which is how I know I probably don't–shouldn't–try out drinking. Alcohol. I mean."

"Sometimes caffeine calms people down," Jacob said.

"I don't *feel* calm," Sydney replied. He did loosen his white-knuckled hold on the mug, and gently set it down.

Jacob considered the statement before speaking again.

"Do you feel better than before, though?"

Sydney looked away and raked his teeth across his upper lip.

"Maybe," he mumbled to himself and re-entered the kitchen. The tea tin wasn't going to empty itself.

"Maybe if you told me what you're trying to *not* tell me, then *maybe* I would," Sydney said, only a little louder than under his breath. He waited a moment in the empty hum of the kitchen. Apparently, he was still quiet enough for Jacob to ignore him, if he'd been heard at all.

Jacob jumped up and rounded the far end of the couch.

"You're right. I gotta go," he said, grabbing his jacket by the hood. "I was just trying to say, maybe you should think of what happened as a good thing. Particularly if you're feeling like you let it happen. There's a reason."

"True," Sydney sighed.

"I had another thought, before I go, though."

Jacob resisted the urge to look down at his phone, if only to avoid Sydney's eyes.

Sydney looked back at the wall of paper, expecting Jacob to pause. He didn't, and rushed the next sentence.

"Are you sure your driver's license is real?"

Sydney did pause. He blinked, making sure to take enough time to consider his answer. The idea wasn't wholly foreign, but opened up whole new branches of reasoning.

"Don't you have to pick up Katrina?"

Jacob drifted over toward the door.

"She's at the salon tonight, which is closer. I can get you a card, if you want," Jacob answered. Sydney absently itched the top of his head.

"Anyway–I looked it up. You can get passport photos pretty much anywhere, and you're not far away from downtown. And if you have a decent scanner–it looks like you have a decent printer–and someone to make it for you, it's possible," Jacob explained.

"Okay, so what?" Sydney shot. "You're saying what? It's fake with an old photo? I don't exactly have old photos of myself to compare," Sydney objected.

"I know, but your coat's in it. If you can talk to Myrna again, that might count for something."

Jacob fought through Sydney's welling upset.

"It could help you narrow down a realistic idea of what happened. Figure out if it's real or not, then you just have to figure out where you would have to be if it's a yes or no. Then, I dunno, take a day trip and see if you see anything you know."

"Jacob," Sydney said.

"What?"

"Go pick up Katrina," he commanded.

"Okay," Jacob conceded. He trudged toward the door. Sydney watched him go–looked forward to it.

Jacob pulled the door open with a crack of the seal.

"Get some sleep though, okay?" Sydney called after him at the last second. The door fell closed with a deep *thud*, and he wasn't sure whether Jacob heard him or not.

He pushed himself to his feet and stepped over to lock the door. He then turned and surveyed the sparse living room, taking a moment to view the house as he had the first time.

The house was quiet again, though slowly, each ambient sound rose out of the void.

And he still felt alone.

He still knew the color of his couch meant he could keep things clean, or that it was brand new. The unruly cushion spring sliced one star off the review, if this was the case.

The table in front of him, flush against the wall, said he didn't have people over for dinner, or many. The angled kitchen was a bit more broken-in but still almost empty of food, and told him he either didn't eat at home much, or he'd found the explanation for his weight and possibly pallor.

So much was obviously unusual, and yet he hadn't left himself much to work with, if this was all his fault in the first place. If this was really remotely going according to plan, how was it even possible?

And worse, what would lead him to do it?

What could be so bad that he'd risk starting everything over?

It's all your fault rang out in his head, though in true memory rather than his own voice.

The wind whistled outside in the dark. The refrigerator hummed from the kitchen, a soft fuzz in the back of his mind. The tree hanging into the tiny excuse for a back yard tapped on the wooden fence underneath.

He sat on the couch again and tapped the track pad. The screen lit up, but only with the neon cat face.

He tapped a few buttons, but the computer was still frozen from earlier. Luckily his phone printed to his hardware upstairs.

The face was one of those familiar things that he remembered, but not in words. The image wasn't frightening, or particularly intimidating, but *annoying*.

Deeper in the dark than anything else, whatever part recognized the neon cat was also withholding the words to describe why he so desperately wanted to punch through his screen. Things may have been his fault, but that face sparked a rage no mere leash would contain.

He closed the computer.

He pushed past the sounds of the house and climbed the staircase. Upstairs, the wallet sat on his desk–containing the driver's license that might eventually tell him more.

Outside, Jacob stood at the driver's side door to his little blue car. He stared down at his phone, reading and re-reading the last screen of text messages there.

You really need to tell him what you found.

What, you want me to do it for you? Bcuz no.

He needs a lead. I don't know what he does all day but he NEEDS. A LEAD.

Did you tell him yet? Katrina had sent last, about twenty minutes ago. Jacob scrolled back up and tapped on the screen shot he'd sent her a few hours before.

It showed a picture of Sydney, but not quite. The image was close enough for the reverse image search to recognize as him, but something was different. Maybe it was because, whoever this was, he was smiling and wearing color.

Underneath, it read:

Benjamin Douglas West, student at the University of Portland, passed away on October 9th at the age of 21. He will be greatly missed for his unique sense of humor and immense care for others. As per request, funeral services will be kept private and for immediate family only. Those wishing to honor his life can make a donation in his name directly to Mothers Against Drunk Driving.

Jacob closed his phone screen and climbed into his car. After a few points in his turn, he finally extracted himself from the slushy curb and disappeared into the quiet, snowy night.

EIGHT

Gizmo's pizza was an eccentric little place set back from the road, a wood-paneled building with blue walls and white trim. The white-painted deck was wrapped with warm white garden lights, all the way up through the stairs and ramp railing.

The enormous window displayed the restaurant name in gigantic irregular, printing-press styled letters in white and copper.

Sydney tried to lose himself in the details, if only to distract himself from the welling panic brought on by impending socialization. His mood didn't improve no matter how much he reminded himself he's the one who agreed to show up.

He just hoped Myrna wasn't going to be there. She didn't exactly have a crush on him, for a variety of reasons.

His private ghost had also been suspiciously quiet since waking up yesterday. Though a welcome silence, the suspicion ate away at him.

He might as well eat pizza.

A little brass bell sounded as Sydney pushed the door open. He was immediately torn.

The air was too warm with his coat on, but he would feel too exposed if he took it off. The dining hall soaked into him as a curiously pleasant déjà vu but, what with the pattern of familiar things, he was on alert.

The Edison bulbs against the blue walls glowed, and his eyes roamed the steel and brass stars hanging from the ceiling. His eyes came to rest on one of the few heads visible over the tall wall, far behind the strangely-vacant greeter's podium.

He made his way over and took a chair opposite Jacob, across the long row of small square tables.

"For someone who doesn't want to come, you're here awfully early," Jacob said as he looked up from his phone. He set it down, then idly flicked a tiny ball of paper napkin across the room.

Sydney pulled out his phone for his clock.

"I'm on time, though?" he half-asked.

"Yeah, I guess. I'm just trying to wrap my head

around why nobody else is. At least Martin's usually so neurotic about being on time."

Jacob looked back down, but not at his phone. His eyes avoided Sydney.

Sydney didn't force him. He slid his coat off and dropped it onto the back of his chair, and the bottom edge gathered into a pile on the floor. His dark red button-down shirt struck an odd compliment to the walls–more like someone performing there instead of dining.

Maybe he was about to.

"I could leave and come back, if you'd like," Sydney said, taking a seat. Jacob's face pinched into the middle, and he looked up. Sydney waited for a reaction, eyebrows raised.

Jacob snickered.

"Still under the weather?" Sydney asked.

"Not really, why?"

"You just seem tired. Where's Katrina?" Sydney answered and asked without pause.

"It's actually closer to her apartment, so she said she'd walk. She doesn't get to a lot lately. I'm giving her a ride back. She might have gotten hung up, or something. I'm just waiting for a text." Jacob sighed. The typically bright-eyed man was uncommonly low-key.

Sydney added Katrina's vague pink nebula of an apartment to his mental map of Colorado Springs. He wasn't sure where it was, but the French rose fog had descended over the general vicinity.

He blinked himself out of pondering over the image.

"I'm… sorry," Sydney choked out. Jacob perked up.

"For what?" he asked.

Sydney sighed before finishing his thought.

"If there's anything I've done, before or after Sunday, that's made life harder for you. I know I'm not the most… pleasant all the time, but I appreciate that it was you who… uh, decided to help."

Jacob shrugged.

"I get it," he said. "Not all of it, but I *get* there are a lot of things that aren't my business. But as long as I know that *you* know I'm not exactly on call, I can deal with hanging out and occasionally helping out. Is that all?"

"No." After that, Sydney wasn't sure, but he thought he might have made a few croaking sounds.

Judging by Jacob's blank, unchanging stare, he guessed it was all in his head.

"Well?" Jacob prompted.

"I'm sorry," Sydney said again. Jacob's shoulders fell, and a warm, welling frustration surfaced to his face.

"You already said tha–"

"Would you just *shut up* for a minute? And let me finish, *please*?" Sydney burst.

Jacob immediately fell silent. He leaned back further in his chair.

Sydney's stomach dropped, his own voice echoing in his ears. There was no re-bottling it, so he pushed himself on.

"I have no idea how I got you into this, but I'm sorry. I have no idea if you were meant to be here, or even what I meant in the first place, but I'd like to apologize if anyone's aware of you that shouldn't be, or thinks it's okay to… thinks it's a good idea, now or in the future, to mess with you to get to me.

"I wish I could say I think we would have gotten along, but I don't really know if I'm anything like I was before. But I'm glad you're here now. Whoever taught you to help other people, I'd like you to tell them thank you, from me."

Jacob's face fell a little.

Sydney heard his own brain tick by a few seconds, finding a place to plug Jacob's changed face into.

"I think my mom would've liked you, honestly. She was a nurse."

Jacob looked away.

"At least as a case study," he spoke again and looked back. A more natural smile leaked out onto his face. Sydney's face barely quirked, and then even that faded.

"What's with the corpse paint without the paint, anyway? I mean you seem okay, but *man,* you do *not* look okay most of the time.

Sydney ran a hand down one side of his face.

"That's one of the few things I don't have a theory

for. Though, when summer rolls around I guess I'll see if I burst into flame." His eyes glazed over, reaching for the distance. What started as a joke quickly flipped over into the horror of imagining his first summer.

Jacob leaned forward again as he laughed, rubbing one eye behind his glasses.

"Whatever happened with Levi," Jacob said, breaking the horrifying bubble of his thoughts, "I'm sorry if that has anything to do with this. He seems like a nice guy, so I have no idea where that came from. Haven't seen him since I dropped him at work Friday. I'll let you know, though."

At least the co-worker part was true.

"He said you wanted to check up on me," Sydney explained. "Caught me while I was… sleeping. Nothing really happened beyond that, though obviously that's enough."

Jacob's eyes widened and he massaged one temple.

"I also… didn't tell you all my theories," Sydney said.

"I assumed so," Jacob answered curtly, willing Sydney to continue.

"Things…" Sydney trailed off, trying to hold eye contact with Jacob, yet losing his words in compensation. He unpleasantly forced it through at the thought of getting it over with.

"…are going to get weirder. I'm not going to tell you all of it, but if there's something you need to know, I promise you'll know it. I want to make sure you don't get dragged into things any more than you might be already. And if you are, I'm sorry. Again."

"Okay, look," Jacob started. Sydney prepared himself to be berated.

"I'm not trying to interfere with anything. But, like I've said *more than once*, I want to help people. I'm just not the kind of person who can do that medically or, you know, financially.

"I don't expect you to share everything, just like I don't expect you to press when I can't do something. You've–you've got a *weird thing* going on." Jacob's eyes widened and he looked away for just a moment.

"But yeah, just let me know if I should be expecting any of the, ah, *weird* to bleed over. But dude, be explicit. No matter what bizarre version of that you think I'm not going to believe. I'd rather be prepared for something completely weird and then scale back if you exaggerated."

Sydney nodded.

"Okay, good. I have no idea if I interrupted anything else you wanted to say," Jacob finished.

Sydney raised his eyes, caught off guard by the opportunity. With permission to tell him as strange a thing as he wanted, there was plenty he might have said.

He knew where his memories were. Turns out, that's where his hallucinations were coming from. Something horrible had happened, which he wasn't allowing himself to tell himself, but the part that knew was still striking out in retaliation for… what?

Sydney didn't think of himself very highly, but the statement was so much more complicated than he would ever state in public, even with a dining hall so empty.

He decided on a half-lie.

"First thing I really, clearly remember is the alarm on my phone for class. The reminder. But, before that, in the hospital, I…"

He looked up to see Jacob was still staring, and didn't appear to have any intention of interrupting.

"There was a mirror. In the right place for me to see myself if I wanted." He left out the part about it being across from the chair, rather than near his bed.

"I don't remember all of it, just that seeing myself was enough where I had to leave."

There was also the part about not recognizing himself immediately, but rather the simple fact that he only saw that person in the mirror, rather than the chair itself.

"Okay. I'm sorry that happened and–well, you *do* look…" Jacob trailed off, and looked Sydney up and down.

"You have a look. But it's not *that* bad," he finished. "Don't people still like the vampire romance thing?"

Sydney hesitated.

"Thanks. I did have one other question, though,"

Sydney said, realizing he had been staring into space.

"Okay," Jacob answered.

"Why are so many people wearing masks?"

Jacob's face drained of color.

"Sydney," he started quietly, with some effort. He leaned forward over the table, to make up for what he lacked in volume.

"Please tell me the year," he finished.

The siren pierced Sydney's attention. His head snapped to the side.

He watched the ambulance, bright red and blue blazing as it sped down the street. The wail coated the inside of his head and wouldn't let go, even as the vehicle completely vanished. He stayed gazing out the window for another long moment, the sense he'd forgotten something trickling back in like water under ice in a spring stream.

"Hey, you okay?" came a third voice.

Sydney blinked.

The room roared to life.

Three friends sat on the other end of the room, talking among themselves. A family of seven wrangled five children under eight. The brick pizza oven fired and crackled, bakers singing something at each other in the kitchens, while a line of five people stood at the buffet. Generic pop-40 rock played from somewhere deep in the ceiling.

Sydney spun around in his chair and spotted the greeter at the podium up front, chatting with an elderly woman and another woman of family resemblance.

Sydney spun back around to face a royal-purple clad waiter, tall and skinny, with a fan of tight black curls over a brown forehead. He must not have hidden his upset very well, based on the step back they took, menus in hand.

"Can I get you anything before, I, you know, get you anything?" The purple-shirted waiter laughed. Nervously.

Sydney reigned his welling panic back inside. Deeper inside.

"Sorry. Fine. I'm fine. Can I get one of those?" Sydney reached out for a menu and it was freely given, though not without a strange look hidden under a customer service smile. They left his side with a shift toward a grimace.

Martin pulled the chair next to him out and sat down.

Sydney tried to ignore his first impulse to move away. He took in the new smells, sights, and sounds of the restaurant in effort to distract himself from the impulse, but found himself overwhelmed again.

He instead tried to shut things out, one by one, like closing tabs in a browser window, and turned toward Martin.

Martin turned toward him and smiled without showing teeth.

Sydney tried to look at him like he'd never seen him before. That almost pushed him toward speaking without restraint. He pulled his efforts back in and did his best, instead, to look at him like he would be comfortable being looked at by someone six inches taller who also didn't want to be there.

Skadi, seated on the other side of Martin, stood back up and reached completely over him to Sydney's menu.

"Not cool. Need pizza," she declared and slid one clear vinyl menu from the top of the other before she sat. She shoved her motorcycle helmet under her seat without taking her eyes off the menu.

Sydney's head snapped left.

Jacob raised his whole arm and waved across the room. By the look in his eye, Sydney assumed Katrina would be hungry from her walk.

Sydney leaned past where Martin would hopefully be content to sit quietly until spoken to.

"What was in that tea you gave me?" Sydney asked across him.

"Just some green tea. And some chamomile. I had some left over from my windowb–why, you didn't like it?" Skadi answered. Sydney looked back down to see an odd, tiny smile threatening to break through Martin's face.

"It's, uh, *strong*," Sydney replied. "Put me out like a light."

"He's asking if there's weed in it," Martin said without looking up.

Skadi smacked him with the long vinyl menu.

"*That's not how that works*," she said louder, across Martin's wider, closed-mouth smile. That smile began to fade just as his eyes didn't seem to focus on what was in front of him.

Jacob wasn't listening for just long enough to be lost when he started paying attention, but Katrina had fully arrived and slid the coat over the back of her chair. His attention to that shard of conversation disappeared again, and he wobbled the menu at her.

She gave a tiny wave to Sydney, silent and shy.

"Do you grow anything else, though?" Sydney asked. Katrina sat with her hands underneath her, thawing her social energy out for use.

"Everything bit the dust at the first snow, but…" her answer met his ears, but he fought with the sudden wave of tension from Martin.

Sydney's skin prickled the harder he tried to ignore it.

"Well, I *could* leave, if you'd like me to," Martin burst. Everyone quieted.

"I'm *joking*," Martin said. "Just don't lean so close. It's weird."

Sydney sat up straight again, squarely in his own chair. He busied himself scanning up and down the menu that he lifted with one hand. The letters wobbled, but not as much as earlier.

"You know what's weird, though?" Sydney started, not looking up until his question was fully freed.

"This, right here. All this."

Sydney waved up and down the table to each member of the two couples her shared the table with.

"Other people are coming, right?" Sydney added. He hardly believed his own ears.

"Yeah, a few others. Dan, then your commune… thing… guy," Martin attempted, still looking down. Skadi again smacked him in the shoulder with her menu and he laughed.

"*Community library*," she corrected.

He almost looked like he wanted to be there, but only for a moment.

Sydney sat at the right angle to see the front doors as people arrived. Once too many of the wrong people looked familiar, he stopped trying so hard. Everyone was starting to blur together.

Dan managed to walk all the way up to the table and sit down before Sydney recognized him. He kept his eyes down once he recognized him from hazy flashes of that day in the library with the migraine.

The music didn't help. He felt he should have recognized it, but it only lent a surreal quality to his efforts to follow conversation, and further efforts to care.

While structure seemed Sydney's strong point, conversation was not. One on one, it all unfolded so much more smoothly. He could keep track and participate at the same time.

"I really don't think–" Martin started, then promptly quieted. No one appeared to have heard.

"Are you…" Sydney hesitated, especially as Martin turned to squarely face him. "Are you okay?" he said quietly.

It wasn't so much that others kept him out of the conversation–more that he and Martin radiated their permission to be left out, whether they meant to do so or not.

"Anything I can–" Sydney chanced again, but stopped short. Martin's eyes, so close, betrayed a bloodshot misery.

"I don't know what you mean," Martin lied. Sydney knew it, but not how he knew.

Skadi leaned into Martin from the other side and grabbed his hand under the table. Whether from invisible eavesdropping or some other sense, he couldn't tell.

The waiter slid into place at the end of their long row of tables. Sydney inched away from Martin, but mumbled a "*hot tea*" when necessary. He insisted it was everything he wanted, also when necessary.

That waiter made a valiant effort against the one hard line their mouth had fallen into, and smiled as the group table was left alone once more.

Sydney leaned across the table to get a better line of sight to Dan. Martin leaned away from him to whisper something to Skadi.

"So, how is… are things?" Sydney croaked. How did normal people talk at these types of things?

"Uh, fine? I don't think we've met. Hey, I'm Dan," he waved from a few seats away.

"I think we did, for a minute. I was in the library a few… days ago." Sydney had paused before choosing his appropriate word for time. Things felt so disproportionate lately.

"I must have missed you. Sorry about that," Dan replied. Sydney sat back, a bitter gnawing in the bottom of his stomach that wasn't hunger.

Sydney also vaguely registered the conversation was turning to video games, so he unplugged himself once more and tried to think about the incoming tea. He caught Katrina making some kind of comment about fisherman's sweaters before he pulled his attention back. He had hardly a moment to rest before it was replanted once again.

Katrina fired excitedly back and forth with Skadi about yarn and dyes, with occasional ghost of a comment from Martin. Jacob added to Katrina's stories of Summer and theater.

Martin seemed to almost smile, as long as he wasn't turned toward Sydney.

Sydney didn't mind, or even notice much. He was suddenly occupied in watching the brown-skinned man in the tan argyle sweater approach the table. He scrambled for a rationale.

Skadi tore herself away from the merits of a national park pass and looked up.

"Ah! William! This is Martin. Katrina, Jacob, Dan, and Sydney. *Sydney!* You look like you just inhaled a bug," Skadi rattled off.

William pulled a chair out at the end of the table, next to Dan. A mischievous spark lit his dark eyes.

"Freaky world, isn't it?" he said with a laugh.

Sydney smiled and hoped he looked genuine. He waved weakly. It could be said he took a few minutes to recover, but a return to his senses only resulted in the decision to leave. He leaned further back in his chair, pushing back a little with his feet but not sliding his seat. He rocked a few times in indecision not whether he should leave, but how best to do so politely.

William, however, didn't look at all disrupted by Sydney's presence.

Sydney looked down to the table in front of him, back up to those at the table, then cast a glance out the large front window of the restaurant. A jolt shot through him, as if he'd suddenly jumped awake.

He looked down to a mug of hot water on a saucer in front of him.

"So, anyway–I still don't think it's a good idea to-" William spoke directly to Dan, who sat with rapt attention. Sydney caught something about graphic medical conversation not sitting well with everyone at the table, considering the context.

He instead placed every last bit of his attention on Jacob. Sydney jumped in surprise once he looked over to find Jacob already staring back.

Martin was missing from his seat. Sydney liked to think people–even the ones he didn't particularly like–were of more importance to him than his tea. A piece of time had been lost. Something important had been skipped.

Jacob leaned in further, over his dark soda. Real food would arrive soon. Hopefully Sydney hadn't ordered anything he didn't remember.

"What did you *say* to him?" Jacob leaned into the table. Sydney mirrored.

"What are you talking about?" he hissed.

Jacob resisted the urge to roll his eyes. He leaned in even further and clasped his hands together.

"You stared into space a second, then tapped him on the shoulder and said something in his ear."

Sydney leaned in even further.

"*Why* would I do that?"

"I don't know, that's *why I'm asking*. But he looked… '*kinda*' angry is a mild way to put it," Jacob explained. His face then fell.

"Why are you looking at me like that?" Sydney shot in the same low tone.

"Because before that, he looked scared," he

answered, then lifted his eyes. "Then ran off toward the bathroom, I think."

Sydney's face fell numb.

He pulled his wallet out and fumbled a moment with the ten-dollar bill from inside. Finally successful, he quietly slid it under his tea mug and pushed his chair away before he stood.

"Sydney?" Dan was the first to call after him as he turned.

"Where are you going?" Katrina called second. Jacob was silent, as was Sydney as he made long strides back toward the front door.

He might have turned and stepped into the bathroom to see if Martin was there, but stepped past. Eyes on the glass-enclosed lobby, Sydney had only a second to notice a pale shape near the restroom door.

Martin hooked his arm around Sydney's opposite elbow and they both swung together with a crash.

"Even if you're right, you come back and I'll kill you," Martin rushed under his breath. With that, Martin walked away back to the table and didn't look back.

Sydney glanced over his shoulder, met Jacob's eyes, then turned away and left the building entirely.

"What was that about?" Skadi asked. The rest of the table was quiet, but Martin didn't seem to notice, or else had lost most of his social anxiety and didn't mind being looked at by several pairs of eyes.

"No idea. Where's he going, anyway?" Martin asked, facing directly to Jacob.

"I don't know," he answered, throwing his hands up. "He's a well-meaning weirdo, but I don't pretend to know how he th–"

"And I've been meaning to ask–what does he do? Like, where does he work, anyway?" Martin interrupted, eyes set against distraction from any onlooker.

"Okay, listen," Jacob began. "I know him, but it's not like I know him."

Jacob's face twisted up in the center as Martin raised an eyebrow.

"I *mean*," Jacob started again, more forcefully to

discourage any further interruption.

"I know him, but he doesn't talk a lot about himself. Or a lot, actually. I met him earlier this week, ah, in class. You're going to ask him about some things yourself–he's got some anxiety over, ah, people talking about him."

Martin held his gaze. After a second, he leaned back into his chair.

"So, uh, pepperoni at this end, right?" the waiter asked from the end of the table, with a lopsided smile.

"Yep, all good!" William answered from underneath the giant round tray over his head.

Skadi looked to Katrina, then to Jacob, who didn't look back. She looked over to Dan instead, who looked back with just as much confusion in his eyes as her own.

Jacob's phone buzzed in his pocket and he took the opportunity to wrench his eyes away from Martin.

Sydney had sent a text.

It's coming back, but not how it should.

I need some time.

Oh, how Sydney hated that house. There were times in his short memory he hated it more than he felt he should have hated any place.

Even when he was seeing himself in every reflection, those first few days were quiet. Now, the stillness was a deafening void, begging to be filled. He held down his shaking hands, which only helped the tremor bubble up and over into an ever-present whisper.

But not of his own voice.

Over and over, he turned the situation around. Over and over, checking for anything he might have seen but subconsciously dismissed. There were still so many pieces of the puzzle missing and one wrong move, realized too late, could destroy something load bearing.

Sydney dropped his jacket onto the usual place over the back of the couch. He pulled each of his boots off as he ascended the stairs, letting them fall where they may down the steps.

He didn't want to be there, but there weren't many other places he felt he could go. Too many thoughts flew through his head, none of them sticking long enough to translate into full sentences. They writhed like threads in the wind, tangling and tying themselves together with no discernible practicality.

Little pieces of missing time now made sense. Those moments he didn't feel fully nested inside his own head, and things moved.

Sydney hadn't changed, he'd just been sectioned off from himself. The original self was still there, as he'd assumed from bits of him trickling through to the present, but he wasn't sure of the extent, whether it was really a ghost or not.

The only question was whether Sydney was supposed to exist, as he did now. And, either way, why he was so angry about it.

He stared vacantly toward the door in front at his left at the top landing. Closer was his bedroom, the laptop computer, and the bed. His eyes focused enough to move from one door to the other several times.

Any painkiller he chose to take for the lurking migraine would merely dull things. It would always return.

He stood there a long time, mental gears gradually slowing as he prolonged making a decision. They started to click, and his eye started to twitch from exhaustion.

The gears started to grind.

Even if you're right, come back and I'll kill you.

Martin's voice came back to him. What was Sydney right about? And who was he, really? He was running out of distractions from having to decide.

Sydney wrapped his hand around his bedroom doorknob and pushed the door further open. He managed a glance to his open laptop, but fell face first onto the bed.

In sleep, he could buy some time to figure things out. There would be nothing immediately vying for his attention, dragging him different directions. Even if he dreamed, it would only consist of what was in front of him, and the rest of him would still.

The healthiest option was to shut down, if only for a few hours. There would be time for more thinking later.

In the last few seconds before he faded to sleep, he

thought he felt something else.

It didn't come as a surprise, or register as any danger. He dimly acknowledged it, but accepted it as a last, calmly pleasant thought before he dropped off.

If he hadn't known any better, he would have thought someone sat down on the end of his bed.

The dim, chilly bubble of what he remembered as his bedroom melted away to a curious contradiction. He walked down the street, pushing his long strides to their utmost potential. Though his skin complained at the icy winter air, inside he was warm, and wrapped up, like his blanket still wrapped around him.

Everything was a blur for several blocks. The dream had unfortunately elected to have him skip the bus stop.

All at once he surfaced from whatever lake had pulled him under and he looked up from his feet, cold inside and out. He found himself standing on a street corner downtown.

The white bricks of a McDonalds greeted him across the corner, with a secondhand store on one side and a tax preparer on the other.

He wasn't familiar with any of it.

He looked up at the street signs and didn't remember seeing them on his phone map before.

The sun was shining, but if there had been any less snow on the ground, he would have been more concerned about whatever time had passed.

Sydney pulled his right glove off with his teeth and opened his phone screen. *Sneetch & Lorax* appeared on his map, right over the dot showing him where he stood.

He scanned the intersection, double-checking the dingy, snow-washed shop signs around him. In a wave of personal embarrassment, thankfully displayed only to an empty street, Sydney looked up.

He felt, rather than heard, someone laughing. He didn't dare turn around, for fear of what he might see.

He instead stared up and the giant, hot purple star.

There was no way his mind was louder than the color of that star on the hanging sign. *Sneetch & Lorax* in bold, antiqued steel was hammered in to the wood with long nails.

It looked like something Katrina might even–

Why are we here? he said to the deep, dark place he used to hear his own voice from. No answer came.

His head lowered to look through the tall windows of the hair salon before him.

The little silver bell above the door rang behind Martin, who stood at the crescent moon-shaped desk, his back turned. He barely heard the sound.

A woman with long eyelashes and longer, glittery black nails took the wad of bills he offered. He leaned in further, head propped up by his elbow, as she counted and made change.

Sydney froze, torn between Martin standing in front of him and the outlandish décor of the salon.

I'm gonna kill you, Martin's voice echoed in his head.

The glare outside the windows muted the artistic license inside. The purple walls and striped, asymmetrical furniture complemented a dozen matte black frames filled with vintage horror movie posters, bright, surreal cartoons, vintage photos, and haircut models in gothic outfits.

Sneetch & Lorax held more of a Dr. Seuss approach to The Addams Family than what he expected from a professional place. He approved.

And, if Katrina was working today, maybe Martin wouldn't kill him in front of her.

Sydney committed. He took a few more steps into the salon. Martin stood and spun around. He looked down to Sydney's shoes, then back up to his face in half a second.

"You'd make a fantastic stalker, you know that?" Martin shot.

Sydney was taken aback with his tone. His own voice wasn't nearly as smooth, and threatened to break.

"I do. Lucky for everybody, I'm lazy." Sydney pulled his other glove off and shoved it into his pocket with the first.

Martin turned back around to receive his change. Even from the back, the tension in his shoulders echoed his face.

It was unusual, then, that Martin didn't seem

particularly angry, though obviously surprised to see him.

Martin struck up a quiet chat with the woman behind the desk, and Sydney was tempted to listen in. Another pang of quiet panic hit, and he turned his attention to the rainbow wall of hair products to try and distract himself. None of them were particularly interesting, but it was a preferable alternative to eavesdropping.

A second perusal of the shelf, he did see one tiny tub of styling wax the same as the one in his otherwise vacant medicine cabinet. The label on the one at home was scratched off.

He thought about opening it to see if it smelled the same, but instead turned back around to the greater part of the salon.

The space was mostly open, without any notable obstruction but for another shelf of hair products dividing the waiting area from work stations. A black and white striped couch with a sweeping curve to the back sat against one of the front windows, across from yet more shampoo and products Sydney didn't even know the use for.

Past there sat eight stations, for at each wall. The two furthest from him on the right included two large, black sinks. The rest sat in front of six enormous mirrors, each decorated with personal trinkets.

Sydney spotted several photographs, dozens of novelty pens, one papier-mache bluebird, three strings of Mardi Gras beads, and a stuffed bat hanging upside-down at the end. Even further back, a utility closet door hung open.

His eyes returned to and lingered on the station with the bat. He looked over the appliances and furniture again before his eyes strayed to the tall product shelf he'd tried and failed to completely ignore.

The black metal fixture held all sorts of strangely shaped bottles that made him uncomfortable the more he looked. Though, one décor choice struck his interest once he forced his attention up rather than away.

He eyed the row of white porcelain heads on top, taking note of the gap where he thought a fifth pale, abstract piece should be.

Then one appeared, lifted from the other side.

Martin, still enveloped in his questionably quiet flirtation with the receptionist, allowed Sydney the opportunity to step beyond the shelf. Katrina stood there on a two-step stool, balancing the fifth porcelain head above her own, pushing herself to cross the top of the shelf.

"Oh!" Katrina said, once she realized who it was. "Hey!"

"*Why* are you still here?" Martin's voice disrupted Sydney's train of thought–mostly having to do with his being somewhat more than a head taller than she was.

"I believe they sell haircuts here, if that's okay with you," Sydney said, forcing his face to drop to blank as he turned. He did his best to hold it that way.

He did, however, note Martin's eyes glance up to his hair and then back down.

"Sorry for running out on everyone yesterd–this morning. Personal things. You're sure Skadi was really okay with you adding to the double date?"

The woman behind Martin made her own face, softly, but with her mouth in one straight line and eyebrows gently raised.

"Why wouldn't she–why are you really here?" Martin stuttered.

The receptionist leaned back in her chair. She pulled a black glittery phone from deeper in the desk and rolled her chair the other way.

"I told you. Haircut. Is Skadi okay with you flirting with your salon receptionist?"

If Martin was going to kill him, Sydney might as well give him a reason.

He heard the step stool rattle behind the shelf. Katrina descended.

Martin didn't deflate in guilt, but he didn't exactly heat up in anger. He just froze.

And then couldn't hold it anymore.

His entire face fell slack, and the color ran away and hid somewhere that for once gave Sydney a bitter pang of concern. Martin, nearly matching his newly bleached hair, struggled to return to himself.

He did so all at once and turned back around to the

receptionist. She still talked on the phone pinned between her ear and shoulder, and wrote in the appointment roster.

Martin snapped back around to Sydney and looked further down next to him a second after.

Sydney turned to Katrin standing there only a foot behind him, holding the fifth porcelain head cradled in her hands. Her mouth was clamped shut, but her eyes had flown wide open.

"Don't talk to me," Martin spat. He made for the entrance with long steps, then vanished with the ringing of the bell.

"See you later, then?" Sydney called after him. He wasn't sure if he really sounded concerned, or merely sarcastic. He may have been both though had attempted the former.

"What was that about?" Katrina asked quietly from below and behind.

"I don't know, but I don't think he realized he was flirting," Sydney answered.

"Then it's not flirting," she answered with a shrug. "Casey, I'm going to cut for Sydney, okay?"

The woman with black sparkly nails frowned and stared after Martin out the window. The ring of her matching telephone snapped her out of the trance.

"Yep, fine," she answered and reached for the phone.

Sydney turned around and held both hands out to Katrina.

"Provided you *did* actually want a haircut, and you're fine with me doing it, mine is on the end. With the bat. But you probably already knew that, so I'm going to just get my–what?"

Sydney silently took the head from her, lifted it a few inches over his own head, and set it on top of the shelf. He turned the face around to face the striped sofa, matching the other four.

"Ah, yeah. Thanks. Take the second to last chair on the left. I'll be with you once I get this put away," she said, hefting the folded stool over her shoulder.

Sydney followed her nearly into the utility closet, but stopped at the station where the stuffed bat lived. He slowly sat.

While faint rumblings emitted from the closet, Sydney stood back up, hung his coat on the peg next to the mirror, then sat back down.

His knees rose uncomfortably high when he put his heels on the footrest bar. He instead set his feet flat in the floor, then laid his head back and stared into the ceiling.

Looking away was the only way he could stop himself, at least by sight, from letting his thoughts run away with him.

Katrina was to be spoken to like a person, not analyzed and picked apart like the plot of a crime thriller. Consciously he was happy to adhere to this obvious fact, but he was finding staying on his train of thought exceptionally difficult.

Finding himself in front of an outlandishly decorated hair salon was evidently one thing that could happen when his consciousness side-stepped to allow–

He stopped that thought right where it sprang up, like the snipping of a rose. Overthinking his latest blackout would lead to dividing attention from the situation at hand.

Katrina flung the black, billowy fabric over his head.

"Sit up straight," she gently commanded.

Sydney bit his tongue from protest and did what he was told.

He was just in time to watch her face twist. She didn't look directly at him, but up and down, then further down. He took a breath to speak when she lifted her foot and stepped down on one of the levers underneath the chair.

He rose into the air, clutching the arm rests.

Katrina's adjustment to the chair didn't satisfy her. Her foot hit another lever. Sydney lowered. She scratched her head.

"Problem?" he asked.

"I'll be right back. Don't go away," she replied.

Sydney turned underneath his big black polyester tent and watched her return to the utility closet. She reappeared with the folding stool.

He rolled his eyes.

She stepped up and the stool rattled. She placed a

hand on top of his head. He looked up to where he felt it, without moving anything but his eyes.

"Please, don't do that."

"I'm sorry," she said and lifted her hand. "How would you like it? Any references?"

Sydney hadn't thought about that part. He didn't have much to work with, except on top. He shuddered at the thought of that disappearing, at least until warmer weather.

"Like this, but… shorter," he said. Even as the words left his mouth, he realized how hesitant he sounded. He blew a lock of straight black hair off his forehead.

Katrina laughed. "I can do that. I'm guessing you don't want a shampoo, though, if, well, y'know."

She wiggled her fingers on either side of his head.

Sydney thought, in horror, of the big black sinks on the other side of the room, as well as her hands running through his hair. She shivered.

"That's what I thought," she said. "I need to get it wet, but I'll spray it instead, if that helps. I obviously need to touch your head a little, but I won't, like, full-on grab you or anything. How much shorter?"

"Ah… like that." Sydney unearthed one hand and pulled that lock of hair back down again, to just above his eyebrows.

"Oh. Keep the undercut, trim on top?" She stepped off the stool and toward the plastic rack of combs and scissors on the chrome counter in front of him.

"Yes?" he answered.

She grabbed the large, lime-green spray bottle, a comb, and hooked a pair of scissors around her little finger. She remounted the stool.

"Gotcha. So, why are you really here?"

"To get a haircut," he blurted, louder than intended, fueled by her sudden spray to the top of his head. She moved through to the front and back. The gentle misting was definitely more tolerable than what he imagined in the gaping sink.

She continued, but pulled her hand away further, combing through each wet patch as she moved.

"No, I mean–well, I'm not sure what I mean. Are you

okay? You left Gizmo's pretty quick," she explained. "You don't seem okay, even considering–"

"You really think I'd be okay with what's going on?" he dodged. He sounded angry, even to himself. He just hoped he was mistaken, and his wet hair accentuated the irritation with himself.

She combed the back of his head straight up, clamped the hair between two fingers, and started cutting. He could feel each snip through his skull.

"Nope. I can't think of anyone who would be. Then again, this doesn't happen much, as far as I know. Or to just anyone."

She cut a little more and Sydney stayed silent, watching her in the mirror.

"I get it. You don't want to talk about it. Except I think you do, because you're here, and you don't strike me as very comfortable with haircuts. What did you want to talk to me about?"

She looked away from him in the mirror.

Sydney stayed silent. Katrina was so many things at once, it was hard to keep track of what he did and didn't want her to know. He definitely didn't want to explain that he'd arrived there after a blackout, probably caused by his memory coming back in spurts of hallucination. He merely hoped whatever part of him was still in control in the middle of all that was still looking out for him, rather than asserting itself in a cruel joke.

He took a gentle, deep breath.

"I can do some pretty weird things with my head. I'm pretty sure all this is my fault, because of… that," he said.

"I guessed."

"What?" Sydney asked, a bit louder.

"I mean, despite all the… weirdness, you still seem pretty functional. I'd really doubt that you're much different than you used to be. It's not like someone else can get plugged into a head that's not theirs. But you can rearrange the furniture."

The top of his head was much lighter, though the length still threatened his vision in the front. He squinted at himself in the mirror. He looked about five years older, and a little less like he was about to get lost in the crowd at a My Chemical Romance concert.

"Oh. Well…" he hesitated. "Thanks."

There was no way to tell her he and his past self didn't quite get along lately. Even if one of them was giving the other the silent treatment.

"I know something happened, and however I did this is tied up in the *why*. Whatever happened, I was willing to start completely over. It just didn't… turn out right."

"You were hanging around in public, too," she said, and continued cutting.

"That's how I know something went wrong. I don't need to tell you I attract attention, I just don't know why I would have–" he stopped and fell silent.

She paused in cutting, but only for a moment. Then, she combed the front of his hair straight up and held it there.

He shivered.

And he was looking for distraction, at least from the sound of his own voice.

The water was cold, the scissors were loud, and he didn't like people being close enough to touch, or to touch him. Katrina had caught onto that quickly, but the effect was still there.

"So, you tried to reboot your head with these brain powers of yours and install a new update, but it didn't go as planned and you got a new operating system instead. But all the files are still there, you just don't know how to access them."

Sydney scrambled to gather words for an answer, but there was none.

"It's not the brain powers, whatever you're not telling me that creeps you out, but the files you can tell are there, but you can't open them, or don't want to."

He nodded slightly, unblinking as he looked back at her in the mirror.

"The only… thing–the only reason I can think that I'd, ah, *reboot*, is if there was a problem with the, ah… original," he attempted.

"Like what?"

"Like there was a… file I couldn't get rid of. Or…

corruption," he answered.

"Well, lucky you, buddy. We all have files we want to be rid of. Though, if you're talking some evil twin with superpowers, you should really be more specific so I can save up for some Kryptonite. Or something."

"I don't think Kryptonite would work. What's that ticking sound, though?"

He was tired of the place this conversation was leading, and the question was the first thing that popped into his head.

"Heh?" Katrina made a strange, vaguely questioning squawk.

"That ticking sound."

He pointed up toward the ceiling.

"Oh, that. I think Casey turned the music back on."

The woman at the front desk bobbed a little in the background. The monotone ticking morphed into an electric slide straight out of the 1980's.

Sydney had heard the song somewhere, but couldn't place it.

"I switched shifts with Sam, who usually works afternoon Saturdays. And Anthony had to jet right after… well, you might understand about Martin. Everything *just so*. He wanted the music off. And he's sort of a good customer, so I'm told, so… but I don't mean in manners."

She cast a glare toward the entrance, as if Martin was still there flirting with Casey.

"He has other things going on," Sydney said quietly.

"Care to share? Because unless he shares that with the class, he seems fine with looking like a controlling prick." Her words came out so fast, there was no opportunity to jump in and change the subject. He just stared at her through the mirror.

And then lightly cleared his throat.

"I get that, but trust me. He has other things going on." He paused, then rushed through his next words.

"How do you know Myrna, by the way?"

Katrina stopped cutting for a second.

"She's pretty regular at the *Cheshire*. We started talking over the counter," she said, resuming.

"The worst lie is a half-truth," he answered, barely audible over Katrina's speedy snipping. The scissors shut decisively, alarmingly close to the top of his ear.

He'd taken a chance based on an invisible thread of instinct. Hopefully the guess wouldn't come with bloodshed.

"The worst lie is coming in for a haircut when you barely have hair to cut, and there's something else you're not telling the girl with the scissors," she shot back.

"I'm an alien, sent here to destroy the planet, but I've decided to protect your primitive race instead," he said, willing his face to still.

Katrina rolled her eyes and ruffled his damp hair. He shuddered.

"Myrna put me through cosmetology school a couple years ago."

Sydney's eyebrows lifted.

"My ex, her brother, asked me to move out here with him. Convinced me even though my family said they wouldn't speak to me again if I did. About six months in, he was arrested for assault," she continued.

"I'm sorry," he said.

"I'm not," she replied. "First time he threw a plate at me, I told Myrna. She talked to him, he threw my Nintendo Switch. And I told her again. And then she told him if he ever laid a hand on me, she'd beat the shit out of him. Turns out that actually scared him, but not enough not to take his frustrations out on someone else."

Katrina paused for a breath.

"She worked three jobs for a while, then moved down from Boulder for school."

"Doesn't Boulder have essentially the same school?" he asked.

"I dunno. There might have been a girl or something, but if you get your privacy, she gets hers. And I *thought* I had mine."

"Still do," he assured, his head oddly lighter though not much had changed. "It's not as if I'd tell anyone, even if I had anyone to tell."

"Well, you have me." She hopped off her stool.

"So tell me all the creepy secrets you want.

Especially the ones you don't want to tell Jacob. Just specify which is which."

She chuckled and stepped around him to pick up her long-bristled brush.

Sydney frowned at her back and hoped she didn't catch him in the mirror. He looked instead over to Casey in the mirror.

She was filing her nails with yet another phone call pinned to her shoulder.

Laughter erupted from her red lips. After another second or two, she laughed again. Good. Sydney was almost certain she was on a personal call, which meant she wasn't paying attention to him.

"How often do you shave?"

"What?"

His attention snapped back to Katrina. She brushed the fallout from his haircut off his neck with a big, soft brush and stepped back around behind him.

"You seem a little red lately. I dunno if it's shaving or what, but–hold that thought."

Sydney imagined unfolding a neat, white paper with "*She's talking too much*" written on it. He shook his head once to be rid of the image.

His other self wasn't fully silent, but had simply changed medium. He didn't like it.

Katrina moved down to his left and reached into the sea of unusually shaped bottles arranged on the black shelf. She returned with the little jar Sydney had recognized earlier.

He took the container in one hand and she reached for the cotton-candy pink hair dryer sitting alongside her arsenal of scissors.

"One thing I've been wondering, though," Katrina began. Sydney set the tin on the chrome counter.

"You've reminded me I already have this one at home. I just haven't been using it," he lied.

She shrugged and lifted the hair dryer.

"Why do you think you were out at the shop, if you were really trying to do something? Like, however you did what you did, if *you* really did it, what's the point of that?"

"I don't know. Judging by that awful drink you said I ordered, I'm obviously not thinking the same. And there's just too much that I could think about all at once, sometimes I just… don't… want to."

"Yeah, that's fair. It just seems to me like whatever you were doing was timed, and went off when it wasn't supposed to. That, or you were waiting for someone else and got Jacob instead."

He gritted his teeth, then let go.

"If I was waiting for someone, they haven't really shown any interest in getting together again." He half-lied.

"Yeah, that's fair. Hope the hair dryer's okay," she answered. "I still don't think you came here for a haircut. Half of what we've been doing is talking, anyway."

"Well, you're a nice person," he informed her. "And competent."

"I still don't get it." Her arms lowered, thankfully removing the hair dryer from close to his head.

Sydney half-groaned. He was quickly running out of words. His ability to use them was still there, but they were losing their meaning and didn't achieve what he wanted to say. Or rather, he wasn't sure what he really wanted to convey.

After all, it wasn't exactly his choice to be there.

He leaned forward out of the chair, spinning the whole contraption around with one foot.

"That I'd want a hair cut from a nice person, or that you're a nice person?" he asked. She blinked in silence.

"How is it, by the way?" she asked.

Sydney wrenched his head around to look in the mirror. It did indeed look like what he'd described, and not too different than before.

He turned again, then jerked his head forward and his hair also fell forward, but not into his eyes.

"Perfect." Then he felt a croak welling up through is throat. "I don't quite know how to say this–"

"Just do," Katrina pushed. He propped himself up off the chair, then fell again when he remembered just how far he would be looking down at her if he stood up to speak.

"Jacob is curious, which is good. He cares about

things–particularly you. Not that you're a *thing*, just–sometimes he wants to know for the sake of knowing, and he puts himself in a position he feels like he ought not be in. I'm grateful for what he did for me, but it's going to get him in trouble one day. He shouldn't stop, he just needs to… prepare. Better."

"And I know people don't always take you seriously, for whatever excuse they make, but he does. If this situation gets out of hand–if I start telling him about some really… odd things, he'll need you to remind him that you two still have real lives. I don't have to interfere with that."

"You're not planning on being around, are you?" Katrina jumped in, all the sparkle gone from her eyes.

Sydney jumped out of the chair as he pulled the neck snaps on the cape open. Katrina flinched.

He balled the fabric up and set the cape on the counter. He stepped over the hair dryer cord and grabbed his coat as he walked past her, utilizing every inch of his long legs.

"Sydney!" Katrina called after him. She lunged forward and set the hair dryer back down before she followed. He didn't look back, but placed a pile of bills on the front desk before he pushed the front door open and strode down the sidewalk in the mid-afternoon sun.

Katrina stood there next to the desk, comb still in her hand, dumbfounded.

In the corner of her eye, Casey stood. The glittery phone fell from its precarious position as the woman's jaw lowered.

Casey picked up the phone from where it fell.

"Oh, yeah. Sorry. I'm *really* sorry about that. But… could I call you back in a minute? Yeah, thanks."

She pulled the bills off the edge of the counter, spread them out, and fanned herself with them.

"I assumed he's a friend of yours, but is there anything else I should know?" she asked.

"Sydney seems like a good guy, but he's absolutely insane. I'm more sure about that part."

Casey gave a sly smile.

"But he tips well," she said, waiving the bills in front

of Katrina's face. There were six twenties for the fifty-dollar hair cut advertised on the door.

Sydney fell into the park bench. It wasn't time to go back to the house, but there was really nowhere else to go, as usual. He was left in a strange gap with nothing to do and nowhere to be. And yet it wasn't quite time to leave.

He didn't fight the pause.

The setting sun cast long shadows, washing the tiny corner park in shades of orange and gold. He felt each person who kept to the sidewalk, and did his best to keep from staring, distracting himself with wondering who they were and what they were going to do. He wanted a moment to himself, to think about nothing.

He did, however, feel an odd shape from the inside chest pocket of his coat.

Hesitant, he slowly reached inside. His fingers closed on it and he rolled his eyes before he pulled it out all at once. *The Hanged Man.*

"You're not funny," he muttered to himself. He looked over the black and white drawing of the man hanging by one foot from a naked, winter tree, then flicked his wrist and cast the card out into the tiny park.

The card disappeared before landing, but he only grimaced.

Shutting his eyes focused every other sense. If he covered his ears, he would only focus his eyes. To do both would have just sent his thoughts toward whatever wood the bench was made of, or how tall the tree behind him was judging by his memory of the shade it threw over several yards of white ground.

He grasped for something to distract him from the distractions, and his mind wandered the park though his head laid back over the bench.

Through closed eyes he counted six silver cars, three motorcyclists and a Volkswagen van before something else caught his attention.

He thought he'd seen Dr. Lorem, but the car passed too quickly for him to get a better look. That car was definitely silver, but whether Lorem was inside was impossible to know. The paint job reminded Sydney of the plain grey suit the professor had worn when they last spoke.

Then again, Sydney hadn't really seen anything. His eyes were closed, and he was imagining it all.

Yet, he was so sure.

An absurd indecision descended on him, and he laughed to himself.

He could stay there all night if he really wanted. He had no obligation to head back to the yellow house.

Night didn't scare him, and neither did being alone. The real debate was whether staying was particularly wise, despite having little concern for his physical safety.

A hand rested on his shoulder, a single word breathed only a few inches from his left ear.

"*Stay*," his own voice said.

Sydney yelled and jumped up, away from the bench.

He was alone in the park.

He lunged forward and grabbed the back of the bench to look over the side. The snow behind the bench was undisturbed, the only footprints yards away.

Sydney gripped the wood even harder to channel his frustrations, but let go once he heard cracking. And then jumped again as his phone started buzzing in his pocket.

He ignored it and took off at a quick walk down the sidewalk. The phone stopped buzzing just as he came to the first crosswalk, and he moved ahead in a few seconds, loping across the road like an enormous black deer.

The phone started buzzing again. This wasn't Jacob's pattern, which meant either something was wrong or someone else was calling. Either way, he had new incentive to extract it from his pocket.

He fished it out of his deep pockets and nearly dropped it in the snow near the curb upon viewing the screen. There, he only read *Private*.

He pulled his glove off under one arm and tapped the screen to answer.

"Hello?"

"*Sydney?*" came a voice he unfortunately recognized.

"Martin, how did you get this number?"

NINE

"Not important," Martin growled back.

Sydney plugged his opposite ear, straining to hear anything in the background of the call that may be of use later. He wasn't sure what that could be without finding it.

"Okay, *fine*. What do you want?" Sydney asked, doing his best to soften the tone. Maybe that would drag the truth out of Martin more easily, but probably not.

"*Meet me at the Red Cheshire at five o'clock.*"

The call cut off.

Sydney pulled the screen away, taking a pause.

The winter sun had sunk low enough for his side of the street to rise up in blocks of shadow. Jagged hills of darkness reached out for him, while the rooftops glowed in the slowly retreating light.

Sydney could have called back. Martin wouldn't have answered.

He sighed and shoved the phone back in his pocket before he turned around to face the street. Looking up and down the road, surveying traffic, he stepped quickly to the corner of the sidewalk and leaned out even further.

Those passing watched him look up to the green light above. The light turned red and he looked back down, straight through to several lights in line down the street.

He was comfortable walking, generally speaking. Jacob and his uncomfortably tiny car were a help, but Sydney preferred the independence, regardless of any smattering of regrets he had in the moment such as weather or people staring up at him.

The sun sank lower behind the buildings, and he pieced together a different kind of map in his head.

The red light turned to green again and Sydney took off at a fast walk. At current speed, density of pedestrian traffic, and his count of the lights between his current location and *The Red Cheshire Coffee Co.*, he thought he should be able to keep up the pace without stopping more than necessary.

The lights were all on timers, after all.

Finally, he ascended the brick steps and peered

through the window-paned door. He stopped, because he suddenly couldn't remember what day it was, but could feel the buzz inside even before he'd stepped onto the porch.

If this was anything other than the weekend, the crowd was absurd. He then decided he was going to ignore the feeling and pretend he was the sort of person who looked forward to the weekends.

The windows glowed in the deepening dark, and he turned the lever handle before pushing the door open. The smell of coffee and bakery blasted him in the face.

He nevertheless crossed the threshold, scanning faces for that unfortunately now-familiar white spiked hair. Ignoring the notes of surprise from those around him, every time they looked to his shoulders and then further up, was almost second nature at this point.

He pushed through to the first step of the staircase, poked his head around the corner to the back room, then turned ahead an started his climb.

The first-floor hum died down a little, but there rose a few pockets of conversation ahead. He swept over the dozen other people in the room, occupied with themselves, then turned to the next flight.

He found the wall.

The staircase had ended, and *The Red Cheshire* had only two floors.

Sydney fell numb. He'd seen only two floors from the outside, but knew he'd been to the third, just like he knew he'd met Dan for the first time in the library despite his comments earlier.

There was no vaulted ceiling. There were no windows looking out onto the back patio. There was no piano, where he'd discovered that hidden talent. The room where he was told *It's all your fault* and met Skadi's friend did not exist.

Sydney raised his hand, reaching out to where the third floor used to be. The wall was solid, and as old as the rest of the paint.

After a deep breath, he turned to the second-floor seating and stepped up to the back window. The back patio was the irresponsible choice at such a time of year but, with the building so busy, it would make the perfect place to speak more privately.

Through the old glass, the layout began to take shape.

The awning frame glowed a soft yellow from the off-white of the string lights wrapped around it, as did the bushes surrounding vacant tables and chairs.

A human shape stirred near the far end, closer to what might have been a stage platform, under the snow. Sydney pressed his face into the cold window and placed his hands on either side of his face to block out more light.

That person shape wore a hat, deforming Martin's most recognizable feature at a distance.

Sydney held down a shiver.

No one else stood near him, but that didn't stop him from feeling like someone was about to reach out and place a hand on his shoulder again.

The shop was so crowded, yet he was still alone in it all.

He pulled away from the glass, muttering a "*Leave me alone*" under his breath as he made for the stairs once again.

The rest of the customers looked away from the very tall, vaguely irritated man who clearly had somewhere to be. A few looked his way, but only as he vanished through the blue-painted door at the back of the room.

Most of them wanted it shut again, and quickly. The end of January had neared, but Winter had made up for its brief lapse in enthusiasm some days before.

Sydney walked a few feet down the frigid path and stopped. The shape at the end of the back garden didn't turn to acknowledge the crunch of the snow under his feet, signaling an approach.

Once he stepped a couple yards closer, he recognized Martin's army green jacket.

Sydney closed the gap and rounded the metal table to get a square look at him. Martin stared at something on the cleared table, between his gloved hands, that wasn't there.

Sydney leaned over to the chair on the opposite side,

poorly swept the snow off, and sat. Martin clenched his jaw, but didn't look up.

Unfortunately, despite the yellow glow of the lights, everything was too dark to see much of what might tell him what Martin was thinking. He only stared into nothing.

"Martin?"

"Go away," the man blurted.

Sydney inwardly flinched.

"But you told me to–"

"I told you to come here so I could tell you to go away. Because apparently you haven't gotten the hint," Martin insisted and looked up without moving his head. Sydney leaned forward and emitted a tiny croak like he was about to speak, but Martin charged ahead.

"You really didn't think I couldn't tell who you are? I know what you *think* you're trying to do, but I'm here to make it clear–*go away.*"

"W-who I am? Sydney stuttered.

"It is *not* that hard!" Martin started, and fell back into his chair, sliding his hands back along the cold table.

"It's just that no one actually cares enough to notice when things are wrong. When things are *off*. Shoddy job, you've done. Absolutely intolerable. You really thought I wouldn't notice?"

Martin's question came as a record scratch at the end of words that didn't seem they would ever end.

"Notice what?" Sydney chanced.

Martin's eyes drifted over Sydney's shoulder, and Sydney resisted the urge to look behind him. Instead, he cleared his throat, then nearly choked as Martin laughed.

"You don't exist, Sydney."

"Excuse me?" he burst.

Martin's eyes drifted again, but this time Sydney turned to look over his shoulder. That corner of the back garden was dark, but he could still clearly see nothing was there. That is, except for the familiar feeling that something was.

The biggest problem was that he couldn't tell if it was the usual ghost, or Martin's unsettling drifting playing tricks on him.

"What are you looking at?"

"Nothing. Why are you here, Sydney? Because you've been lying to me," Martin said, tilting his head to the side. His eyes weren't wide, but oddly round. His pupils hovered in the center, locked onto him.

"I thought you said you knew why I'm here? I don't know what's going on."

With his left hand, Martin drew something from his belt that rattled slightly, then clicked. Sydney took a second to recognize what he held, probably because of the shock.

Martin held a wild-west style pistol, which glimmered as it caught the soft glow of the string lights. The garden was suddenly colder.

Sydney didn't look at Martin, but at the end of the gun.

"Are you drunk?"

Martin gave a chuckle, more nerves than amusement. He abruptly stopped.

"I can't drink," he said.

"Why not?" Sydney shot back.

Martin rolled his eyes so hard his head tilted back and the gun wavered. He righted his head and his eyes were still strangely wide without getting bigger.

"Super-secret personal reasons, all right?"

"Oh."

"Tell me where you were born," Martin commanded, even before Sydney could take a breath. Still, without more light, Sydney didn't have much to go on for whatever was happening. He might have been wrong, but having more pieces to put together might have calmed the welling panic of staring down a gun that looked more like it belonged in a saloon than the icy back yard of a coffee shop.

"Seattle," Sydney said.

"Liar."

Sydney blinked a few times.

"I can see it in your eyes. Or, I don't know, I just know it some other way. Where did you live before Colorado Springs?" Martin continued.

"Martin, I–"

"Don't bother lying about that one, either. Though,

while I'm at it, where do your parents live?" The gun began to shake, but not from the cold.

Sydney was about to answer, but Martin couldn't be contained.

"Because I'd love to know how to get that back. Hometown, parents, anything really. I don't remember Brighton. I don't know my parents' names. I don't remember meeting Skadi, and I don't know when I moved here, or why. Hell, I don't even know why I *sound* like this! You're *not* taking me back!"

He ended in crescendo and threw his hands up so violently, Sydney was concerned he might pull the trigger.

Sydney broke through the internal freeze and reached forward almost before he knew what he was doing.

"Martin, put the gun down."

Martin pointed it at him again, and Sydney sat back in his chair, hand resting on the cold metal table.

"Or what, we'll start all over again?"

Martin's eyes bounced over Sydney's shoulder and back.

"No, *seriously*, what are you looking at?"

"*Please* don't look over there," Martin insisted.

"What did I say to you at lunch?"

"Don't play stupid, Sydney," he hissed.

"I'm *not* playing!" Sydney took a moment to realize the implication of what he just said. "Humor me! I'm stupid!"

"You said '*They know we're here*."

They sat in silence for what felt an eternity, but had to have been under a minute.

"What?" Sydney breathed.

"Oh will you *stop it!*" Martin yelled, voice cracking.

"I don't know where parts of myself went. But I know this happens to people. The brain gets screwed up chemically and makes up whatever it wants, all because it connects what shouldn't really be connected. Which is why people get little white pills in little orange bottles," he ended in a singsong voice, then paused, as if to take in the reality of his confession, however sideways.

Sydney didn't dare move a muscle.

"But there's one thing I do know, and I have to do something about it, even if it's not real. Because if it is, and I could have changed something, it'll be all my fault. The worst that could happen is I just go back to… things I do remember.

"I've seen you somewhere before, Sydney, and you told me they know I'm here. That's why I know you've been lying to me all week, and to everybody else. And that you're lying to me now, playing stupid. So, before either of us get hurt, you need to leave."

The gun was shaking again.

Sydney watched it vibrate, and something about it felt… *off*. As much as he wanted to figure out what that was, he pulled his eyes away from the dark hole in front of him and looked at Martin, instead.

"I woke up Monday morning in the hospital," Sydney started, and watched Martin's face flicker.

"I don't know where I'm from–why I'm here. I don't know what's going on, but I do know I have no intention of hurting anyone, you included. I have no idea who you are or where you've seen me."

"That doesn't matter," he answered. The faint sparkle in Martin's eyes turned out to be gathering moisture.

"Because if you're here, they know I'm here–you're right," he continued. "And if they know, it doesn't matter anymore what you do and don't want. I just–I just can't…" Martin's voice trailed off, and he lifted the gun to point up as his eyes wandered again.

Sydney's heart jumped as Martin seemed to wake back up, re-aiming the gun.

"I can't do nothing," he finished.

"Then do something else," Sydney rasped. The cold air accentuated his poor attempt at convincing. The several seconds Martin stared back at him stretched on.

"That's easy to say, but you have no idea what that really–"

"Then *explain it to me*," Sydney blurted.

"That's not how this works! That's not how *any* of this works!" Martin shouted.

"*What*?"

"*Schi-zo-phren-i-a!*"

Martin's roar rang out in the empty back yard, his eyes wide at the sound of his own voice. He quickly set down the pistol and looked away, though it didn't leave his hand.

The ghost of Martin's voice faded.

"Okay, listen–" Sydney said after a gulp of icy air. "I don't know you. You can believe that or not, not my problem. But if you want to have any chance of getting help, for anything that's going on, no matter what that is, you need to pretend like you believe I'm going to believe every word you say. Just get it out. Listen to yourself say it, and I *might* believe you. If I don't, it's just us here. And who am I going to tell? If you haven't noticed, I don't exactly make a lot of friends."

"You'd tell Jacob," Martin answered quietly.

"You really think I've told him even half of what's going on in my life? The absolute ins–*insanity* of this? Rewinding my own brain? My own voice in my head saying things I did *not* know, or even think? I nearly got hit by a *truck* because a ghost wanted me to hit up a *witch shop!*" Sydney found himself out of breath, but continued once any fraction of it returned.

"I have some kind of supervillain ex who's insisted this is all because of *me*, and I don't know what to do, either, Martin. So, you can start being clear with me, or *you* can go away."

Martin was silent, but their eyes held.

After a moment, he sat up straighter.

"I need to test something," Martin said.

Sydney threw his hands up.

"Fine, just don't shout again," he answered.

Martin let go of the pistol, then grabbed the barrel-end and held the grip out to Sydney.

Sydney looked down at it in suspicion, but Martin shook the gun a little and Sydney hesitantly took it in hand.

The wave of nausea passed as quickly as it had come, but Sydney's skin crawled.

He held Martin's clear plastic AirSoft pistol in his hand, the barrel pointed down at the table.

"It's the plastic one, right? Not the Colt?" Martin

asked.

Sydney turned it on its side. The gun wasn't even the same shape as the one he saw Martin holding. The plastic still reflected, but not like metal. There was no way it was the same gun.

He noted the safety switch on the side, in the on position, and bit back a spike of hot irritation before he set it down in front of him, out of Martin's reach.

"Then there's that," Martin said, a head flick to his left toward the empty chair.

Sydney looked over, then jumped out of his chair with a screech. His jaw had clenched so hard his teeth still hurt.

Sydney looked at himself sitting there in what had been an empty chair. He knew Martin was also looking at him where he stood in the snow, but couldn't pry his eyes away from his own face.

He looked back at himself, hair slightly longer, face clean-shaven. And there was silence, except for the crackling of resentment behind the seated Sydney's eyes.

The seated Sydney crossed his arms, then bounced a few times on the back of the chair before looking to Martin.

"I see a lot of things, like you probably guessed. And I wish I could say it happens less than it used to, but it's just–it's just different." He paused and looked the Sydney in the third chair up and down.

"I don't remember everything I'd like to, but I know I've changed medication four times in the last year. This part–" he gestured vaguely to the seated Sydney, who still watched him as he spoke "– this part doesn't change. Not you specifically, just… extra people.

He tore his eyes away from the Sydney that shouldn't have been there.

"And, lately, I've realized it also goes along with what people are about to talk about, or get particularly… annoyed that I ask about. I've seen people fantasize about things that would make the latest slasher look like a Disney Channel special. Accid–incidents before they happen. People thinking about all sorts of other people, sometimes people who aren't alive anymore. Those ones look back at me… occasionally.”

Sydney let himself look directly at Martin, who held down a grimace. In the corner of his eye, the seated Sydney suddenly looked different. When he looked back up, Jacob sat there instead.

He took his glasses off and cleaned them on the red plaid shirt under his open parka, like nothing was out of the ordinary.

Martin pointed one hand at the ambivalent Jacob, but didn’t look directly at him.

Sydney took a breath to speak, but the seated shape changed again. He looked back up to Levi sitting there, staring daggers into Sydney’s eyes.

He almost wished it would go back to his possibly-evil twin.

“Wait, you know him?” Martin’s voice rose.

“Not really. I–”

“You really have no idea what’s going on, do you? You didn’t see the plastic one before I handed it to you?” Martin interrupted.

Sydney clamped his mouth shut to allow himself time to organize his thoughts so the first irritated one didn’t jump out before he found his control. The image of Levi still stared into him like he was looking forward to a snack.

“Why didn’t you say something about this before?” was the nearest to helpful thing Sydney could come up with.

“I’m crazy, not stupid,” was all Martin said. “What do you remember about that evil ex of yours?”

“Nothing! Other things are familiar, but I just can’t–I can’t…” Sydney ran his gloves through his hair and looked away from them both.

“Can you get rid of this guy? Please?” Sydney pled.

“No. That’s all on you. It’s definitely more interesting than when Skadi’s thinking about anime characters, but I understand the distaste.”

Levi turned back into Sydney, though a significantly paler version than before. He still stared daggers, but even sharper than Levi had.

“I don’t know what that person looks like–whoever’s been watching, but they know about however I got myself into this mess. They're someone who's been here, and someone who wants me to know they can see me. If I could just–"

Katrina sat there, swinging her feet. Sydney's eyes widened, and Martin's did in reply before his head snapped left to see what Sydney was looking at.

Martin took a breath to speak, and then Katrina was Skadi.

"I'm guessing you don't have a name instead of a face, do you?" he asked Sydney, though turned toward the image of his girlfriend who also stared into Sydney like something was about to happen.

"The Cat. Long story."

Martin's eyebrows twisted.

"What?" Sydney asked. Skadi was then a double of Martin. This time, looking at the real Martin.

"I just–" he turned back to the empty chair full of himself and flinched before he looked to Sydney, brows raised.

"None of this feels real. None of this ever feels real, which is why I'm not screaming right now," he said with a little nod. He swept a hand over the lower half of his face

"But, two things that really concern me are that I have no idea who you're talking about. The other is that the thing I did with the gun, that thing only works on people who can't… who aren't… who haven't seen… what…"

The Martin that wasn't really there started to smile and the real Martin silenced to look back.

Sydney looked between them. Though Sydney was no longer the object of scrutiny, the second Martin looked at the original in a way that had Sydney start wondering what would happen if Martin were to join him standing.

"Well, I'm aware something's going on," Sydney explained. "It's just… complicated how much. I do know, if I have anything to do with you, then the Cat is the person who's causing all this. I have nothing to do with–"

"No, it isn't," Martin shot.

"What?"

The second Martin seemed to shift into another shape before Sydney looked back to him. What might have been a tall woman with long blonde hair was Martin again.

"That's my… ah, where my concerns *overlap*. If I could show you the Colt, you're technically not who you were, but you can still see part of… things going on. And then you're telling me the person causing all this is called The Cat, and I have no idea who that is. You're *you* and *not you*, at the same time.

"Which *means*, if we're both telling the truth, there's a lot more people involved in this than I originally thought, and this is a lot more complicated than I thought. There's your–the *Cat*, and the *Foundation*, where we had volunteered for th–"

Sydney doubled over as lights flashed behind his eyes. All senses dulled, but still the pain tore through his head like microphone feedback. The images rushed through in an explosive mosaic, each emotion of the moment as real and raw as reality.

The white walls spun and he ran over tile even as he collapsed over and over onto the cold floor. Feet and murmuring voices and mirrors and rubber cart wheels and somewhere in there came Martin's voice asking him if he was alright, even as Martin sitting across an entirely different table flashed like a grain of sand through a thunderstorm.

He found the ground in the back garden but wasn't sure the floor under his hands was real, or where his hands were in relation to everything else. He sat across the table from so many people in rapid succession, in a tsunami of senses turning his head inside out.

His head was full of open fields while his body sat in a straightjacket, inside a house behind his eyes that refused to see.

The tall wooden gate leading back to the street banged against itself. Sydney found himself on his hands and knees in the snow, his face cold with sweat. Over his shoulder, Martin's chair was empty and so were the others.

His head snapped back forward and he traced the frantic, messy footprints through the snow back out to the front of the *Red Cheshire*.

On instinct, Sydney snatched the pistol up and darted

after Martin, slowing only as he fought the sensation he was about to snap back–that his feet were chained somewhere else. He looked back, broke through that feeling as he forced himself to confirm the contrary, then shoved the gun in his coat pocket–there would be time to think about what had just happened later.

By the time he pulled the faded red gate open, Martin stepped into his low black sports car. In one last, hopeful effort toward nothing practical, Sydney lunged forward to catch the door. He missed.

Martin lurched away from the curb without a glance up and sped away. Sydney watched him go, as well as each drift correction as the dark, red-eyed vehicle centered and re-centered itself in the lane. He took a wide turn several blocks down and vanished.

Sydney finally resigned and fell numb. He shoved his hands in his pockets, fingers curling around the gun there. It still felt wrong, compared to what he originally saw, and the defensive haze held off for that much longer.

He took a look up and down the street and stepped back behind the wooden gate.

There, he pulled the gun out for a better look.

Sydney held the clear plastic Airsoft pistol with a bright orange tip on the barrel. He had plenty of experience with things shifting on him, but this was the first instance confirmed by anyone else.

And this time, someone had anticipated his reaction.

Meaning? came his own voice in his head.

I was wondering where you went, Sydney thought to himself. He left through the gate once again, walking slowly in the same direction Martin's car had disappeared.

He came to the turn he would have taken to get back home, but kept on. The streets were timeless, the infinite snowfall set aglow by warm white street lamps and colored traffic lights.

He found himself in a daze, staring up into a bare tree, tracing the pattern of its shadows when his phone buzzed in his pocket.

He sat down on the park bench and set the phone on his knee. He buttoned the top button of his coat and flipped the collar up against his neck.

The cold had started to get in again.

The message was from Jacob.

Katrina says Myrna wants your phone number. Can she have it?

Sydney sighed, then settled deeper into the bench, sticking his legs out far enough to pose substantial tripping hazard.

He might have said yes, if he was planning to stay. He might poke around and see how Martin was doing later, but the conversation was enough for him to deal with, without inflicting anything on someone else. Time had come to explore, if only to clear his head a little more. Or to fill it with something useful, for once.

He searched in the dark for a reason to say no to Jacob, one that wouldn't start a conversation about when he would talk to Myrna again.

Instead, he decided to ignore him.

The street was nearly vacant for a long distance around, but he noted a few stragglers. It was odd for a Saturday night, which put him on edge almost as much as the scene he had just left. He instead turned his attention to counting the windows he could see from where he sat.

It was time to just sit alone for a while.

Counting windows didn't kill his anxiety–just let it build up. He'd have to think about Martin's words sooner or later.

Snow began to fall harder, and he was finding it harder and harder to think about leaving the bench. He crossed his arms and closed his eyes.

Somewhere down the street behind him, a motorcycle approached, slowed, and sped past, while sirens blew on the distant wind.

Sydney didn't flinch as his ghost began to congeal next to him. He'd seen his own face just a while before, and without reflection this time–it was time to stop jumping every time he felt he wasn't alone.

His eyes stayed shut and he stayed still. That feeling solidified even further.

It wasn't just a ghost, because he sensed a definite

height and structure. Someone had sat down next to him–a solid weight.

He heard the cold creak of the bench and the faint whisper of shoe soles on the ground.

Sydney opened his eyes and pushed away with a start as soon as recognizing his own left hand to the right of his right hand. He sat alone in the deepening snow, in the empty park.

If anyone had been tucked away in the long shadows, they would have seen Sydney take off at a quick walk down the street.

Occupying his body sadly didn't distract his mind well enough.

All this had begun due to something Sydney wanted. He didn't even know what he was like before–there was no telling what he really wanted enough to risk wiping things away. Then again, with how strongly certain tendencies asserted themselves, he couldn't think of why he would want to be in such a crowded place to begin with.

That is, unless he was taunting someone who wanted him to keep to himself. Unless the buzz of commotion had something to do with the process.

Martin had confirmed not all hallucinations were true hallucinations. Thankfully there were no killer clowns or talking furniture, but things were happening for a reason. The validity of that reason was locked away in the back of his head along with the part of himself he didn't understand why it was so angry all the time.

Then there was *The Foundation.*

The whole story had multiple sides–an obvious thought, but terrifying in application.

He looked over his shoulder out of instinct. His second self still followed, though no one was there but a couple further down and a man in a tailored suit he couldn't afford.

Sydney turned forward and shook his head once.

He didn't know where that thought had come from, but it was so strong. It came to him like a tall drink on a hot day. It was simply a fact, and one he accepted implicitly.

Sydney turned his head inches to the left, down the

crossing street. Even further down, flashing red and blue lights reflected off the buildings, while road flares dotted the pavement, sending hot orange sparks into the air. He looked back and forth, confirmed traffic stood still, and stepped into the middle of the road.

He walked slowly closer, torn between forcing what he'd seen back out of his head, or giving in to his desperate need for some kind of progress. To accept what he was experiencing was really happening.

With acceptance came the responsibility of doing something. Just like Martin had said.

He crossed through the black skid marks cross-ways over the black road, counting one squad car, two ambulances and one low, black sports car with its front-end smashed in.

There was also, at the end of one set of the skid marks, a little blue mini cooper with a shattered windshield and crumpled passenger side door. It was nearly bent into a complete U- shape. What remained of the back windshield, including the University of Colorado Springs sticker, faced him.

Sydney shut out all other thoughts and continued making his way down the center of the road, toward the lights.

TEN

Jacob heard something ticking. The sound was irregular, and slightly plastic. No, more like periodic *clicking*.

Hard rubber squeaked on linoleum. He sensed light through his eyelids.

The clicking continued as feeling melted back into him, and he woke enough to register further annoyance. A squeak came again. He lifted his heavy eyelids.

The hospital room was dim, but he still squinted against the warm yellow lamp over his head. He heard a beeping from behind him, but ignored it in favor of his effort trying to recognize the person who sat in the chair in the corner, next to the light blue curtain.

The human shape held what might have been a Rubik's cube, explaining away the periodic plastic clicking. They also held it absurdly close to their face, as if trying to see inside rather than just the colors on the surface.

Sydney turned the pieces of the puzzle with another smattering of clicking sounds. He dragged his foot across the linoleum. Another squeak pierced Jacob's tenuous patience.

He opened his eyes wider, then jerked. He tried to look down, directly at Sydney from where he laid on the angled head of the bed, but found he couldn't move his head at all. His neck was oddly stiff, wrapped in a gray plastic brace, and his right arm felt the same.

"Oh, you're back," Sydney said and turned, but still held the cube only a few inches from his face. Without looking, he twisted one side and two of the blue columns lined up.

Jacob struggled to sit up and bashed his long arm cast on the bed rail in the process. The groaned at the dull ache and closed his eyes, waiting for the pain to dissipate. It did quickly, due to the IV line taped into his opposite hand.

Jacob opened his eyes again and Sydney stood at the bed rail, the toy sitting on the chair in the corner.

"Did I just…" Jacob mumbled.

"Yeah, just a little nap," Sydney answered. "You want to sit up?"

Jacob half-shrugged, but thought better of the other

half.

"Yeah, sure," he said, instead. Sydney hesitated.

Jacob looked up at him without moving his head.

Sydney's eyes lingered, then looked to whatever button he was about to press. The head of the bed rose with an electrical buzz.

"Your car is totaled," Sydney blurted, just as Jacob took a breath.

"You were about to ask what happened."

Jacob clenched his jaw, winced, and let go. He geared up again, but Sydney cut him off once more as he turned back to his seat.

"Martin's could be fine."

He stopped, looked over to the empty end of the room as if he heard something, then took his seat again. He picked up the cube and turned it quickly a few times. More colors lined up.

Jacob stayed silent, but winced as Sydney's shoe squeaked across the floor again. The man just didn't fit neatly in the chair, and repositioned himself as much as necessary.

"And I was just telling Katrina I thought he was avoiding me," Jacob said. Silence fell back into place, except for the persistent beeping of whatever monitors he couldn't see and the clicking of Sydney's cube.

Jacob was awake enough to then feel the cast extended to his upper arm. He vaguely remembered raising his elbow at a sudden, blinding light.

"Dan gave Katrina a ride back from work–don't worry about it. Martin's probably getting at least six months, though," Sydney said, still focused on the plastic in his hands.

Jacob almost managed to sit back up, powered by shock at the last sentence.

"Six months?" he asked.

"Initial DUI charges dictate a year, at most."

"*What?*"

Sydney waited calmly while the pulse monitor overtook the moment.

"He's fine. Ish. But they told me he was drunk,"

Sydney explained.

"Martin doesn't drink."

"I know," Sydney shot back.

"Uh… how?"

Sydney looked up from the cube to the wall, then slowly over to Jacob.

"Psychic powers," he said, one eyebrow raised. Jacob squinted.

Sydney's resolve broke and he looked back into the cube in his hands.

"With that weird little network Katrina has," Sydney lifted one hand and traced the invisible web of contacts in front of him, "Skadi told Myrna she was taking her bike down to the police station with Martin's medication as proof of bogus charges. She didn't tell me what it was, exactly, just that it was evidence enough that he *definitely* didn't drink, or things would have been noticeably… *not good* long before now."

Jacob would have let his jaw gape, except for the neck brace. He mulled over the implications of this information.

Sydney picked up his coat from the seat next to him and slid into it. He dropped the cube in his pocket, where it knocked against something else plastic.

"I'll be around tomorrow morning," he said as he flipped his collar the right way out from where it had hidden down inside.

"Where have you been, anyway? I called you, like, eight times," Jacob asked.

"Texted. Three times." His gloved hand grasped around the bar at the end of the bed.

"I'll tell you about it later. I promise."

"If you think I really want to know, sure," Jacob said, pointing sternly with his left hand. A smile flickered over Sydney's face.

"Fair enough."

With that, he moved quickly to the edge of the curtain, where he nearly collided with a red-haired female nurse. Jacob noted the seconds worth of deeper alarm on his face before he vanished.

She looked over her shoulder after he passed, then gave a little shrug and turned back to the bed.

"Hi! I'm Chloe, and I'll be checking in with you for tonight. You're doing well, but we need to make sure it stays that way."

Jacob stared at her blankly.

"Yeah, uh. Hi. Did my glasses survive? If so, I'd really like to have them back, particularly if anyone else stops by."

Sydney strode back through the halls of the hospital at a speed somewhat above gentlemanly. He paid just enough attention to keep from crashing into anything, but the rest of his focus was placed on reaching the lobby doors before the spreading numbness overtook his ability to stay upright.

Keeping momentum, he took the stairs instead of the elevator. He also had no patience for standing in a little mirrored room with strangers, trapped even for a moment.

Before him was a straight shot to the outside world, anticipation blocking nearly every other thought. He walked past the front desk so quickly the receptionist looked up, squinted, then shrugged and looked back down.

Sydney pierced through and was again under the night sky. He only stopped long enough to catch his breath in the cold, open air, then started off again back to the yellow townhouse on West Barrow Street.

The shadow of his former self had been silent, no voice and no noted shifts in reality for the last several hours–since Sydney was lost in the scene of the crash. That was worse than he'd expected.

He walked home alone.

Sydney threw his coat over the back of the sofa and pulled his cell phone out of the side pocket. He tossed it onto the coffee table next to his open laptop computer. The tremor jarred the computer awake.

Both the clock on the stove and the clock on the desktop read minutes to midnight. It had been running a virus scan for the last few hours. He didn't really think anything would come of it, but he couldn't think of what else to do. They wouldn't let him see Jacob immediately.

He'd spent some time between then and the hospital phone call plugging his library into a spreadsheet, for no other reason than curiosity and containing his panic. The virus scan was nearly done.

He ignored the pop-up only long enough to make himself another cup of tea. He wasn't going to sleep, anyway, so he might as well caffeinate.

Sydney set his tea down next to the computer, taking a moment to lean forward and close out his browser windows. He had toyed with the idea of getting Jacob a Get Well Soon card, but had rather gravitated toward some kind of gift.

The embarrassment of such a thought pushed him in the direction of some sort of stuffed tarantula, just so he could say it was a joke.

That's what friends did, right? Silly jokes?

To cheer each other up?

Some part of him had shorted out at the sight of Jacob's car, and he didn't even begin to understand where to repair it.

He clicked on the virus scan with a mixed sense of satisfaction. There were a total of four instances the computer was accessed–once from Mumbai, once from Sao Paolo, and twice from McMurdo station.

Sydney opened another browser tab and typed into the search engine. He had just opened a list of results explaining internet access in Antarctica when there came an unsettling squelch from the virus scan window.

He navigated back and clicked the *Next* button, then jumped as the file browser opened. In that folder was a video, the title only a long series of numbers and letters.

The pathway itself was a complicated series of numbers and letters that hurt his eyes to look at. Yet, in the folder, there was only one file–a movie.

Without a second thought, he double-clicked on it.

The whole system froze. He lifted his hands from the keyboard and waited. Nothing changed.

Sydney lifted his mug and sighed, then stood from the couch. He leaned over to flick the kitchen light off, then turned toward the stairs.

If the computer wasn't going to cooperate, and he was being so reckless as to click something from a virus scan, he might as well get some reading in. There was nothing on the computer he was particularly attached to, so he might just end up buying another.

The screen itself dropped to black, and he sighed again.

He took his first step up the stairs when he heard a voice and jumped so high he nearly spilled tea up his sleeve.

In his surprise he didn't catch the precise words, but it definitely came from outside his own head.

He carefully stepped back to the floor, then hooked his free hand around the side of the wall, where he felt around for the light switch. The laundry room light came on. It wasn't much, but let him find the coffee table again without falling over himself.

The sound from the laptop was fuzzy, like music through an AM frequency from far off.

"*Or, we can just sit here*," the male voice spoke again. It was oddly familiar, holding a hint of fear under calm confidence.

Sydney gently took a seat on the couch, squarely in front of the black screen. An idea struck him and he set down his tea, then tapped the keyboard shortcut to adjust the brightness.

The screen flashed with glitchy lines and stabbed through his ears with a pop and more electrical fuzz. He frantically tapped the brightness back down, luckily just in time for more lines and pixels to pierce through before a cut to black again.

A video was there, but corrupted.

"*Please focus*," came George Lorem's voice. Sydney sat up straighter.

"*Make me*," said the first man.

"*Don't tempt me*," Lorem said with a squelch.

Sydney reached for his tea as the other man snickered, somewhere behind the veil of audio static.

"*You were introduced to the full network about a week ago, I'm told,*" Lorem started again. Sydney squinted against a few more flashes of light.

"*I'd like to talk about your experience,*" Lorem went on. The first man scoffed, then there came a metallic bang.

"*Ow,*" he said several seconds later, quite lethargically.

Lorem drew in a breath. "*We can do a scan, or you can tell me verbally. Due to your... aversion to the former, I suggested what we're doing now.*"

"*And what are we doing, exactly?*"

They both fell silent for a long moment.

"*You realize he can talk back, right? Your* 'network*'?*" the first man finally spoke. The voice was more and more familiar with each word.

"*He told me all about you people. Most of it, I'd caught onto, but he told me all about what you'd done to him. What you're trying to do to other people. How you... sawed him in half and glued him back together with his own blood and started doing it to everyone else. Damn vampires.*"

Sydney's eyes widened in the dark room.

Something solid shifted out of the corner of his eye and he turned his head with a loud beat of his heart. The couch was still empty on either side of him.

He was beginning to gain ground on recognizing that man's voice, but his emotional response was more enthusiastic than finding a name. He felt the answer before thinking it.

His hands started to shake and he set his tea down.

Lorem was still silent, but there came a tapping, most likely fingers on something metal.

"*I saw the inside, George.* You *showed me the inside. And I can tell you right now, you're so far in over your head I can't even* begin *to describe how much you're going to regret what you've done. Or maybe not, I suppose.*"

"*You of all people know what we do helps people,*" Lorem began. "*If you're not going to share the results of your exercise, we're going to have to go take a scan. I can't keep–*"

"*Oh, I'm sharing,*" Sydney on video said. He sounded like he'd never heard himself speak before. The same kind of anger he heard in that intrusive voice in his head was finally coming to his physical ears in more than fits and starts.

"*I've learned a few things while I was plugged in. Everywhere you see, he can see, too, you know. He can talk to anyone. If only there was someone to talk to.*" He began breathing heavier, holding back his anger in favor of getting the words out.

"*I know your program. I know your tests, your games, how you think you're making the world a better place, so long as it's in your own image. I also know what you're going to do to me if I'm not the one you've been looking for. Like all the others you burned out along the way.*

"*You want my* results, *so I'm giving them to you.*"

The screen flashed a few more times but, on the last burst of light, Sydney spotted a human shape. Unfortunately, it was also bright enough to reflect off the sudden glimpse of his own right hand sitting next to his left, a tiny flash of the image of himself sitting next to himself on the couch.

He found himself leaning away from the empty space where he'd seen himself. The fragmented video continued.

"*I talked to your blessed little brother, all about how he was pulled apart and put back together. Hoping he'd be more compliant. All about how you keep calling him special, trying to make others just like him, but not* too *much. That's why he's here, not out there, after all.*

"*You've killed people, George. Or worse. And maybe not with your own hands but the hands you've assisted. You can't fix the world with control, or calculate the soul.*"

Lorem did not reply in the long silence.

"*I've seen the future, and you're not in it. You, or your little friends. But you've made monsters–*" Sydney on the video laughed. "*So many of them who, in turn, make monsters. And, whatever happens, yes–this is your fault.*

"*You're trying to grow, when you shouldn't even be alive. You sick, arrogant people are going to give someone a double dose of what you think makes them* special *one day, all because you thought they were ordinary to begin with.*

Everyone's ordinary, to you. Even the most messed-up ones you take advantage of. You have no idea what people already have inside, because you never bother to look. You don't look harder than you have to. That's your first mistake."

"*But, you know your biggest one? Even if you did manage to double up on someone on purpose? Ratchet things up?*"

The finger tapping resumed. Someone leaned forward in a metal chair.

"*Even if... you did this on purpose... you still think you're in control!*" Sydney roared with a high, digital screech.

Sydney sat back on the couch, covered his ears and squinted through the flashing light and partial images. The metal table clanged, as did the chairs, audio screech still going strong.

He pushed himself back into the arm of the couch, the screen continuing to flash in pixels and glitchy smears.

The video ended; the screech cut.

Sydney listened to his ears ringing, staring at the black screen. Once his ears toned down, though hadn't fully calmed, he leaned forward to the computer.

He tapped the volume key and used the track pad to move the slider down to the lowest setting without being muted. He moved the progress bar over to the last ten seconds of video.

"*That's your first mistake. But, you know your biggest one? Even if you did manage to double up on someone on purpose? Ratchet things up?*"

Someone tapped on metal.

"*Even if... you did this on purpose... you still think you're in control!*" Sydney roared with a high, digital screech.

The flurry of nauseating images assaulted him, but he persevered.

He hit pause and found one of the human shapes, surrounded by neon pixels as if the man was dissolving into basic data.

Sydney hit the arrow key and was dismayed to find the video backed up further than he wanted

"*...double dose of what you think makes them* special, *all because you thought they were ordinary to begin with. Everyone's ordinary, to you. Even the most messed-up ones you take advantage of. You have no idea what people already have inside, because you never bother to look. You don't look harder than you have to. That's your first mistake.*"

"*But, you know your biggest one? Even if you did manage to double up on someone on purpose? Ratchet things up?*"

Someone tapped.

"*Even if... you did this on purpose... you still think you're in control!*"

Sydney impulsively tapped pause. He couldn't breathe, and couldn't find it in himself to blink.

On the screen, he saw himself in what might have been white scrubs. The pale room was mostly white tiles, and large–more than enough room for the wide metal table in the center, across from which sat George Lorem.

At least, he had been sitting a moment before. He'd shoved himself back, out of Sydney's reach as he lunged over the table with unnaturally long arms, a scream of rage distorting every part, but particularly his teeth–his mouth was full of long, sharp points. His eyes glinted like a cat.

He stared at the screen a little longer.

It looked like him.

It sounded like him.

And, deep down, it also felt like him.

"That wasn't a video, was it?" he said aloud, eyes still wide in the stark light of the screen. It cut to black on its own.

His own hands appeared to his left, the body attached to it propped up by the elbows on the back of the couch. He looked into the black laptop screen and saw himself there, next to him.

"No," the ghost said.

Sydney half-turned to look directly at him.

"*Don't turn,*" he growled. Sydney did as he was told and looked back into the black screen before he fully laid eyes on the man next to him.

"That was a memory," the ghost explained.

"Oh, what, you can play back my own memories now? Why not earlier?" Sydney complained. The ghost met his eyes and sighed in annoyance.

"What about that was HD to you? Turns out I did a pretty good job, even considering, well, *I'm me*."

"What did you even do? To begin with?" Sydney pled. The ghost paused and watched him through the screen.

"I turned off a memory," he said.

"Which created me."

"Yeah."

Sydney rubbed one eye.

"How do you even do that?" he asked, the time of night catching up to him despite caffeine.

"Do what?"

"Just… *shut off* part of your–*our*–and you know what? If you can't push the memories through without it looking like that, why are you here right now? I can see you there," Sydney said as he pointed to the screen. "But I can also see you there."

He looked over to the hands next to him and on impulse turned a bit further.

"*Don't turn*," the ghost hissed.

Sydney did as he was told and faced forward. The faint scent of blood wafted through, but he rubbed his nose and it was gone.

"I'm here because Martin's curse has to do with images–perception. He can suggest you see what he wants you to see, or show you something you're ignoring. Unfortunately, that also comes with being particularly in tune with the signals of others, and even more complex with someone like… us. You can see this," the ghost stretched his fingers out, "because you saw me earlier. You've already accepted this is possible, but you'll lose grip on it, eventually. The longer it goes on. Which is why now, not earlier."

Sydney sat in silence, looking back at himself.

"Is he actually schizophrenic?"

"Yes," the ghost answered. Sydney hesitated again, reminding himself to breathe. The temptation to turn was so much stronger, and he glanced at the ghost's–his–hands out of the corner of his eye.

The ghost sighed and dropped his head before looking back up.

"Medicine and psychology pretend to understand anomalous neurology, but all they can do is chart patterns and make correspondences. There are objective facts, such as '*Martin Gardiner is schizophrenic.*' But what that means in application can be subjective."

"He's experienced hallucinations and delusions for a long time. It's how they slipped this little, ah, *quirk* in. His connectivity was already so high."

Sydney sat straighter.

"You knew him before this?"

The ghost stared back at him through the computer.

"But, a shared experience is what moves something from subjectivity, a little closer to reality. And, in this situation, acceptance has a lot to do with ability. Show someone something they can put complete faith in, and it becomes real for them. In a religious sense, it changes nothing. In a psychological sense, however– and that's what really holds weight, here."

"You're saying I *accepted* what he was doing, which made it easier for him to do. Beyond that gun thing, which he did on purpose. Told me what it was, and so it was." Sydney rubbed both eyes.

"Essentially."

"That's interesting, because I'm pretty sure I don't *accept* that we're some kind of monster of the week abomination like I saw in that vid–memory you pushed."

The ghost tilted his head.

"*Rude*."

Sydney dropped his hands.

"And you were trying to escape your handlers, is that it?"

The ghost merely stared. The reflection of his companion in the screen began to look a little blurry. Sydney took a deep breath.

"Martin and I were involved in some kind of *brain* experiments, which Lorem worked–works for. They either made us into this, or brought it out, but you–I wanted to leave. They didn't catch onto that idea but I left anyway, and the Cat is in there somewhere in our band of weirdos who should probably get cast in the next *Suicide Squad*.

"Only, something about the Cat was *off*, so I left there too, and they knew I was going to try and turn part of my brain off and sabotaged it. Or I'm not as clever as I think I am. Or I didn't care, because that part was–what would be so bad that I'd risk being right here, right now, talking to myself about psychic powers? About seeing something because a *schizophrenic man* showed it to me?"

The ghost stared back through the screen. A small smile did flicker at the edge of his mouth.

"What would *you* do if you were handed a weapon and were told to hurt someone?"

Sydney squinted.

"Depends on a lot of things. You can't just–"

"Say you decided to bury this weapon and come back for it later. Burying takes time, but you have time. And you can come back for it later, after those people stopped telling you what to do?" the ghost interrupted.

"Is that what you did? Buried you in me, for later?"

"Now imagine, just as you're finishing up burying this weapon, someone–" the ghost coughed and looked away with wide eyes. Sydney caught himself turning and pushed himself back toward the screen.

"You okay?" Sydney asked. The ghost looked even paler than Sydney ever had–paper white with sunken eyes. Sydney blinked and the change was reversed.

"Just as you're burying that weapon, a child comes up and is friendly to you. You're friendly back. You're told if you bury this weapon, that child will suffer."

"What, you mean Jacob?" Sydney replied.

"But it's too late. You can't unbury it–the process has to finish. No undoing it now. You try to find it again, but it's been moved. You thought you knew where to dig, but the solution isn't there. You reach out to the new… landlord, but you don't speak his language so well. You were successful and failed at the same time." If Sydney hadn't known any better, he would have thought the ghost's eyes were wet. And yet, his spectral companion pushed ahead.

"The people telling you to use that weapon try to send you a map to where it is–to make you remember–"

"I was supposed to remember Martin, and then everything else?" Sydney interrupted. "How does that even work? I saw him once before, in the library, and I didn't remem-"

"The plan has changed. I can't force you to remember, anymore. And there are more people involved than I can–than I can expl–" the ghost distorted momentarily in Sydney's screen like someone had cut his video tape and glued it back together.

"–explain right now. We're running out of time, but I'll still be here. To push you in the right direction."

"Okay, what did I change? And *how?* You've put in all this effort, at least tell me that," Sydney asked.

The ghost took a breath, which Sydney felt more than he'd ever felt that voice before.

"What's the biggest difference between you and me?"

"I'm in control," Sydney said.

"Are you, though?"

Sydney threw up a hand.

"Everyone *else* seems to think so," he answered. "And it's *my* body right now, so don't get clever."

The ghost didn't miss a beat.

"Why does what other people think make you in control? Make you real?"

Sydney stared back. He blinked a few times. No satisfactory answer was coming.

"You seem to want me to remember, and I want to remember, but I'm not remembering. *They* want me to remember," he said and cast a hand toward his laptop screen, "but you're saying you can't help that anymore. Why? What did I–you try and change?"

The ghost didn't bat an eye.

"Again, what's the biggest difference between you and me?"

"We are... the same... *person!*" Sydney shouted. He tasted blood at the back of his throat and coughed with wide eyes.

"When why do you treat me like we're not?"

Sydney threw his hands up, fighting the metallic taste.

"*What* is so bad about you, if it's not the fangs and sass, that you'd risk being me?"

Sydney turned to face him. His blood ran cold.

The ghost stood there, identical to him in every way, looking back at him like nothing was amiss. The corners of his mouth, however, were downturned.

His coat was gone and his white shirt was more red than white, still-wet blood showered over one shoulder like he'd only just turned from some moment of carnage. Blood from his sleeve cuff at his elbow seeped into the white fabric of the couch.

The ghost reached up and wiped a long smear of blood off the side of his face–so much that it quickly dripped off his hand and onto the couch cushion. He looked down at the spot in annoyance, then back up to Sydney like nothing had happened.

Sydney found the energy to look him up and down. His knuckles were bruised, cut, and bloody on their own, as well as a series of small gashes across the right side of his face, but there were no injuries to explain what he was seeing. He did however wonder why he continued to blur.

Particles began wandering awa y, like grains of sand in the tide.

"We're the same. You just haven't accepted it," said the ghost, as calmly as if he'd announced he'd just finished the dishes. "When you do, maybe we'll get somewhere."

The grains of sand were larger, like embers from a fire drifting away.

"In the meantime, you should probably go to bed. Our time's up," he finished. His outline had begun to come away in larger pixels, every color tone that comprised him shifting away with the squares.

Sydney forced himself to breathe again, however shallow. Without blinking, he stood and backed away toward the kitchen.

There, he made himself another cup of tea, never looking up. He pulled the tea from the tin Martin had given him from Skadi and threw the leaves loose into the cup. He ran hot water from the tap, up to the top, then vanished up the staircase.

The room was once again empty, the white couch pristine. Sydney West was not seen again while there was still snow on the ground.

The Hanged Man

www.ingramcontent.com/pod-product-compliance
Lightning Source LLC
Chambersburg PA
CBHW070553310726
48982CB00011B/1568/J

* 9 7 9 8 9 8 7 3 0 1 3 1 9 *